THE PERSIMMION SEQUENCE

PART I
of
the
OLEANDRE TRILOGY

A SCIENCE FICTION EPIC
by
D. JOHN FRETLAND

APOLLO BOOKS
Woodbridge, Conn.

For Tryscha
   Brightener of the dismal,
     looking glass.
   Flaxen-haired Muse. . .
     trader of Time
  and love.
    – D.

Printed in the United States of America

PROLOGICA
THE SENKA SEEDS

. . .with the evolvement of tactical biological weapons and their recent aggressive use against the People's Tribunal of Upper Manchuria, I, in protest and in personal disgust, hereby second the motion of the distinguished delegate from East Molandzia for the permanent disbandment of the International Health Organization. . .and may God help us all!

— Harmon Tertzov, I.H.O. delegate,
Republic of Free Slavia.

Ann. I.H.O. 477:1343, (1997).

CHAPTER 1

The young man wore the rank of "INVESTIGATOR" on the etched nameplate that glowed in platinum luster on his white tunic. He was well muscled, and his defiant black eyes hid an underlying gentleness. Pausing in a hallway that intersected two concentric corridors crowded with admiring colleagues, he fumbled nervously with the tape cartridge unit under his arm, aware of their approving glances. The tape module was simply marked: ANTIMATTER INTER-CONVERSIONS – 57.

He was not physically aware of the pull of artificial gravity on his body, nor could his sense detect that the Oleandre had, that day, exceeded the galactic pleat and was traveling out of the galaxy at a rate sequential of three point seven. (The word "speed," as related to velocity or, incidentally, as a term with psychomimetic connotations, no longer existed. Rate sequential was merely the exponent of ten multiplied by the speed of light in vacuum. . .in this case, the speed of light times ten to the three point seven power [$c \times 10^{3.7}$]).

It was *his* achievement and would, no doubt, result in his promotion to the rank of "SCIENTIFIC FELLOW," and there were only nineteen living SCIENTIFIC FELLOWs at that time. A slight, self-satisfied smile curled at the edges of his mouth, and Sean Eric Senka felt the warm, heady pleasure spread over his mind. Around the gentle continuous curve of the passageway-transporter came the girl, wearing a "jumpsuit" of metallic silver leaf, sheer as zeelon, yet almost wear resistant. Her tawny red hair was closely cropped, and over her shoulder was slung a black leather satchel.

"Diahna, over here!"

She spotted Sean through the bustling mass of people and made her way over to him. His extended hand clasped hers lightly for just an instant.

"I'm so glad you could meet me, Diahna," he said. There was a trace of nervousness in his voice, not only from the excitement of the day's events, but from his equally stimulating anticipation of their meeting.

"Oh Sean, I'm. . .well, I'm glad too!"

"What's in the satchel?"

"Some wine, for a celebration." Her green eyes stared deeply into his. "This is an extremely momentous evening. . .the first hours man has exceeded the speed of light. I can't tell you how pleased I am that you've asked me to share your victory with you."

"On the contrary, *I'm* the one who's honored," he said, looking out at the passing crowds, yet seeing nothing.

The projection tram accelerated swiftly after he had pressed the appropriate code into its memory banks. It soon stopped in front of his quarters, on Deck AC-33, deep in the interior of Oleandre.

He walked up to the translucent door, Diahna lagging a few

steps behind. With nothing more than his thought command, the door silently flew open and the white glare of the interior illuminated them, casting long shadows back down the curved corridor. The door and, for that matter, every service device in his area was attuned to his thought transmission. It was not even necessary for him to think the word "open" hard enough so that it could be heard in his "mind's ear." He had only to complete the neural connections necessary for the encoding to occur, and the door would indeed open. Usually, Sean was unconscious of the fact that he had actually thought "open." It was working. . .the complete subjugation of unconscious thought to servile use, freeing the mind for constructive creation.

"Please come in."

"Thank you, Sean," she replied, looking dubiously into the glare. "You certainly don't have much room. I thought. . .I mean, after all, you're an INVESTIGATOR, so naturally I thought you'd have a large suite and. . ."

"I really don't need much room. Just enough space to think and record my thoughts. . .and, of course, access to the Prime Computer Memory Banks. You'll have to excuse the mess." He picked up some celucel tapes and tossed them carelessly under the Dichroic telescanner.

"I'll put the wine in your cryogenic unit if you show me where it is."

"Oh, yes, by all means." He laughed almost embarrassingly and, pointing to a magnetic shelf suspended behind the black pullout couch, said, "It's *actually* hidden behind that pile of recordings under the shelf."

She cleared away the mound of tapes and memory modules (noticing that their subject was nucleonic energy systems) and opened the small, rectangular door. Immediately, vapors began to swirl out of the orifice. Inserting the bottle, she slid the door shut and depressed the black button on the handle. In a few seconds the yellow light flashed and the white wine was thoroughly chilled. A sonicator effortlessly removed the cork and Diahna poured the spirits into two long, tubular crystal glasses. And lifting her glass to his, she said, "Here's to you Sean, and to the Mission."

"Thank you. Here's to the Mission — *and* to us." He clicked her glass.

The dry white wine had a slight yeasty bouquet and just a hint of an earthy taste. After a few draughts, an alcoholic warmth spread over their bodies and freed their minds of any formalities and shyness that remained. They sat close on the couch, her head leaning on his shoulder, her hand bound gently in his. His thought dimmed the lighting and encouraged the audio module to play a Bach recording: the 5th Brandenburg Concerto.

Sitting silently as the symphony continued, Diahna noticed that the niche over Sean's writing table brimmed with loosely bound copies of his father's works. One title in particular stood out: Senka and Horvitz, AN INTRODUCTORY TEXTAPE OF NEURAL TRANSPLANTATION TECHNIQUE.

"Sean?"

"Uh-huh."

"What was he like?"

"What was *who* like?" he replied, head resting on the back of the couch and his glassy eyes only half open.

"Your father, silly."

"Why would you even care about that?"

He looked down at her; his vision blurred.

"Well, he's so. . .so famous. I mean, he'll soon be in the history tapes, and I'm just interested as hell!"

He looked at her dark strawberry hair and smiled. . .a drunken smile.

"OK, I'm nosey!"

"If you're really that damn interested. . ."

"I am. I never knew him and everyone says that you are his image."

"All right," Sean got up and stumbled toward the suite's master console. "I have some very old tapes. . .tapes of my father's diary, or rather, his journal. I haven't played them in over three years."

He pushed several panels on the module, but a red indicator flashed to signal an error. Sean tried again, and static was immediately heard in the audio system, followed by a scratchy, whirring noise.

"That's it," said Sean, returning to the couch and flopping down beside Diahna. He leaned over and kissed her wetly on the ear; and she responded by squeezing his hand in hers. Together, they listened as the crackling voice emanated from the audio banks.

* * *

". . .*the area near the innermost Martian satellite, Phobos, has been teeming with activity for nearly a decade now. The concluding phases of the work have been carried out with practically no secrecy since the undertaking seems too ludicrous to be believable.*

But, unbelievable as it sounds, the Oleandre Project is within one Earth-Lunar cycle of completion.

If I am to keep this diary, it must be done in such a manner as to be sensible to future generations.

This then, is my record and journal of the coming voyage. . .the trek of the Oleandre to deep hyperspace. I am Eric Carnovon Senka, Chief Life Investigating Coordinator. . . data retrieval system code sequence: CLIC-1A.

I keep this record because it is my most sacred belief that civilization has gone utterly berserk, and that there are sinister forces lurking to destroy the Mission, even though our lax security arrangements seem to negate the latter assumption. I will not date these preliminary entries since history will simultaneously end and begin anew with the launching of the Oleandre.

"Oleandre" is the vehicle that will transport myself and my fifteen-thousand four-hundred ninety-four courageous, yet desperate, colleagues to new frontiers. . .away and safe from the madness we created in the name of civilization. Fifty great nuclear engines, operating on the principle of matter-antimatter interconversion, and generating approximately ten billion megawatts of power, will propel the entire satellite of Phobos out of its orbit and into a course designed to circle the solar system twice, building the velocity necessary to fling it out into oblivion or paradise – it does not matter which.

I must explain that I have not been trained as a writer; but I am hopeful that the style of this journal will improve with time. The events leading up to the conception of the Oleandre Project are indeed complex, and I will go into them in detail later; however, I feel some opening remarks are in order:

The failure of the major powers on Earth to extricate themselves from the faulty logic of the Asian Mainland Wars led to the ultimate economic and spiritual decline of their power structure. But, of course, this is all common knowledge, and an excellent synopsis is available at Data Retrieval Coordinate 3.078 by 3.117. Anarchy was rampant among the intelligentsia and peonage alike. The subsequent repression of the student classes and the complete censorship of the universities resulted in the decline, and near extinction, of creativity in the world.

The remaining intellectuals were forced to carry on their activities in secrecy. The highly sophisticated military intelligence network quickly uncovered their ranks, and the authorities gave the captive a choice. . .slow painful extermination, or planetary colonization. Many accepted the latter alternative and they, and their children, are here on the Oleandre today.

Five years passed before the completion of the great metallurgical complexes on the Martian surface; and it was *there that we and our parents began the construction of Oleandre. Meanwhile, the military control of this space sector became virtually nonexistent due to the advent of the General Recall. Officers and men of the Extraterrestrial Services returned to Earth by the tens of thousands. The United States of the Western Hemisphere and their Slavic Allies had faced off against the Asian Coalition on the Siberian wastelands. . .it was senseless slaughter. A billion casualties resulted, in a single campaign that lasted only six days. With seemingly unlimited human resources, Imperial General Kim van Traum threw army after army of the disciplined, well-armed Sons and Daughters of the People's Guard at the Westerner's position, balanced them on the brink of victory, only to be repulsed by the millions of robotoid shock-troopers who vengefully fought even with their limbs hacked off. These were supported by thousands of laser battalions rocketed in from Free Slavia in the crucial final hours. The Battle of the Kierov Valley was the worst single disaster in the Earth's history, the record prior to this being held by a natural geologic cataclysm that rocked the Shensi Province in the area once called China. Over three quarters of a million humans died and countless others were injured in that holocaust, which occurred in January, 1556, the Year of the Dragon.*

Even after the cries of fury and agonized death had been dissipated by the biting, subzero winds in the Kierov Valley, and the vaporized blood had congealed and crystallized on the frozen steppe, and the crushed tissues and shattered bones were ground under by the spiked balloon treads of the retreating attack vehicles, the land was restless with shrieking blizzards. Still, both sides held back their thermonuclear devices.

Then, about ten years ago, a great political polarization and coalescence took place. The so-called Westernizers grouped into what came to be known as the Alliance. The fractious tribes of the orient were united into the K'uang Fong.

Of the six thousand-odd languages and their various dialects spoken in the late twentieth century, seven were used by over fifty percent of the Earth's population. Fifteen percent spoke Mandarin; ten percent, English; while Spanish, Russian, Japanese and German accounted for about six percent each; and Hindustani, one percent. But, in the early twenty-first century, during the period of the great political confrontation, a strange, and still unexplained, linguistic shift occurred. Mandarin as a spoken language declined, even with the rise of the K'uang Fong, mainly because many of the East's great leaders (notably, Edward Kaisan, Regent Stoeckenius Lampert and Q. E. D'Thue) had been educated in Western universities. At this time it was estimated that seventy-five percent of the world's peoples spoke English; five percent, Mandarin; and fifteen percent, Mundanlingua, a crude yet constantly improving attempt at a common international language. It is strange that as the Earth's people grew farther and farther apart ideologically, they grew closer together linguistically. The slavic and postlatin tongues were almost dead, used only by dissident bands of monks who lived under a loose coalition in the foothills of the Ural Mountains, and studied the illuminated manuscripts that contained the essence of their faith. . .Barthsword, a kind of existential metaphysics overlaid with a primitive and rather pagan form of goat worship.

A year ago, the strategy of the world's great powers changed decisively. Nuclear duels have taken place, but the technology is so evenly matched that most warheads are intercepted and destroyed outside the atmosphere by orbiting antiballistic missiles. Still, a few of the devices get through, and we receive occasional sketchy news reports of entire populations being vaporized by horrendous, searing explosions. Unfortunately, neither side has used its neutrino capability!

DO THEY WIPE OUT ONLY THE ENEMY SOLDIERS AND ROBOTOIDS? NO, THEY INSIST ON THE TOTAL DESTRUCTION OF CIVILIZATION!

They will be thrown back into a stone age! IT IS MADNESS! Recovery would surely occur. Some would survive. . .but they could never rebuild a technological society because they will have totally depleted the planet's natural resources. And because they are genetically ill, the evil would rise again. This must not happen, and it will *not. The Oleandre Project, of which this vehicle is only one part, will ensure this.*

I have so very little time now. The endpoint in the countdown is so near that I dare not take the time to record any more until we are well underway. I will return to this journal in a few days when the Oleandre flight has begun, and the Earth has been destroyed."

". . .today history begins. It is Oleandre Day One. I am transcribing these preliminary notes into the private memory banks in my quarters on Deck 63, Subarea Z-8. This is a period of great exhilaration for me, yet, I have an overwhelming feeling of loss and foreboding. All links with our birthplace have been destroyed. . .our ties with the rest of humanity severed. Even though we were persecuted, departure is still a severe psychic blow. We have executed our world. . .our Earth. . .our heritage, and begun anew. . .it is frightening!

Two Earth days ago, I accompanied Harlin Willoughby to the Hoverport, which lies on the smoothed out surface in the gamma sector of Phobos. It was all very mysterious. We had filed a flight schedule indicating our destination to be the Primary Particle Analysis Chamber at the Basic Sciences Complex, called Phlogoston, on the Martian surface. After boarding the two-seater Hovercraft and lifting effortlessly from the Phobian surface, Willoughby revealed that due to my expressed interest, I would be shown the thermonuclear offensive devices that he and his colleagues had designed and installed without the slightest security leak. Even though we had hardly exchanged a word, I felt a natural empathy and thought I had an understanding with Willoughby, an unspoken coalition.

Willoughby flicked the time-phase programmer next to the communications console, and the Hovercraft's speed slowed from 2.9 to 1.3 miles per second as we approached the surface. At an altitude of three hundred miles, the entire orange disc of the planet seemed to fill the port. At one hundred miles, we pulled into Retrograde Pattern-758, and wide hollow wings unfolded from the upper side of the Hovercraft. They were webbed and batlike to provide the necessary lift in the rarified Martian atmosphere. We sped across the Sinus Meridiani, only a thousand feet above its surface, to the Margaritifer Sinus, where the great, sprawling, underground metallurgical complex is located. I noticed a huge yellow dust storm raging in the distance, in the area of the Sinus Aurorae. Turning south with a power upsurge, we landed on a small strip in the region of the Mountains of Mitchell at the south pole.

As we walked down a dry path, which was heated from beneath by nuclear fire, I looked back and saw that the frozen ice crystals on the summit of Mount Brahe had a lavendar tinge. Brahe, at thirty-five hundred feet and the highest of the Mountains of Mitchell, stood sharply outlined against the pale blue sky.

Before us, housed in protective silos, were fifty boosters. Each was armed with a cluster of three megamegaton thermonuclear warheads. These would do the job, Willoughby told me; and I nodded solemnly. He told me many things that day, most of which were incomprehensible to me. . .complex mathematical theorems, guidance devices and advanced concepts in telemetry. I understood only one thing: that in these shining tubes were the agents of our answer to the depraved violators.

After thanking Willoughby, I bid him good-bye, saying that I hoped to meet with him again, aboard Oleandre. The air screens slid silently shut and I felt the raw evening air attack

my face. Walking down a pathway cut into the rocky hillside,
a whirling gust of bright white snow streaked the ledge ahead
of me. The eroded rocks, reddish-brown, black and violet,
were abundant with the various polymers of carbon suboxide,
which accounted for the multitude of hues. It was with a pang
of hesitation that I picked out the Earth shining in the stars of
the constellation Leo.

It is ironic, I thought, that the Earth is in the House of the
Lion. The light disc of Phobos was just rising on the western
horizon. I pulled off the respirator for a second. Although it
was not a necessity, I had never adjusted to the thin Martian
atmosphere and had always worn a small breathing device that
fit just over my nose and mouth, its refresher unit being hung
on my belt. The crisp air gave a dry, yet curiously burning
sensation to my throat that slowly migrated to my lungs,
leaving my chest heaving in hot pain. But, I thought, this may
be the last breath of 'fresh' air I would respire for many
years. . .perhaps forever.

The Hovercraft's airlock opened and I entered. I removed
the respirator and my heavy, fleece-lined gloves. Almost
without thinking, I started the single engine and sped down
the short silver-foil runway with sprays of purple snow being
thrown up behind me. I turned the controls over to the
onboard computer, and the Hovercraft was inserted into
Soarpath B-128, which would take me to Phobos.

Above the Martian surface, the planet's half disc hung in a
bluish haze; and, looking back toward the area I had just
visited, I saw waves of bright, dazzling pinpoints of light
leaving the surface. It has begun, I thought.

The fleet of deadly missiles sped Earthward at speeds
approaching five hundred miles per second, closing in on a
course that kept the Earth's moon between them and the
target. .,.this as a shield, an admittedly ineffective one, against
the Earth's detection systems. I tuned in our central control
center and heard a report that as the fleet of warheads

*approached the Moon, antiballistic missiles were launched
from somewhere in the Arrhenius region. Our lead warheads
were immediately diverted; but the decoys and the majority of
the missiles passed unscathed. We were not aware of this ABM
emplacement, nor have we any positive proof as to whose it
was; although the K'uang Fong occupied most of the Moon,
with the Alliance restricting its activities there to guerrilla
operations. Lu Chio's forces on Lunare must have been more
advanced than we ever imagined.*

*We did know that a nuclear duel was taking place over the
Artic wastes and most of the Alliance's ABM capability was
already committed to use. We doubt that they could have
intercepted us.*

*The first wave of warheads spread into a vile umbrella that
burst at an altitude of four miles. The panorama unfolded in
all its beautiful horror before me, since I could receive visual
impulses from satellite cameras orbiting the Earth. My
unblinking eyes stuck to the telescanner monitor as great
rolling balls of orange and yellow and waxy red flame spread
across the continental United States of the Western
Hemisphere, scorching the land and turning the oceans and
lakes and brooks and streams to massive rippling clouds of
steam.*

*The second wave of multiple warheads suddenly came into
a compact formation as they entered the atmosphere.
Designed to penetrate the Earth's crust, they detonated
simultaneously deep within the San Andreas Fault.*

*The Earth split in a single, fantastic explosion, leaving only
a myriad of small glowing fragments. Great shock and energy
waves were sent in all directions, turning my screen black as
they hit and destroyed the satellite cameras.*

*I was not even aware that the Hovercraft had landed. I
noticed that my hands were perspiring and my knees shook,
while the craft was drawn into its berth by the inhuman
magnetic grapplers."*

"...It was, I suppose, a necessary thing. By all that is holy, they had tried to destroy us...the creative ones. There is not a doubt in my mind that the most valuable humans from the Earth civilization are on the Oleandre today. They are the creators, the innovators. We...I...have but one true and sacred love, that of man's will to project itself into an objective. The objective may either be concrete or abstract, as long as something has been created from man's own consciousness. The men and women who have this ability are the greatest among humans.

Yet such people were neither recognized nor rewarded for their creative activities. No, just the opposite was true. Their ideas and inventions were stolen by mindless corrupters whose only ends were to use that creativity for their own evil purpose. The inventor was merely patted on the head, or given a golden medal on a satin ribbon, and then sent back to his laboratory. The creator had no control over the destiny of his innovation.

This is the way it was on the Earth at the beginning of the middle decades of the Twenty-First Century. God, what it did to Ernst!

Perhaps I will use the story of Ernst Scheider to illustrate the depravity we destroyed. Ernst was twice Nobel laureate in Medicine, and a member of the Directorate of the International Academy of Sciences. I worked as a meager assistant to the master, in his laboratory at the IAS Research Institute, a complex that covered fifty square miles of green rolling ground just outside the Boston Megalopolis. In a brilliant series of biochemical experiments, Scheider isolated an inhibitor enzyme from malignant cells that supressed the repressor operons for cellular division. The inhibitor was called adenylglyoxalase, and was found be common to all types of cancerous cells. This was his greatest discovery. After that, his students purified the AGase, as it was called, and produced antibodies that would destroy the inhibitor. Thus, an effective

*general therapy for carcinoma was produced. It did not seem
to prevent the onset of cancer, but, once a malignancy started,
it could be halted indefinitely by use of the antibody to
AGase. Scheider received a lifetime stipend from the IAS and
the Order of Merit from the Leningrad Institute, but was he to
see his momentous discovery used to alleviate the suffering of
mankind? NO!*

*The military authorities confiscated the records of his
isolation and purification processes and, in the name of
"national security," made Dr. Scheider a virtual prisoner in his
own institute. Then, the decadent thieves put Scheider's
discovery to the vilest of uses. Great quantities of antibody to
AGase were prepared and made available to the citizenry and
military personnel of the Alliance. Then a biological compaign
was undertaken against the Asians. Literally tons of a bacterial
extract that causes liver cancer were spread over the sprawling
military and industrial plexes in the Gobi Desert. That single
raid resulted in five million deaths, while our military
government stood by with the antidote. It was hailed as a great
moral and ethical victory for the Alliance, with banners and
public ceremonies announcing the destruction of the K'uang
Fong world conspiracy. As for Ernst, it was more than he
could stand. He was found slumped at a bench in his
laboratory. . .a bullet in his brain. Communiques subsequently
released by the government press told of the capture and
supposed confession of the K'uang Fong "assassin" who had
murdered the great man.*

*So, you see the illness that was spreading among us. Even
Ernst's protein could not halt the metastasis of **that** kind of
malignancy. They were like mad dogs, foaming and rabid; and
like mad dogs, they had to be destroyed.*

*The creators had to be saved. I had to be saved for I am an
innovator, an originator of ideas and technique. . .in my field
of brain transplantation and molecular memory transcription.*

Today, we all have a paradox of feelings: great fear and anxiety, yet extreme elation and hope. We are setting out to create a place for man somewhere in the universe, where we can be free to use our creative powers to their epitome. The endeavor is grantedly utopian in scope, but I have confidence in its success. Now, if we can only follow the Oleandre Directive!

I had not truly realized the impact of what we had done until this evening when I was up in the observation bubble. Looking around, I picked out some of my favorite astronomical objects. . .the Great Andromeda Galaxy. . .Algol; but something was definitely wrong. . .a shiny disc was missing from the constellation of Leo.

". . .On this, Oleandre Day Four, I decided that I have left this journal unattended for too long. The pace has been frantic. You can imagine the vast scope of mere logistics. Adding the human element multiplies this factor a million fold. Most of the menial duties are carried out by the servomechanins, a kind of mongoloid robot having no judgment powers. It has gone relatively smoothly though, considering that more than fifteen thousand individuals are involved. Of course, we have been briefed for over a year now; because of this, only minor accidents have occurred. . .servomechanin collisions in passageways, misplaced provisions. . .nothing time won't ameliorate.

One situation, however, has come up that warrants my concern. Yesterday, O.D.-3, there were two suicides. One person jumped into a laser-pulse channel and was instantly vaporized; the other, and this is most strange, merely hanged himself in his quarters with a length of bed-sheet. Not very ingenious, but nonetheless effective. These two suicides were unexpected since every member underwent a most intense and sophisticated orthomolecular-psychiatric examination before

*being considered for the Mission. I suppose the trauma of the
Earth's destruction had more adverse effects than we had
planned. Even I, the cynic, feel a gnawing sense of loss.*

*I had better clear up one thing immediately, though it may
seem trivial. Even though we are heading for deep space, out
of the Solar System, and eventually out of the galaxy, we will
continue to use the conventional units of time. . .hours, days,
seconds, etc. This is because our biological regulatory
mechanisms — biological clocks, if you will — are accustomed
to this system. It is not for any great love of heritage! The
continual rhythm of pi-meson antipi-meson interconversion is
translated into precise electrical units and factored into a
sequence. that will approximate our former method of time
keeping.*

*A beeping had announced someone at the entrance to my
quarters. In my viewer, I see it is my personal servomechanin,
bringing the evening meal. It seems so illogical to say 'evening'
since evening is only a portion of time now, having nothing to
do with the approach of night.*

*I have named my servomechanin Pseudomonius, a name
that just came to me, without obvious meaning or rational
derivation. It is probably a psychical composite of sociological
and microbiological terminology. Who knows? I have inserted
a null-initiate sequence into the servomechanin's master
program, and Pseudomonius will bring this food at precisely
this time, every day. . .every day for an eternity. Notice, I've
already masculinized it. My privilege! You must forgive this
digression while I eat my meal.*

*Perhaps some background, specific to the Mission, is in
order now. The basic conception of our adventure was
formulated at the Jason Oleandre Foundation on Earth in*

June 2007. The Foundation was a private group of dedicated, world renowned intellectuals. Formed under the guise of an ultrapatriotic organization, the membership was truly multifaceted, comprised of eminent physicists, sociologists, physicians, lawyers, chemists, urban renovators and representatives of every aspect of man's creative endeavor. All joined with the ultimate oath and single aim: extinguishing the de facto repression of the creators. Under the direction and guidance of Jason Oleandre, Alliance funds were clandestinely diverted into the Foundation's coffers and the facilities of those members from both academic and the industrial-military complexes alike, were put to the utmost use. Two years after its inception, the Oleandre groups had tangible assets of over two hundred billion Alliance dollars. Security was undertaken by a well-paid force of professional counter-insurgency experts rivaled only by the MSD's network of agents. MSD was the Ministry of Subversive Detection, the assassination arm of the Alliance's Internal Security Agency headed by the infamous Nathaniel L. Marsten.

I speak of Marsten, not with total repugnance, but with a sense of pity, of waste, for the man possessed qualities admirable in a normal human. His brilliant handling of the hundred thousand MSD operatives and counterespionage agents was the perfect equilibrium of enlightened planning and expert administration coupled with a ruthless, savage requirement for total commitment, complete loyalty. The act of animal depravity that brought upon him the title of "Nathan the Terrible" arose out of the state arrest of the Bishops of the Methovite Church. The hundred and three aged scholars were interned at the MSD Indoctrination Center that occupied Key Largo, where they were personally martyred by Marsten, who had each kneel before him with head bowed, whereupon he touched the victim on each shoulder with a high-voltage sceptre.

*As always seems to happen in this type of operation, there
was a security leak. It is said that the arrests and execution of
the Foundation leaders occurred in a matter of hours. Jason
Oleandre received the horrid, but not wholly unexpected
news, while speeding across Old-Montana in the Northern
United States of the Western Hemisphere. Toward the red ball
rapidly disappearing into the west, the sleek silver Jaguar
XK-750 cruised on Route 2 at an effortless hundred and
eighty miles per hour. The turbine engine purred in its housing
behind the cockpit.*

*Oleandre was headed toward Havre, and a meeting with the
Canadian Council. The communications console, which sat
under the tachometer buzzed and the telescreen activated. He
heard the worst from Hendrik Fergis, a close associate and
founder of the Peoria Rocket Propulsion Corporation that had
initiated the first practical intercontinental rocket passenger
service, and whose facilities were used by the Alliance in
military operations. Jason Oleandre watched helplessly, as
MSD agents broke into the room and unceremoniously shot
Fergis then beheaded him with a rather dull, double-edged axe.*

*Having foreseen this eventuality, Oleandre initiated the
launching of the three deep-space probes. At a secret site in
the Grand Teton Mountains, three giant boosters had been
constructed with a technology exceeding even that of the
Alliance. The first probe was placed in heliocentric orbit
somewhere in the vicinity of the planetoid Pluto, and perhaps
in orbit around Pluto itself. The second is supposedly just
outside our solar system, but we are not exactly sure where.
The third? THAT IS THE RUB! We have the celestial
coordinates for the first two probes from tapes made by Jason
Oleandre; but the location of the third was lost in the
accidental nuclear holocaust that ravaged the Southwestern
United States sector of the Alliance in the last month of the
year 2011.*

Our Mission reflects Jason Oleandre's convictions, and we now search for the instructions he left for us in the three probes. Before his laboratories and organization were destroyed, great advances had been made...advances and discoveries never divulged to the Alliance. These technological and social concepts he left to us, his heirs. But to claim our inheritance we must find the first two probes, and hope that clues as to the location of the third will be contained within them.

This journal will divulge little about the activities and philosophy of the K'uang Fong, since my knowledge of them is limited mostly to propaganda tirades. Neither the Alliance nor the Foundation had any success in penetrating their territory. Crack agents, prepared by years of training and surgical reconstruction were never heard from again. Saboteurs stratopulted into China, for example, or the Forbidden City of Johansberg, were simply swallowed up as if they had never existed. Life inside East World, as the land of the K'uang Fong was popularly called, remains a great mystery.

I think I said earlier that the Oleandre will make several large orbits about the Sun to build momentum. Because the Oleandre has been completely hollowed out, and only the surface remains intact, it could not withstand instant acceleration to its ultimate speeds. Our first arcing post-orbital swing is calculated to take up into the area where Jason Oleandre's first probe is located. An Ultrahovercraft will sprint ahead of Oleandre to pick it up. I am fortunate enough to be among the crew going out. There will be two of us, the other being Harlin Willoughby. We are to meet with Commander Hayakawa at twenty hundred hours today and discuss the project.

Our speed has built to over a thousand mi.. ...er second now; but there is no sensation of movement. I am surprised the gravity mechanisms have worked so well. Of course, we are all accustomed to the lighter gravity of Mars. Just under

Oleandre's rocky crust is a huge sphere of pure Tholomite metal, and concentrically within this, a second rotating sphere, producing artificial gravity. All passageways and quarters are located on concentric circles around the major axis. In order to get to the surface of Oleandre, one travels the long corridor running along the rotational axis, emerging at the Hoverport on one end, or the power sources at the other. The observation bubble and guidance instrumentation are close by the Hoverport. There is a constant stream of activity at these locations.

A most difficult engineering problem presented itself soon after the theoretical antimatter conversion engine became a reality: how and where to store the antimatter, since the ship would be instantly destroyed if the antimatter were housed in a material chamber. This dilemma was ultimately solved by Georgii Berbergovoy of the Fieldion Astrophysics Group. The antimatter is suspended in a powerful magnetic field which forms a huge invisible donut around the engines. The fuel (in this case, antiproton) is then channeled into the fusion modules and thrusting units by magnetic fluxars, in a nill-grav environment.

Of course, if the whole craft rotated at a constant rate, decks closer to the surface would have a different gravity than those decks close to the major axis, deep in Oleandre. However, each deck has its own rotation controlled so that the outer decks spin slower than the inner levels and thus, the gravitational effect is constant throughout. Horizontors and tramways, naturally, run parallel and between decks.

It will all take scme time to smooth out the defects; but we have plenty of that stable commodity. For now, I have experiments to begin and the meeting with Commander Seth Hayakawa. . ."

". . .many exciting events have occurred, and we have only been on our journey a full week.

The briefing with Commander Hayakawa was extremely enlightening. Seth is a very stern person. . .a man in whose presence one feels a warming security. I believe him to be a just man and do not in the least envy the pressure and responsibility of his position. Willoughby accompanied me to the Commander's private suite which lies just under the main Mission Regulation complex: Oleandre Control. The Commander greeted us dressed in sandals and a white, satin tunic belted at the waist with a black sash. The room is rather spartan, dominated by two huge telescreens on which is projected the fields of view directly ahead of and behind the Oleandre. The latter is filled by the now-dulled brilliance of our former star, the Sun, Sol.

Commander Hayakawa briefed Harlin and myself as to what was expected of us when the time came to lock-on to Jason Oleandre's First Probe.

The capsule is in orbit around the small planet called Pluto, although our most learned astrophysicists do not accept Pluto as a true planet, believing it to be a long lost satellite of Neptune. We shall be able to receive, if it is still functioning, the electromagnetic signal from the First Probe at a distance of ten million miles. As soon as we return the precise code required, the probe will activate a pulsed-laser beam that will give us both visual and directional contact. The procedures for contact, verification and picking up the capsule leave little margin for error. The Oleandre will then be traveling at fifteen thousand miles per second.

It is amazing that with the great trauma and excitement of the Mission, people can still settle into a routine so quickly. Perhaps it is because we are now free to pursue the things we have always wanted to do. We are not restricted. Well, that isn't exactly true. There are certainly logistical restrictions. For example, I wanted a cerebrally activated circulatory probe constructed; and I had to wait my turn to get on the materiel-request computer. But, once I had programmed the *proper instructions, it was only a matter of two days until Pseudomonius received the signal to pick up the device at my area's local instrumentation distribution point.*

I might point out that we have decided to try the "total immersion" concept of our work; that is, each of us lives right in the area in which we work. My laboratory, for example, is adjacent to my living quarters, and, on the other side, is my private microdot library. It contains all the literature references I might need for my experiments. I can sit in my library and punch out the coded data for anything in the field of neurochemistry, as far back as the early 1930's; and the article will appear almost instantaneously on the telescreen in front of me or on any of the subsidiary visors in the laboratory. If I require a copy of a particular journal article, I merely depress another copying stud and a celucel reproduction is immediately in my hands.

It would seem then, that most people are too involved in their own work to have time for any other activities, but a vigorous schedule of physical exercise is advocated and encouraged. However, apart from the many athletic and social facilities available, there is a weekly teletape delivered to each person. On it are short summaries of every group's endeavor. . .their discoveries and problems.

Even this early, there are exciting reports. Jonathan Fischer is our librarian; and he and his staff have just announced that over a million titles are now available. Think of it – a million works of literature, science, philosophy, theology, sociology and history are stored in the microcircuits of his massive, internally linked computer system! Now, anyone can press the appropriate selector in any of Oleandre's multivisored reading rooms and the particular work of choice will appear, either visually or on audio. Fischer is busy cataloging and sorting out another hundred million works. He believes it will be a good ten years work. It is especially difficult, I am told, to work out a sequence for the myriad degenerate works published during the time of the Alliance. Some of these vile things are already available, on a limited basis.

There is no restriction per se, but children under the age of fifteen years have no access to them without the consent of a parent. Each of these books is prefaced with an analysis of the work and with critical opinions. Otherwise adults are free to form their own conclusions. I must emphasize that in order for our system to work, THERE MUST BE NO CENSORSHIP!

Ordinarily, these distasteful and inaccurate works of propaganda would not have been included in the Great Receptacle of Knowledge. However, many sociologists and historians aboard Oleandre are studying the reasons behind the decline of the Earth civilization. That this ultimate disaster cannot recur, it was at our colleague's urging that all the Alliance publications be included. Our children and their offspring must know what it was like then so that they will appreciate their new heritage.

Yesterday, I had the 'midday' meal with Dr. McCartney. Maggie is a dear friend and former classmate from the days when we attended the Post-Graduate Institute at the Free University. Those were good times! She was, and is, a brilliant astrophysicist. It was unfortunate that her work was set back by the General Recall and its accompanying lack of funds. She has had a sad life. . .with the disruption of her career and, the hideous murder of her husband in MegaLondon by Alliance agents, who delivered his grisly fragments to her doorstep.

However, I am pleased to record here that I have never seen her happier, as Maggie is totally involved in trying to make up for lost time. Using the compact radio telescope on Oleandre's surface, she is scanning the edges of our galaxy for new pulsar sources, as she firmly believes in communication attempts by other civilizations. Not being too successful in pinpointing any new sources, she has recently scanned known pulsar sources and compared her results with the old data in the literature.

Much of our food is synthetic; but we do grow natural

*foods in immense tanks. The green algae, **Photohypnea carbohydreas**, has been used for decades as a dietary supplement. Now, by adding certain enzymes and enzyme precursors to the broth, and by removing others, it has been possible to increase the algae's growth cycles a thousand fold. This process was developed during the time of the Alliance by marine biochemists at the Boca Raton Institute of Marine Ecology, and it would have practically eliminated starvation on the Earth. The Alliance, however, withheld the food lest THE ENEMY obtain it. The Alliance was so foolish. People do not rebel on full stomachs!*

The algae-derived food is actually very tasty. After the algae's photosynthetic appartus is removed, various procedures produce a white or tan powder which eventually is made into bread.

Attempts at a synthetic wine have been atrocious, and I must admit I commit the most sinful act...that of hoarding. I have two cases of old wine and champagne...Chateau Lascombes-Jiu, 1972, and Piper-Heidsieck, 2002. I am saving them for a very special occasion. Some abominable Scotch-whiskey has been made, too. However, we've produced a concoction called "SN999, Sergei Nemisis' 999th," a synthetic brew equivalent in taste and bouquet to the best Olde-English gins.

Today, O.D.7, we are in the process of making a flyby of the planet Uranus, partly to glean scientific data, but mostly to use the planet's gravitational field to gain velocity.

We approached this greenish frozen sphere and passed at a distance of twenty thousand miles. A scientific probe was launched and I watched it from the observation bubble. As it plunged to the surface, the small thruster was lost in the blue-green glare that illuminated the entire chamber. Telemetry revealed that a much lower content of methane, which supposedly accounts for Uranus' color, to be present in its atmosphere. Some ammonia was detected and, although the temperature of the outer atmosphere and the surface registered about two hundred twenty degrees below zero Centigrade, a strange phenomenon was noted.

When the scout probe was about eighty miles from the icy surface, the temperature telemetry circuits showed a reading of only minus fifteen degrees Centigrade. This lasted for only about six miles and then the temperature plummeted again. This was thought to only occur on the giant planets Jupiter and Saturn. The astronomers specializing in planetary atmosphere are certainly very puzzled and they will have to revise some of their theories.

This strange world is certainly an oddity.. Its axis of rotation lies practically in the plane of both its orbit and its axial rotation. The rotations of its satellites are the reverse of others in the Solar system, although Uranus itself does rotate similiarly around the Sun. I am always amazed, having been a serious amateur astronomer, that the ancients never recorded Uranus as one of their 'wonders'. . .it was faint, but certainly visible to them under the best atmospheric conditions on the antidiluvian Earth.

The flyby produced another bit of strictly academic information: no less than six new satellites of Uranus were cataloged, one over two hundred miles in diameter and lying in a circular orbit six thousand miles from the Uranian surface. There had previously been recorded only seven moons. It is really of no matter, for if all goes well, Oleandre is not likely to come this way again.

As I mentioned in earlier centimeters of this journal, the purpose of the transuranian passage is to gain speed. I am pleased to record that this is precisely what has been accomplished. We are traveling through the void at fifteen thousand miles per second. It is utterly unbelievable, fantastic!

I am extremely tired now, and think I will retire, since I must be up early tomorrow. It is most gratifying to me that at this morning's General Sciences meeting, the Behavioral Group's representative reports no more cases of abnormal behavior and claims there is an upturn in attendance of daily nonsectarian religious services. Since I have a goodly amount of contact with the Behavioral Group, I stopped Kermit Willer after the meeting and asked him for his candid reactions to his own report. He replied that the spiritual episodes had been totally unexpected, and that the Oleandre population, by its very nature, would logically lean toward agnosticism and even atheism, especially due to the destruction of all their aspirations by the Alliance and their total personal alienation. Perhaps, we concluded, the intellectual has more fear of the unknown than does the ordinary man. The great uncertainty of the Oleandre Mission, then, could be drawing them toward the start of a new faith, both in themselves and for humanity.

I will dine tomorrow evening with Dr. McCartney, and I look forward to talking with her again with great expectation.
E n d   t r a n s m i s s i o n . .   .c o d e A. . .Z. . .one. . .three. . .dash. . .seven. . ."

CHAPTER 2

At the first misty stimulations of waking, his tongue crept unconsciously from between his dry lips, wetting them, then exploring the grainy roughness of his unshaven upper lip. Dull consciousness seeped into his mind, and he reveled in these warm drowsy moments of wakening. . .a limbo between reality and the primeval womb.

He was only vaguely aware of a rustling sound near the bed. Christ! It can't be time to get up, he thought.

With a matter-of-fact movement, a metal claw twice touched his foot, then the servomechanin turned on silent bearings and, with a whirring noise, went over to the small table to prepare the morning meal.

"Is it *that* time already? Oh, Christ," Eric Senka groaned as he flopped over, pulling the blankets over his face. The painful light setting off convulsions deep in his brain. Then, with a quick jerk, he tore the covers from him and in an instant was sitting on the side of the bed, rubbing his head and the knotted muscles of his neck, looking at the vibrating dancing pattern on the patternless floor with vacant eyes.

"Good morning Pseudomonius," he mumbled.

"YES. . .IT IS MORNING, DOCTOR SENKA. SIX THIRTY-FIVE HOURS TO BE PRECISE. . .AS FOR THE TIME BEING GOOD. . .I CANNOT SAY. . .GOOD IS A SUBJECTIVE VALUE AND I AM UNABLE TO REGISTER ANY COMPREHENSION OF THE WORD FROM DATA SAMPLED FROM MY RELEVANCY COILS. . .YOU SEE DOCTOR SENKA. . ."

"Oh sure, sure, but not *now*. Please, it's much too early for any of your polemic, much too early."

"YES, DR. SENKA," replied the servomechanin in its monotone voice.

"And, Christ, must you call me *Doctor*? Can't you say Eric or sir, or even shithead?"

"DR. SENKA, I SHALL BE ONLY TOO PLEASED TO ADDRESS YOU AS ANYTHING YOU WISH, BUT YOU MUST INSERT THAT INTO MY MASTER PROGRAMMING WHAT IS THIS WORD: SHITHEAD?"

"Never mind — is my meal ready?"

"YES, DR. SENKA. . .AS USUAL."

After splashing some cold water in his face, Eric hurriedly ate his rare, synthetic steak and gulped down a glass of apricot juice. The morning's work program was fed into the computer while he dressed. He would not shave until just before the evening meal, since shaving more than once a day was one of the most revulsive things he could think of.

By seven-fifteen hours, the door to the Neural Phenomenon Laboratory slid open and Eric Senka burst into its sterile brightness. Radiation counters blinked in one corner. On another bench, a protein solution was being separated into fractions by molecular weights each fraction's protein content calculated, and the amino acid sequence of each protein determined. . .all automatically. All of this data would then be deposited in the computer in Eric's quarters where he would evaluate it at the end of the work day.

"Seven-twenty," he muttered, and thought, where is that Goddamned Horvitz?

Five seconds later, a young man with a gleaming bare head and infectious smile strolled casually into the laboratory and calmly said, "Morning, Herr Senka."

"Well, well, Meister Horvitz, I am *certainly* glad that you are able to bless me with your presence today."

"Sir?"

"Let's begin. We've plenty to do today. The brain of that old orangutan was removed yesterday after its neural program was put into computer storage. . .right?"

"Yes, Dr. Senka."

"Oh, God, even *you* sound like that damn brainless, aluminum cretin, and if you say 'as usual,' I shall, with a great deal of pleasure, kick you squarely in the ass."

"What?" Jesse looked truly bewildered.

"It's nothing. Now, the first thing for you to do is see if the body has been well maintained overnight. Meanwhile, I'll strip the electrical activity from the young orangutan and nullify its chemically coded memory. Then we'll insert the new brain. I'll need your help for that — oh, before I forget, I have to attend a meeting from ten 'til eleven-hundred this morning."

While Jesse Horvitz was checking the heart and respiratory rates and the acid-base balance of the brainless ape, Eric went into the adjoining animal room.

Covered with long, orange wispy hair, the great ape looked up momentarily, then returned to contemplating a toe and picking at an ear.

Eric returned and leveled an anesthesia-gun at the ape's flank. With a pop, the jetstream of liquid penetrated the beast's skin. The animal looked down quizzically and slowly toppled over into almost a fetal position.

Breathing heavily and perspiring somewhat, Eric hoisted the orangutan onto the surgical module and quickly cannulated a vein in the animal's forearm into which an oxygen-enriched nutrient began to seep. Eric covered the ape with a sterile green sheet and rolled the portable module into the surgical suite.

"That cadaver is doing fine," said Jesse from across the room: lights from a computer bank flashed.

"Good. . .let's get these electrodals attached. While I'm getting this telemetry wiring untangled, you set the linear temperature programmer for a decrease of one degree per minute, leveling at twenty-seven degrees Centigrade."

"Yes sir, one degree per minute."

While Eric was rearranging the many orange and green and blue electrodal wires, Jesse lowered the orangutan's body temperature. Then, while his assistant was carefully shaving patches of scalp with a sonic depilator, Eric applied the electrodals to the animal's head. The fruity odor of the electrodal telemetrical lubricant permeated the room and, while not exactly nauseating, the smell was most unpleasant.

Not much time had passed until the simian head was covered with wires that led up to a panel across the room.

"What's the temperature?"

"Leveled at twenty-seven," replied Jesse.

"Very well, seal off this area!"

They went outside, and while Jesse sealed the pneumatic doors, Eric sat himself at the master control. He first touched a series of levers. A light panel jumping to life signaling that the surgical suite was now under completely aseptic conditions.

All that remained was to activate an unimportant-looking microswitch. Aluminum iodide memory banks pulsated, microdot tapes spun, and, in a matter of a few minutes, the entirety of the animal's memory responses were stored in the matrix of the computer's memory cores.

Noting that it was nine-fifty-five hours, Eric gave Jesse instructions to remove the monkey's brain and prepare it for reinsertion. Then he turned and stepped out of the laboratory, the door sliding closed behind him.

Using the gallium-arsenide laser, Jesse Horvitz easily removed the bones of the ape's skull. The laser device had a built-in sensor that allowed the burning beam to cut only through the bone portion, leaving the delicate meninges intact over the orangutan's brain. He dropped the domed, hemispherical skullcap into a beaker of warm nutrient and attached several gassing hoses, then proceeded to isolate the major arteries in the neck that led up to the monkey's brain, connecting them to a maintainance device that would keep cold nutrient broth, supplemented with an anti-coagulant, running through the isolated brain. It was a relatively easy procedure to sever the spinal cord and the cranial ganglia. Soon, the perfused brain lay in its bath of bubbling brine.

Jesse went over to the televisor.

"Seven, four, two, seven. ,."

A pause.

"Yes?"

"Anatole? Jesse here. Say, do you want a pair of ape adrenals? I have a fresh cadaver and I could remove them."

"I would certainly appreciate it Jesse."

"Fine, I'll freeze them for you. How about some multi-dimensional chess later this evening?"

"I think I could make it. What time?"

"Oh, about twenty-hundred at my quarters."

"Yes, that would be fine. See you then, and thanks."

Jesse made two great red arcs low on the cadaver's back with an ordinary crystal scapel. He held back the layers of outer skin with autoretractors, cut through the delicate-looking, yet very tough, peritoneum, quickly dissected the two glands from atop the kidneys, and put them in a shiny aluminum tube. Setting it in the freezing compartment, he mentally noted that he would label the tube later, but, of course never did. The remainder of the animal was tossed like a rag doll into an opening that appeared in the floor at the touch of a phobosensor. The orangutan vaporized in the greenish iridescent light of the positron stream.

Jesse checked the perfusing brain, took a sample of the media for future biophysical determinations, cleaned up the laboratory a little and then relaxed with a beaker of hot coffee.

Standing in front of the urinal, Eric chuckled to himself as he thought of the ancient adage about more than three shakes and you were playing with yourself. His urine was instantly vaporized by the pulse field.

Eric's mind wandered as he thought of the coming committee meeting. The committee was in charge of organizing and administering Oleandre University. This was the first meeting and several general ideas were to be discussed. There were four other committee members aside from himself; and the meeting would be held via the telescanner hookup while each was in their respective quarters. Harvey McMaster, head of the Linguistics Section, had been appointed interim chairman.

Seating himself in the reclining black chair and making sure he had a pad of celucel sheets handy and that the telescanner was properly focused on him, Eric pushed the green panel in the arm of the chair as the digits of his watch clicked off ten-hundred hours.

Immediately, the color televisor screen in front of him brightened and then divided into four sections. McMaster, Lee Fields and Rheinhardt Schmidt were already in place, but one portion of the screen showed an empty room cluttered with papers and celucel tapes. Presently, the entrance opened and in stumbled Benedict Fu, fumbling for a moment with an armload of memory modules.

"So sorry to be late gentlemen," said Fu. He peered so closely into the telescanner lens that his image was hideously distorted.

"Let us begin then." McMaster's voice showed an obvious irritation with Fu's lack of punctuality. "Gentlemen, since I have been appointed interim chairman, I have prepared a general summary of *my* ideas on the structure of Oleandre University."

Of course, thought Eric, the son-of-a-bitch always has to be so damned efficient; first day in the reign of Harvey the Magnificent.

Harvey McMaster began: "Ours is not an easy undertaking. We have acquired a great responsibility which is not to be taken lightly. The very success of the Mission is dependent. . .and let me make this very clear. . .dependent on our being able to educate our brightest young minds to the epitome of reason. They must learn, through our example, to develop and nurture a love of knowledge and a love for their new heritage. . .the wisdom of Jason Oleandre and what he represented."

He paused as if awaiting applause, and then started again. "I suggest that we organize Oleandre University loosely based on classical Earth university concept. I have created six colleges within the university proper: The College of Socio-economics, The College of Creative Arts, The College of History and Neolinguistics, The College of Pure Physical Science, The College of Life Science, which will include medicine and clinical research, and finally, an innovation: The College of Applied and Interdisciplinary Study, which will of course, encompass the engineering sciences and the Bauhausian Institute. Any questions thus far?"

"Yes," said Rheinhardt Schmidt, "is there any estimation as to the maximum number of students, in all years and classifications, that will be able to attend?"

"I have some figures," Fu interjected. "If the University were to open in six months, there would be just over four thousand people eligible for training. I have estimated that, minimally, a faculty of two hundred will be needed. According to my manpower survey, we are in good condition in the physical sciences, particularly in pure physics and astronomy, and adequate in all other disciplines except sociology and parapsychology. It would seem the Alliance took quite a toll in these latter areas. Perhaps we can fill some of the gaps with overlapping appointments. For example, Eric, you would have a joint appointment as Professor of Neurosciences and Professor of Behavior."

"Yes, I'd be damn happy to. In fact, I was going to suggest it. But *full* professor? I never rose above the rank of instructor at Free University. Professor. . .hot damn!"

"And, I trust, the rest of you would be willing to hold similar positions," McMaster announced, in a tone allowing no one the opportunity to refuse, and as if the whole idea was his in the first place.

All nodded.

After about forty minutes of similar dialogue, McMaster attempted to close the meeting.

"So, if we are all agreed, that curriculum should generally follow that of Earth Free University, and that the subcommittee chairmen know their assignments, I propose to adjourn this meeting until a week from today at the same time. Of course, a recording has been made of this meeting and copies will be sent to each committee member and a permanent record set in the central retrieval banks. If that is all, I bid this, the first meeting of the Committee on Oleandre University, closed."

The screen went blank.

Thank Christ that's over, Eric thought. The organization of Oleandre University is an important task, but that damn McMaster is too smug. He wouldn't be so cock-sure if he knew how close he came to being excluded from the Mission and exterminated, for there were and are, those who claim he was more than sympathetic to the Alliance.

Eric Senka gave the combination air pillow and sonic

temple massager a kick across the room. "God *damn*it," he grumbled, and went into the laboratory.

The greyish white brain lay regally in the beaker of frothing nutrient solution. Many brightly colored sutures marked areas that were to be matched up with similar threads inside the now empty skull of the receptor cadaver, which now lay on a gleaming table and covered with green, disposable surgical cloth. All that was visible was the empty skull covered with a transparent bag and a bare, but hairy arm. Attached to the arm was an arterio-venous shunt to the life-support console. The great ape's chest moved effortlessly up and down under the module's control and its heart beat perfectly.

All was in readiness.

"How's it going Jesse-me-lad?"

"Excellent. No trouble. The old fellow's temp is twenty-seven...heart and respiration stabilized; acid-base balance: normal. I just checked the spinal fluid glyoxyase and its up a little, just borderline high-normal."

"And the clotting time?"

"Thirteen minutes."

"All right, give it an injection of a hundred micrograms of polyinositol sulfate, and give it intramuscularly. That will form a pool and allow the drug to diffuse slowly into the orangutan and *should* keep his clotting time stabilized."

"Yes sir."

Eric completed a circuit, and the energy unit moved down from the ceiling. Its conical nose caught the light from the blinking computer and reflected it in a pulsating rainbow around the room. The iridium laser micro-beam was adjusted by computer to his precise specifications, and was much more delicate than the gallium-arsenide laser Jesse used to remove the brain.

Keeper of essence, organizer of thought, the initiator of all volition, the brain had been removed from the primordial ooze and laid loosely in the open cavity of the orangutan's skull. Eric matched up several of the colored sutures and tied them off. This made a primitive connection of brain to body. Now, working via a magnifying televisor, Eric pulled up a tiny, fragile white thread of neural tissue, a descending neuron, and touched it to several points on the severed spinal column. When a certain pattern, indicating the proper connection, appeared on the edge of the scanner, he welded the neuron in place with the laser beam. This procedure was reproduced many hundreds of times in the next five hours. Finally, when the spinal cord rehabilitated and all the cranial nerves were reunited, Eric replaced the meninges, sealing them with a wide, hyperbolic blast from the laser. The bone of the skull was set back and the flaps of the scalp thermosealed together. After waiting a few minutes, the life support system was disconnected and all metabolic monitors proclaimed that the new brain was perfectly guiding its body's autonomic functions.

"Jesse, arrange to keep him under light anesthesia for several days and feed him I.V. until recovery is complete."

It would be several days until the ape had sufficiently recovered from the surgical trauma, and Eric would be able to evaluate the success of the transplant.

The ape that had received the brain transplant had been taught a simple task: to avoid shock by pressing a red button. The long-term memory of this function was etched in the myriad isomeric sequences of the brain. Now, the molecular memory had been converted into electrical impulses stored in the banks of Eric's computer. Then, the brain itself had been removed and discarded as if it were diseased; and the brain of a young orangutan, electrically stripped of all but its basal functions, was reprogrammed with the recorded data including the memory of the shock-avoidance. Eric's theory was, that the new brain would exhibit the shock-avoidance pattern of the old. A transplant of mind and memory. It was certainly plausible; but only time could reveal its practicality.

It was a few minutes after fifteen-hundred hours when Eric Senka removed his surgical helmet and shut down the laser power source. He flopped down into a chair in front of a desk covered with data tapes, papers and calculators.

"We did a good job on that one," he said, wiping the back of his wrist over his perspiring forehead. "Damn good. Some coffee, Jesse?"

"Sure, Dr. Senka."

"You get it, OK?"

Jesse poured the dark brew from the gleaming reservoir that was powered by a tiny, almost invisible, pellet of Plutonium-238. The atomic coffee perculator would run fifty years on the milligram of the decaying isotope.

The coffee was strong and black, reminding Eric of the expresso he used to buy in his student days. This avenue of thought led him to address Jesse Horvitz: "Jesse, you can have the rest of the day off — what little there is left of it. But first, I have something to tell you. In a few months, you will work for me only half a day."

Jesse's face screwed up into a contortion of obvious displeasure.

"No, no, it's nothing like *that*," said Eric, "the University will be opening soon, and I'll be happy to sponsor you."

"Really? That's great. . .hot shit. . .I mean, thank you Dr. Senka."

"Not at all, don't get feeling too full of piss and protons. I have selfish motives. You have real talent, but you need discipline. If you apply yourself, you could make really important contributions."

Jesse merely nodded unbelievingly, for he had long ago resigned himself to a lifetime as a laboratory assistant.

"Furthermore," Eric continued, "since you have no parents

and if I'm to sponsor you, you'll be *my* responsibility. Now, I'm willing to take you on only if you're willing to work hard. Do I make myself clear?"

"Yes sir. You'd never regret it sir. I'd work my bloody ass off. . .I mean. ,."

"Bloody ass is certainly an apt description. Now get your tail out of here! I have an early dinner engagement."

"With Dr. McCartney?" Jesse asked, in a tone which indicated that Eric's interest in her was more than platonic.

"Yes, as a matter of fact. . .if it's any of your damn business. And what's the implication of *that* tone of voice?"

"Oh, please, Dr. Senka, the way you look at her," Jesse replied. He tried to suppress a laugh as he went through the door and the air screen energized behind him.

It's preposterous, thought Eric.

Eric showered slowly and, after drying himself in a hot air blast, flicked a tiny micro-switch at the base of the nozzle. A faint but high-pitched hum occurred, and then the sonic messager bombarded his body with pulses of sound waves that made his skin palpitate like a tiny, probing fingers. He could feel the tensions leave his body and mind. Pseudomonius had layed-out his best white slacks, polished silver boots, and a luminescent black tunic that bore the insignia of Scientific Officer.

He was pleased with his sartorial appearance; but something vaguely disturbed him. Eric would not accept it as nervousness, and dismissed the pain under his ribs as pangs of hunger.

Taking an express tram to Area 7 of E-Deck, he alighted about a hundred feet from Maggie's quarters. He walked up to the entrance, noting with pleasure the confident spring in his step. He passed his hand through the phobocepter and heard a soft distant buzzing from within.

"Yes?"

"Dr. Eric Carnovon Senka to see Dr. Margaret Ann McCartney, please. Summon your mistress servomechanin!"

"Oh Eric, you idiot," she laughed as the air curtain sprang open.

"Good evening madam. . .and how be ye lassie?"

"Marvelous, kind sir. But really, Eric, you're wonderful. Please come in; I've been so looking forward to this evening since our last meeting."

"As have I Maggie."

Her shear white sheath was transluscent when the light was behind her. Under this, Maggie wore a golden body-stocking and tan sandals. Her light brown hair was not tied up in the usual severe hairdo, but rather, hung softly and flowing over one shoulder.

"Sit down, Eric. How is your work going?"

"Fairly well. We finished a transplant today but won't know if we're successful for a few more days. . .but I'm. . .we're hopeful."

"Good, that deserves a toast. Vodkasyn?"

"Please, but very cold!"

Before raising the frosted elliptical glass to his lips, he said, "Oh, before I forget or drink too much — please Maggie — throw me out at twenty-two hundred. I have to be ready to pick up the Oleandre Probe by one-thirty hours."

"Well then, a double toast is in order: to your work *and* the rendezvous."

As the evening progressed and more iced vodka and the meal had been consumed their light conversation had turned to more serious dialogue: the terror of the Alliance. . .her husband's death. . .how the feminine emotion had wavered, then died within her. . .her fears of the future.

She had cried. He had touched her shoulder, then her hand. Her wet eyes had looked up into his. They were filled with loneliness and want. Her shaking hand had covered his.

"It's almost twenty-two hundred Maggie."

"I know."

"I *must* go now. . .I don't want to."

"Yes. . .yes, good night my darling," she said, softly pressing his hand a little tighter.

Eric Senka stepped into the passageway and did not hear the air curtain shut behind him. He rode the tram back to his quarters unaware of the people around him.

Having quickly dressed, he emerged in a standard silver-leaf, pressurized ExtraVehicular-Activity suit. With his priority clearance, he procured a tram that transported him directly to the Hoverport. Flashing red letters suspended in the corridor read: EYE SHIELDS IN PLACE.

The face of Commander Hayakawa filled the televisor screen; Eric could see the master control center behind Seth, with personnel busily going about their duties.

An airway marked DIGITAL SPINOUT CHAMBER-43 loomed ahead. This would transport him from Oleandre's moving interior to the airless, weightless waste that was its surface.

Eric Senka stepped through the entranceway and into the multicolored, pulsating transportoscrambler. Instantly, his mind began to float, and his body rushed toward destination.

CHAPTER THREE

Emerging from the Exterior Transition Chambers into the cold, pale starlight, Eric Senka was slightly disoriented in his weightlessness. He could feel the tiny microgrippers on the soles of his insulated boots interlock with their counterparts that covered the entire surface of the launching area. Having never got used to null-gravity movement, he literally had to will each step, clumsy as they were. After a few paces and finding that he did not have to look at his feet any longer, Eric moved toward the ultrahovercraft that stood in its magnetic launching pad.

Bathed in white light at the entrance to the small silver ship stood Harlin Willoughby, similarly dressed and with one foot resting jauntily on one of the ultrahovercraft's ion propulsion pods. Eric waved, and in the process lost his balance, but checked himself before falling over completely.

"Well, Senka, are you well prepared?"

"Of course. I've been briefed. By the way, this is all very exciting. . .sort of like being in on history, you know."

"You are not merely being *in* on history, you're helping to *make* history. . .we all are."

The ultrahovercraft was a globe about twenty feet in diameter. On the end of one axis protruded a transparent bubble from which the craft was flown. At the opposite end was a cluster of four elliptical pods which were the ion propulsion engines. The ultrahovercraft was not designed to penetrate atmospheres, but to cruise in the endless vacuum of space. . .thus its nonaerodynamic construction. Several antennae protruded from orifices in its side and a gold foil disc spun silently in a mounting on the port side.

Willoughby and Senka stood on a circular platform beneath the open underbelly, Harlin's fist resting on a suspended control box. Upon passing his hand through a sensor beam, the platform quietly and without the slightest jerk, moved upward, bringing them into the ship and simultaneously sealing the cabin. The internal environment system immediately energized and pressurized the cabin, permitting the crew members to remove their helmets.

"I wish they'd get that permanent boarding dock completed so we wouldn't have to wear pressure suits," said Willoughby. He was obviously irritated.

"They *are* a damn nuisance."

Willoughby activated the power systems and a maze of control panels blinked in multicolored array. As the propulsion units slowly lifted the ultrahovercraft from its berth, the televisor on the command module in front of Willoughby flashed to life. On it was the image of the Commander.

"Our sensors have you on 'LOCK IN' and your course projection looks fine. You may start your acceleration pattern any time."

"Yes, Seth," replied Harlin Willoughby as he ran a program into the onboard computer. Instantly the ultrahovercraft's speed began to increase at a rate that would eventually level off and stablize at twenty-thousand miles per second. The ion engines had finished their pulse, and the ship seemed to drift. Eric looked back to see the now dull spheroid of Oleandre fading in the distance. . .fading in both size and brilliance. He could detect the pulsating curvature of the antimatter storage base near the ship's engines, and, up ahead of Oleandre, the shimmering, yet transparent shield of antiprotons. As one exceeded velocities of a thousand miles per second, the danger of collision increased dramatically, almost exponentially, as one approached the speed of light. Even at fifteen-thousand miles per second, less than one tenth the craft's limit, impact with a microscopic grain of interstellar dust would generate enough energy to vaporize Oleandre and its occupants into a jellied mass of subatomic particles. The RAM, as it was popularly called, a pocket of antiprotons held in a magnetic field that continually danced ahead of the ship, instantly annihilated any piece of matter that lay in its path. The ultrahovercraft, too, was equipped with a microRAM.

Commander Hayakawa's voice crackled over the audio monitor again. "Gentlemen, we received the electromagnetic signal from the first probe about ten minutes ago, and I am now having it fed into your computer, and into your audio monitors."

A faint but steady whining was heard inside the ultrahovercraft, and Eric felt strangely uneasy as if an unwanted noise, a remnant of the past was accosting him.

"Are you receiving the signal?" asked the Commander.

"Yes," replied Willoughby, who was a very precise person, always using a minimum of dialogue.

"Now I will begin to return the code that will nullify the probe's defensive systems, and that should activate a laser beam to give you visual contact. Do not, DO NOT, attempt a rendezvous until that visual contact is confirmed, because the probe may be armed with missiles and I don't want to get you vaporized."

Thanks, you're really a prince, thought Eric.

Commander Seth Hayakawa produced a small platinum key that hung on a brown hide thong around his neck. Placing it in a slot in a control panel, a high-pitched humming occurred; and when it ceased, he turned the key sharply. A single indicator glowed. Then he spoke into the audio receptor. The series of number sequences had been given to him personally by Jason Oleandre.

Memory banks and tapes spun into action as the proper code was transmitted. And, although they were eight million miles away and could not see it, a faint but steady red pulsation began to emanate from an aging metallic shell that circled the airless, barren and freezing rock. . .dark Pluto.

Traveling at this speed, they would reach their destination in just under seven minutes. Eric activated the Orbital Tangential Mixing System that would perfectly match the velocity and orbit of the ultrahovercraft with that of the probe. The sensors quickly picked up the probe's signal and automatically took over the ultrahovercraft's controls. Looking out the oval port, Willoughby was able to spot a flashing red point in the distance, as bright as a second magnitude star.

The ship was perfectly inserted into orbit just behind and a little below the First Oleandre Probe.

Willoughby touched the appropriate sensors that nulled the microRAM and put the ship back under his control; and slowly, very slowly, the ultrahovercraft closed the distance between it and the apparatus suspended ahead in the starry background. The probe appeared to be a cylinder about four feet in length and a foot in diameter. From the end facing them, came the intense crimson laser pulsation. On three sides were sets of panels, equally spaced, that expended outward like fins and seemed to be covered with small squares of crystalline material. Probably solar power cells, thought Eric.

The cabin lights were dimmed. Willoughby was outlined by the eerie greenish glow of the instrumentation. Outside the port hung the Oleandre Probe, and beyond, the paradoxically dark yet light-filled universe. Willoughby seemed a spectre among them.

An opening appeared in the underside of their craft and the probe was gently moved inside. Eric quickly repressurized the storage module, while Willoughby contacted Commander Hayakawa.

"Pickup completed, Seth, and. . .wait. . .one moment please."

Eric notified Harlin that a quick internal scan of the probe in the lower compartment showed no appreciable emission of radiation. Although the continuing pulse of the weak laser beam was creating a rise in temperature, it was nothing critical. Willoughby conveyed these facts to the Commander.

"Good. Excellent, Harlin. I will meet you and Senka at the Hoverport. McMaster will be with me. . .no one else."

Harlin shot a puzzled look at Eric.

"Why the secrecy?" asked Eric.

"What's that?" said the Commander.

"Nothing, Seth," replied Willoughby. "We will come under your control as we approach to within five thousand miles of Oleandre."

"Excellent. . .HAYAKAWA OUT. . .OLEANDRE TRANSMISSIONS INTERNAL."

Willoughby executed a directional velocity shift and the ultrahovercraft made a smooth, yet rather abrupt, turn and quickly accelerated to fifteen thousand miles per second. A steady blue stream of intense light pulsed from the ion propulsion pods as the power cells sped them homeward.

Although he could see nothing out of the port other than the stars of the constellation — Scorpius, with Antares shining as a brilliant ruby in the arachnid's heart — Eric knew Oleandre was somewhere in the field. He switched the telescanner to high magnification, and a dark disc appeared. The distance readout was 8,600. At five thousand miles out, Willoughby decelerated to a hundred miles per second and, at a thousand miles, to one mile per second. Oleandre Control then maneuvered the ship clear of the antimatter fields, and settled it softly onto the deck of the Hoverport.

It was several minutes until they had put on their EVA-suits and the hatch of the craft was slid open. The surface of the Hoverport was devoid of spectators except for McMaster's servomechanin.

Humph, thought Eric, some royal welcome this is. They could see the images of McMaster and Commander Hayakawa still inside the Interior Transition Chambers.

As they sat in the tram that carried them toward Willoughby's laboratory, with the bulky servomechanin clumsily holding the probe with magnetic grapplers, Eric spoke to Seth Hayakawa. "Why all the cloak and dagger silence? I would have thought this to be a time of some rejoicing."

"Under ordinary circumstances, I couldn't agree with you more," Hayakawa began, "but these are extraordinary times. Even though things appear to be functioning smoothly, there's a great deal of psychic tension on Oleandre. If the probe should have nothing to reveal, or have malfunctioned, I am not at all sure the people would take it well."

Commander Hayakawa's fears were reinforced when the primitive tape-modules from inside the probe proved to contain nothing but nonsensical mathematical symbols and a rather crude version of the "Anthem of the Alliance." The Commander, Willoughby and Eric Senka were silent. But McMaster, who had become quite pale could only wail, "Goddamn! What in blazes are we going to do now? Ooooh Jesus!"

"You see what I meant," said Hayakawa turning to Eric.

"Yes I do," he replied, but deep in the substance of his soul he felt about the same as McMaster.

He walked out of Harlin's laboratory, lit up a pipe, and turned for a moment to look back. To the left of the entrance was an etched platinum plate that read: HARLIN K. WILLOUGHBY — APPLIED KINOPHYSICS. He saw the sign; but it did not register in his fearful mind.

Willoughby and McMaster worked frantically all morning trying to extract some clue from the probe's contents, but to no avail. Commander Hayakawa was called away to deal with a technical problem in Oleandre Control. Even though only a comparative few knew that the probe had been picked up, *one* knew that a vital message had not been obtained. At the lack of any official announcement, however, rumors began to circulate and, in this case, the rumors were undeniably true.

Eric paced about his quarters, his mind unconscious of his body's actions. He twirled a communications wand in his fingers, felt the texture of the walls, touched the stem of each pipe in its rack, thrust his hand into the humid beaker of tobacco and let it filter through his fingers, not even noticing the aroma. In his mind, he relived the pickup of the probe. . .Willoughby's outline against the port, Antares, the solar panels, the ruby laser beam. . .the. . .the SOLAR PANELS! It hit him like a thermonuclear hyperpile. Eric Senka ran for the communications console, shaking his head and muttering, "Of course, how simple!"

"Harlin. . .Harlin. . ."

"ERROR. . .YOU ARE IN ERROR. . .PLEASE USE CORRECT. . ."

"Oh Jesus," Senka said, punching out the correct communications code.

"Willoughby," said a tired and distraught voice.

"Harlin, damn it man! I have it. . .be right down."

"But. . ."

Eric had no time to wait for the tram. He sprinted down the bright curved corridor and burst in on Willoughby and Harvey McMaster.

"Eric, what. . .," said Harlin; and McMaster simultaneously grumbled, "Senka, what in hell!"

"Listen," said Eric out of breath, "it's in the panels. They're solar cells, right?"

"Yes, but. . ."

"Don't you see, once the probe is out as far as a Plutonian orbit, solar cells are of no use. The Sun is too far away."

"By Sargon's testicles! You may be right," shouted McMaster, as if *he* suggested it.

And it was indeed true. The tapes had been intended to confuse, should the probe fall into the clutches of the Alliance. Jason Oleandre had made certain that his message would come only into the hands of the creative ones. He had known that it would take ingenious, and desperate men to discover the code on the solar vanes.

It seemed that every twentieth solar cell was askew in its bracket. A code was embedded in the lattice of its nobelium-isoprenoid crystals. It took about six hours for the molecule's asymmetric vibrations to be scanned by the fourth generation sesquianalogue computer, deciphered, and recorded into the printed language that spewed forth on a celucel ribbon.

"It's not much of a message I'm afraid. . .gives details for some rather sophisticated weaponry. . .and the celestial coordinates of the second probe."

Commander Seth Hayakawa put down the slender strip of celucel. A look of distress spread across his face.

"Seth?" Eric's voice had an anxious tone.

"I am concerned, gentlemen, and do not mind admitting it. If the location of the Third Oleandre Probe is not contained in the second, I am afraid the Mission is in real danger of failure. I could never say this publicly, but some instructions from Jason Oleandre were lost in transmission during the nuclear holocausts on Earth. Some of you knew this. . ."

"So? What *is* the point," interrupted McMaster.

"The Third Probe is to contain the Powers Equation. Without it, we shall never be able to attain the capability of intergalactic travel."

It's very clear, Eric Senka thought to himself, that we're. . .the Mission. . .is in serious trouble. The concept of the Oleandre is invalid if we cannot attain the ability to travel quickly across this galaxy to other galaxies. The Third Oleandre Probe contains the Powers Equation that holds the basic formula for speeds beyond that of light. Without it, we might as well give up the Mission. Traveling lesser speeds would take generations merely to cross the local stellar system. The essence of the Mission, to establish a base of human creativity in another galaxy and then branch out to contact other life forms if they exist, is negated if the Third Probe is lost.

"Goddamn the fuckin' Alliance," Eric said outloud to himself, and looked around sheepishly.

Luckily no one happened in the corridor at the time, and as he walked slowly past the entrance to the Bibliophilic Research Institute, his mind continued to wander.

"Damn them" is right, he thought, they and their militant technology. They *had* to have their AOM system. The Anti Orbiting Missile system had been built by both sides in the early nineteen eighties. It had been tested only in a limited sense; and neither of the antagonists had a dependable system when the saturation raids of nineteen eighty-eight simultaneously devasted western Canada and parts of the Gobi Desert. And the cost! God, not in lives, so much, but how the economy suffered! It eventually cost the Alliance over nine hundred billion Freedom Dollars for a "thick" AOM system that never really worked. Perhaps the military never really expected the system to perform, but with all the output, the citizenry could feel safe and protected, what with the Asian claims of perfecting the neutron device.

If only the people could have risen with the indignation they had felt in the early nineteen seventies, when they pressured the American government into stopping construction of the primitive antiballistic missile network that was meant to counter the first crude Chinese missiles.

Eric believed *that* is what gave the Alliance its real power. With the population's acceptance of the AOM defense system came public apathy and the rise of the military class. When the common man realized what had transpired, it was too late, for the private citizen, as such, had ceased to exist. The State existed for itself; and the individual existed only by decree of the State. The Alliance and its ultramilitary counterpart, the K'uang Fong, the Furious Winds, had become all powerful in their respective territories. . .

He practically bowled over Jesse Horvitz coming around a corner.

"Dr. Senka. . .well. . .it's just come over the televisor. . .the Probe has been deciphered. Great news isn't it?"

"Yes, yes, of course," replied Eric sharply. "Let's get on with the work at hand." They moved down a short lateral corridor to their laboratory.

The orangutan with the new brain seemed to have made good progress toward a total recovery. It moved about slowly, but freely, in its small restraining cage. It was being fed intravenously in the scalp by long spring-coiled tubes to permit movement. A single green capsule covered the top of its head. Telemetry of vital functions showed normal responses. . .as normal as one could expect after the most radical of neurosurgery. Automatic samplers made forty basic biochemical analyses of the blood, urine, feces and cerebrospinal fluid. This was performed without fail every fifteen minutes. A wonder of miniaturization, the NKVD-27 needed only twenty microliters of fluid to make its determinations. A continuous flow of metabolic data was fed into the computer storage banks, and the analysis instantly flashed on a visual monitor: GLUCOSE-110*****LDH(7)-205*****GLYOXYLASE(CSF)-003. . .

"Well," said Eric, "he seems to be coming along."

"Splendidly, sir."

"I think he'll be ready for testing tomorrow, Jesse, so get here as early as possible."

Looking toward the weary ape, Eric said, "You may become a very famous fellow. I believe you should have a name. Any suggestions, Mister Horvitz?"

Jesse pondered the question a minute and then replied, "Aristophanes."

"Aristophanes! Excellent, Aristophanes, it is."

The night had come quickly and Eric dined alone in his quarters. Maggie had been detained to make some important computations since her computer time was designated, this time, in the evening hours. Accepting this stoically, he made a few short entries in his journal and settled back in his black lounging chair, which he called his sleeping chair, and listened to a recording of W. B. Yeats' lesser poems that Jonathan Fischer had been able to obtain for him. They were rather old, scratchy tapes as they had not yet been entered in the Great Receptacle of Knowledge. These poems were considered minor works at best. But the verses were among Eric's favorites, and the Irish brogue flowed easily into his consciousness, numbing it. Gentle waves of sleep overcame him, and thrust him into deeper and deeper substrata of sleep.

When Eric awoke, it was after three hundred hours, and without removing his garments, he staggered to the bed.

Arising at precisely six hundred and eating a quick breakfast, Eric made his way into the laboratory. He glanced at several instruments. Crossing the room, he chanced to look into the next chamber. . .the sterile animal room. He froze. He charged into the little room.

"Oh Jesus," he shouted, "NO!"

The great orange ape was crumpled over at a strange and unnatural angle. Its fur was dry and matted, and a large patch of black blood lay in crusty clots at the base of its skull. Hemorrhage was Eric's first thought.

The monitoring system had come to a halt when there was no more fluid to sample and had burned itself out.

"Goddamn it to bloody hell," he said disgustedly, almost

vomiting with frustration, "daughter of an effing bitch!" With
this, he threw an empty beaker across the laboratory and it hit
the wall in a shower of glass that reverberated like a distant
Martian thunderclap. Then, seeing the humor of his tantrum,
he thought, "thunderclap": a Zeusian social disease. . .oh
Jesus, that's bad, bad, you perverted devil, Senka.

Eric laughed out loud and, feeling somewhat better,
investigated the situation. It was, as he had suspected, an
intracranial hemorrhage that had killed the orangutan.

Later, after Jesse had arrived, they autopsied the monkey
and found that one of the surgical vascular connections had
loosened, leading to the rapid and fatal loss of blood. Eric
immediately decided that if his experimentation was to
continue, the first thing that had to be done was to fabricate
an alarm module, connected to some kind of life-sustaining
system. He would give Jesse this assignment and a week to
complete it. Meanwhile, he would prepare other animals,
check the breeding progress of the orangutan colony, and set
up further follow-up experiments.

He would also want to devote more time to Maggie. Much
more time.

Jesse Horvitz, though he was very young and inexperienced,
had done his job with great skill and precision. Not only had
his device been constructed to adjust respiration, cardiac
function and electroencephalographic regulation in an
emergency, but he had gotten some portable alarms that were
compact enough to put in a tunic sleeve pocket. They could be
conveniently carried anywhere in Oleandre or on its surface.

These alarms did not merely monitor heartbeat: it had been
found, more than a decade before that the level of a certain
enzyme in the blood plasma was a sensitive indicator of
metabolic integrity. It was of little diagnostic use, since the
slightest variation in *any* bodily function affected this

enzyme's blood level. This was, however, just what Jesse Horvitz needed. The ape's plasma was continually monitored and if any of the monkey's metabolic functions changed, it would be reflected in the enzyme, and the alarm would sound.

Extremely proud and defensive of having found a practical use for a hitherto useless and academic technique, Jesse presented the HOLIMOR (Horvitz-Life-Monitor-and-Resuscitation) system to Eric on a morning when Senka was feeling poorly due to a bout with intestinal flu.

He had ordered an emetic, but Pseudomonius had brought an ordinary FLUROSELZER tablet that made him feel even worse, which he thought was well-nigh impossible. After curtly dismissing Jesse Horvitz, an act which he later regretted and eventually apologized for, Eric Senka's FLUROSELZERed miseries made him think about, of all things, fluoride: Fluoride, Goddamned stuff. Fluoride, hmm? It's a good example of Alliance government regulations. He remembered reading about the stink that was made about water fluoridation in the early nineteen seventies, after it was proven that a definite link existed between fluoride content of drinking water and bone neoplasia in children. Hell of a stink. So, to pacify the damned right-wingers, the government outlawed all fluoridation. To replace it, however, their Advisory Committee on National Science clandestinely added cobalt! Damn idiots! The Alliance saved face, though. It executed most of the clowns responsible for the cobalt infusions, and most of the ultraright-wing was put away as undesirables. . .

The next day, after Eric's head and bowels had cleared, and following his apology to Jesse, he resumed his research with renewed vigor. A new set of animals was prepared, and the brains of the first select pair of orangutans were quickly processed. Even the programming tasks went more smoothly than expected.

The transplantation of a five-year-old brain into the aging anthropoid named Aristophanes II, had been accomplished without a mishap. Even though Horvitz's life-maintaining and alarm systems functioned perfectly — it had been critically tested in an emergency situation earlier — it was not really needed. The ape's recovery from the surgical trauma was uneventful and the reprogramming of its new brain with its old mind was complete.

Several days were allocated for preliminary testing while the orangutan was still in restraint. The beast, covered with wispy auburn hair, was able to feed itself, scratch (which is very important to an orangutan), and was generally aware of its surroundings. Routine neurological tests were all normal, and even the delicate Strovinowski Reflex Arcs were intact.

On the morning of the fourth postoperative day Eric was in the laboratory well before six-hundred. He had not been able to sleep at all that night because of his anticipation of the coming tests.

Jesse came in shortly after with a nervous "morning, sir."

"You here so early?"

"Yes Dr. Senka. . .couldn't sleep."

"Neither could I. . .kept wanting to rush in here to check on him. Well, let's get on with it. If we're unsuccessful we'll have all day to get rip-roaring drunk. Or you can go and make vengeful perverted love to that little girl with the more than ample bosom I've seen you with lately."

"What?" Crimson was spreading across Jesse's cheeks.

"Never mind. You set the chromatic sequencer and *I'll* bring in the illustrious Aristophanes the Second."

Jesse rolled a portable light panel over to the training module and made certain telemetrical connections. Meanwhile, Eric carried the docile orangutan in his arms, the monkey clutching him lovingly and quizzically looking around. Sitting him gently in a sturdy, straight-backed chair of gray metal Eric checked the bandage cap that swathed the ape's skull. Through the transparent wrappings could be seen the deep purple cuts, crosshatched by tiny red scars made by the thermal suture device. Assuring himself that all was in readiness, they began.

Before the experiment, this orangutan had been taught to read a certain light pattern that was flashed on the oscillating light board in front of it. The pattern was a four color sequence displayed at certain intervals in an otherwise continuous flow of light changes. When the monkey perceived the pattern, he had learned to depress a simple lever. Only after he had seen the correct pattern and pushed the lever was he rewarded by an electrical stimulation to his neurosexual brain centers. It was elementary conditioning coupled with a complicated perception-recognition sequence.

Now they would see if this memory was transferred into the new brain by the computer.

All the lights were dimmed in the laboratory and the shadows danced in eerie exchanges of color as the light panels throbbed in front of the beast's eyes.

For at least two hours the patterns were presented, with only random response from the subject. But when Eric had just about convinced himself that he had expected too much, Jesse called out from his seat at the telemetry integrator that responses were coming in sets of two. Soon the first triplet and correct response occurred. Of course, no reward was given, for the reward was to be remembered. Aristophanes the Second ejaculated. After that first remembrance of the past neuro-sexual reward, the ape registered an abnormally high number of significant responses. The computer proclaimed that Aristophanes' reactions were statistically valid.

It was obvious that the memory of a past event had been successfully transferred electrically into a new brain.

Almost with a mist in his eyes and his heart rebounding off his ribcage, Eric walked over to the entrance of his quarters and called Pseudomonius. The mechanical wizard whirred into motion, and Eric ordered two double, very dry martinis.

"YES DOCTOR SENKA...BY ALL MEANS SIR," croaked the mechanical voice.

After they had taken a great sip of the cold, volatile brew, Eric turned to Jesse and said, "This is a great day, lad, savor it! It's not often that a scientific breakthrough of this magnitude occurs. Think of the ramifications. Damn!"

"I have, sir, and I must really tell you how exciting it's been working with you and how much...well...how much I admire you Dr. Senka."

"Nonsense," replied Eric sharply; but he was secretly proud to be the subject of this hero worship.

"We will attempt to repeat this work?"

"Of course; we must be sure. But I'm confident enough to send out a preliminary report to the Central Coordinating Staff right now. Why don't you take the rest of the day off, even a couple of days: you've earned it. Don't worry, I'll fudge your time-input tape."

"Are you sure?"

"Oh hell, yes. I'll clean up here. You go ahead. Go look up that little Rafferty girl?"

Upon returning Aristophanes II to his restraining cage, giving it an extra ration of fruit and patting it approvingly on the flank, Eric walked to the communicatons console and said, "three...zero...one...seven."

Maggie McCartney was busy making some preliminary calibrations on the infrared scanner. The visual hookup to the prime focus of the Rasai telescope on Oleandre's surface pulsated with the rhythmic glow of the visible pulsar in the Crab nebula. The three-hundred-centimeter Rasai instrument, which was a combination of the old Maksutov optics coupled with Rasai's holographic etching technique, compensated perfectly with Oleandre's movement. Only when a rapid acceleration was made, which rarely happened, were any perturbations in the telescope noticed.

Maggie was so involved with her calculations that when the televisor buzzed she practically jumped from her chair.

"Yes," she answered in a tone that indicated that her mind was still on her work.

"You have an errored connection," replied the exaggerated nasal tone.

"What? I made no call. . .Oh Eric, for God's sake!"

"I call to give you great tidings of joy that shall come to. . ."

"Oh Eric, the experiment. It was a success?"

"Yes, isn't it great? I'm really excited: this is an important breakthrough."

"Oh, it *is*."

"Dinner at my quarters?"

"Of course, but what about this: I'm getting nowhere with these calibrations today. Why don't you come up here. We could have some lunch or a late breakfast. Jonathan Fischer is giving a seminar this afternoon on some aspect of the decline of literature during the Alliance. I'm sort of interested in hearing him. Could we go?"

"I'd be delighted to accept, kind madam. And I shall have my loyal chromium butler prepare the dinner later. . .seriously Maggie, I'll be up in about twenty minutes."

"Good-bye Eric," she said softly, "and again, congratulations. I'm very happy for you."

Eric sent a short summary of the experiments to date to the Central Coordinating Staff, then changed into a maroon turtleneck shirt with light tan stretch slacks and dark brown boots. His paper-lab uniform was tossed in the positron disposer. Slipping all his ID cards into the pocket of the left sleeve and lighting an electric pipe, Eric Senka emerged from his quarters feeling better than he could ever remember. The smoke from the bowl of his metal pipe flowed in faint white swirling wisps ahead of him as he stepped onto the moving part of the corridor that ran one-way in a continuous belt. Back of space prohibited a two-way transporter; but it was circular so that if one really wanted a ride, you could eventually get to any part of the passage. This did not seem like much, but on upper levels, the corridors were many miles in circumference.

However, Eric rode only a minute, stepped off and into an Upper Level Tram, then caught an Express in the central tube to Sub-Deck Two on which Maggie's laboratory was situated.

Strolling leisurely around the hall that led to her lab, and feeling damn self-satisfied, he stopped to look into a large, cavernous room that was filled from deck to ceiling with huge tubes. They were filled with a greenish, opalescent fluid that bubbled and frothed.

This was the PRIME NOURISHMENT CENTER, or actually, centers, since twenty-five similar facilities were scattered throughout Oleandre. In these gurgling tanks literally billions of tiny photosynthetic algae lived in continuous culture. They were a mutant form, especially produced through a brilliant series of genetic manipulations by Akira Que Kishimoto, and equally brilliant molecular geneticist. These minute green plants, once inhabitants of the Earth's south China Sea, continually reproduced themselves at an increasing rate, and through the effects of the artificial "sunlight" provided by the nuclear engines, were able to produce more than a thousand times their normal amount of carbohydrate. The mature organisms were siphoned off and automatically processed into food by special servomechanins located deep in the bowels of Oleandre. After the green pigments were removed, a good grade of flour could be produced. Not only did the algae provide food, they were a major life-sustaining factor on the ship. The carbon dioxide exhaled by the human and other animal personnel all over the craft was carefully collected and bubbled into the algal broth, where it was utilized by the microorganisms. In the end, the

lgae gave off vital oxygen which was pumped throughout
)leandre. Since their metabolic rates were vastly increased,
hanks to Kishimoto's techniques, the algae gave off enough
oxygen to meet the needs of the entire animal population.
"here were, however, backup systems which could produce
oxygen electrochemically with nuclear energy; but since they
equired vast amounts of power, these devices would be used
only in an emergency.

Dr. Kishimoto, it was reported, was working on a method
of specific genetic mutation that would encourage the algae to
urnish a new type of hormonallipid process that would allow
hem to function "photosynthetically" without light. This
vould be a tremendous achievement for future generations in
erms of energy conservation.

If anything was to be worshipped with all one's soul, it was
he PRIME NOURISHMENT CENTER, for on it all life
lepended.

As he began to turn from the slotted window of polarized
ozmyglass, Eric chanced to see the shimmering reflection of
omeone approaching him from behind. It was Maggie.

"Well," she said in a tone of false anger, "I never expected
o be stood up by the likes of *you*!"

"Oh hell," he laughed, "I've just been. . .

"I can see exactly what you're doing. Being damn nosey
gain."

She took a quick look into the slot and said in complete
eriousness, "I just can't help being a little awed every time I
ook in there. So much depends on Kishimoto's system
unctioning perfectly."

A zany look appeared on Eric's face and one eye squinted
lightly.

"Pretty soon, you'll start bringing in a lamb to sacrifice or,
etter yet, a servomechanin which you'll place on
computerized altar, null it by depolarizing its motorans, and

toss it helplessly into the broth, you pagan! Or even better —
Jesus, this is marvelous — people will start paying homage t
the algae, trying to get special favors by sneaking them littl
vials of carbon dioxide. Fantastic!"

"Eric, my God, you're a madman," she laughed, and the
walked hand in hand down the corridor, not caring in the leas
who saw them.

Oleandre, in spite of the vastness of its facilities, lacke
certain things, among which was the aesthetic pleasure o
elegant dinning. Of course, this had almost disappeared durin
the time of the Alliance anyway, due to the war effort. In tha
period, one could obtain entertainment cards once a year
Even then, it was subject to strict regulation so that n
Alliance citizen would be exposed to softening decadence. /
privileged few, however, had been exempted from tha
provision; but only through the application of graft in th
right places.

Maggie and Eric ate the midday meal at one of the many
public food-dispensing units. They sat in a small booth an
ordered from the rather limited menu that flashed on a smal
televisor. Their selection was indicated by touching th
appropriate square on the screen, heat sensors picking up th
signal and, within a few minutes, a slot opened at the end o
the short table and their food came sliding out on a celuce
conveyor.

Maggie had ordered a hard roll and greens, that were grow
in the hydroponics astroagricultural facilities, while Eric ha
beer, a roll and liver paste, which was in limited supply since i
was prepared from the dead laboratory animals on board. N
one paid, since money had no particular value on Oleandre
However, they were required to put their ID cards through
computer niche when leaving, which aided planning for foo
logistics.

The theory of the Oleandre Mission made it clear that in

creative society such as this, the system could survive without capital. . .at least until a new and permanent home could be found. Oleandre did carry a vast supply of what Earthlings considered valuable commodities: diamonds, gold and platinum metal, plutonium, Malovium Alloy, pure interferon and others. These would be used to barter with other civilizations, if they existed, although one could only speculate as to what other beings valued. Perhaps some alien life forms would value oxygen or cellulose more than all the platinum in the universe. No one could tell.

"Would you like a sip of beer Maggie?"

"Yes, it looks good and cold for a change."

"It is, have some."

As he held the tall purple glass over toward her, Maggie's fingers brushed lightly over his knuckles. His eyes gazed far through her irises, penetrating her being. There was a long warm silence.

"When does Fischer's colloquium begin?" he finally asked, his voice cracking slightly.

Maggie glanced at the digital clock across the room. "In about twenty minutes."

The discussion by Jonathan Fischer was given in a small auditorium that held about a hundred people. It was situated inside a vast complex that housed the Great Receptacle of Knowledge.

The entrance to the Receptacle, as it was usually called, was an unimpressive aircurtain, and Maggie and Eric followed several other people toward the small auditorium, past banks of flashing lights and whirling tape reels. Servomechanins carrying reams of celucel sheets scurried about. Fischer's seminar was not expected to attract much of an audience since it was held at a busy time of the work day. However, when they arrived, Maggie and Eric were hard pressed to find seats. They eventually found two seats together in one high corner of the sloping room.

Each clear red plastic recliner was equipped with audio
devices that were connected to the main amplification system,
so that any discourse could easily be heard by all that were
present. There was no need for translation facilities since
English had been the "human" language for over five
decades. . .even K'uang Fong had spoken English most of the
time.

Jonathan Fischer emerged from an entrance at the front of
the room near the speaker's module. He was dressed in a
simple gray tunic of harsh looking cloth and walked very
mechanically.

Jonathan Fischer was totally and irreversibly blind. He had
been visionless since birth, never feeling the sensation of light
impinge upon his neural matter. Fischer was afflicted with
congenital neurogenetic cortical blindness, yet Jonathan
Fischer *could* see. He was able to walk into the room, proceed
to the speaker's area, look up into the audience and recognize
colleagues. This event of almost miraculous ramifications was
by now commonplace. If neurological science had not yet
been able to repair or replace neurons deep in the brain,
another branch of technology had made a wonderful
discovery. Beginning in the late nineteen sixties in diverse
academic circles, until the work culminated in The Institute of
Advanced Tactile Research, the discipline of tactile science
had been developing a device that mimicked vision.

On the inside of each thigh, Jonathan Fischer wore a small
maleable sheet of Malovium Metal upon which was sealed a
microcircuit-telemetry device. Resting on each ear was a
miniature telescanner transmitter which was the size of an
old-type cigarette filter. The telescanners picked up the actual
visual environment and transmitted it as tiny impulses of
pressure on Fischer's thigh. The sensitive area of his inner
thigh was thus actually able to record an image. . .various
pressures indicating contrasting shades of light and dark.
Fischer's brain was actually receiving a tactile image of the real

world. He was "seeing." He had spent over a thousand hours in training, learning to differentiate the various pressures, training his skin to become a keen receptor. He eventually learned to read, and the reading helped him to gain the skill in tactile perception that had enabled him to become one of the "Free" world's most authoritative bibliophiles.

The perfector of the Tactile Representation Unit or TRU, was William J. Starley who had, at age eighty, invented the method of mimicking depth perception. Each telescanner transmitter was led first to an image scrambler, and then to the thighs. Starley, who was then feeble and harmless, was executed as a state criminal by the Alliance for giving his device to the world. The Alliance had not wanted the millions of Asians, blinded in the two great Mongolian laser battles, to benefit from Starley's genius.

It was to be noted that a group of Visual Electromolecular biologists was working on Oleandre to add color perception to the Starley device.

Even though he was sightless, Fischer had been exiled by the Alliance to a life of forced labor in the tungsten mills on Lunare, imbedded deep in the Alps near Mare Imbrium. He had committed the "crime" of writing public critiques of Alliance literature, and had referred to them as "obscenely degenerate." Eventually he had escaped his lunar imprisonment during the mayhem of the General Recall; and Jonathan Fischer was subsequently recruited for the Oleandre Mission. Fischer had operated several clandestine broadcasting stations which transmitted propaganda of peace to both sides during the Earth's last days. The stations were located, for confusion's sake, in the large expanse of space between Mars and Jupiter. . .the asteroid belt containing the myriad dark, jagged fragments of the ancient planet Nimrrah, as it was known to the Sumerians. It was the perfect place for undetectable broadcasting operations.

Jonathan Fischer began his discussion on the role of the Receptacle in the Oleandre Mission. He sometimes became distracted enough to preach against the degeneracy of the literature during the time of the Alliance. Toward the end of the hour, a lively and totally unexpected debate had developed as to the actual definitions of creativity. Harvey McMaster was his usual half-assed self, Eric thought later.

"Damnit Fischer, you're just being stubborn, admit it! The creative ones are a class unto themselves. . .a group that should be worshipped by the peasantry."

There are no more masses, much less any peasantry, thought Eric. He raised his eyebrows at Maggie who nodded in agreement.

"Oh, come now, Harvard," replied Fischer with a kind of knowing chuckle and in a tone that recognized McMaster to be the selfrighteous and pompous fool that he was, "you know that the essense of creativity is fixed, but that in reality it is applicable to every human. The peon in the field *could* be creative, just as any university president *could* be a mindless imbecile. Creativity in the real world is always relative."

"Gentlemen? I-I-I-If I-I may interrupt," a voice stuttered from the rear of the room. Several people squirmed in their seats and twisted their necks to see who was speaking.

Jesse Horvitz, sitting nervously in his chair and fidgeting with his sleeve, began, "creativity is the act of producing *something* by one's talents uh. . .uh, without the uh. . .direct influence of another. There are two words in this statement I must emphasize. The. . ."

"See here, young man," interrupted McMaster.

"Let the boy finish," echoed down from somewhere on the side of the auditorium. McMaster's eyes darted over the area looking for the offender.

"Thank you," replied Horvitz, "*whoever* that was. Now, as I was saying, two words in my statement need clarification. First I said the '*direct* influence of another.' You see, no one acts truly of his own volition. You know, every person is influenced both consciously and unconsciously by previous experiences. I also referred to 'producing *something.*' That 'something' created can be several entities or combination of entities. The something can be a theory. . .an abstraction if you will, or a solid object. The typical result of creation is a combination of abstraction and reality. Take the painter's canvas or a sculpture, for example, or a bridgespan, some mechanical device, *or* the object of today's discussion. . .a work of writing."

"That's just it," said Jonathan Fischer. "I refuse to compliment them with that term. . .*works* of writing. . .are the degeneracies of the Alliance literature the acts of creation?"

"No, sir, they are not," said Horvitz. "You see, that's just *my* point. Most of the writers during that time were not creating out of their own talents. They were told exactly what to write by the Communications Media Review Board and, in some cases, by the Ministry of Mukluhanism itself. They were directed in their efforts. Thus, it was not creative work."

"But," said McMaster in a voice indicating his displeasure with Horvitz for entering *his* private discourse with Fischer, "once they got their subject from the State, it was their own literary talent that created the final product."

"No, it wasn't," replied Horvitz. "With the subject matter and content assigned, any raving idiot could use the common literary devices to tie everything up. . .no sir, it was *definitely* not creation."

His last statement came out with such an air of finality and sureness that McMaster was only able to come up with a feeble, "But. . ." Sensing this to be a good closing time, Jonathan Fischer thanked everyone for attending — especially Horvitz whom he asked to see later — and announced that on a week from this day a second colloquium would be held to discuss in detail, the Alliance's particularly disgusting literary efforts.

There were one or two scattered attempts at applause. People began to rise and the intensity of the murmuring sounds grew larger. Eric just looked at Maggie with a sense of disbelief.

"I think my young assistant is in the wrong field."

Jesse Horvitz was making his way down to the front against the crush of people leaving. When he got next to them, Eric gave him an approving wink and Jesse broke into a big grin.

"I hope I wasn't out of line," Jesse whispered.

"Hell no, boy, any time McMaster catches it in the rump is just fine with me."

As they filed out the way they came in, Eric and Maggie stopped to admire a display of literary works. . .real books, some from the early twentieth century. This particular set dealt with the collected poetry of Harry Crosby. The yellowing, tattered pages of the Black Sun Press limited editions lay almost regally behind the ozmyglass panels which reflected the blinking computer lights behind them. Eric thought it strangely ironic that these aged works were held in such high esteem, when all around them automation reigned.

They walked arm in arm down the glittering translucent corridors and soon arrived at Eric's personal quarters. Pseudomonius had done his task well. The small white table ha ' been pulled out of the wall and two black chairs had risen from the deck and were sitting in place. The square white plates and shiny eating utensils were ready, and the food compartment's light was on indicating that dinner was prepared and waiting. On the corner of the table stood a clear, purple beaker from which protruded the neck of a dark green bottle surrounded with tarnished and torn foil. The vapors of the cooling solution swirled and caressed the container.

"Oh, Eric. . .champagne?"

"Yes, I told you I was hoarding it."

"Marvelous. I can hardly wait to try it."

The lights and music were low. After peeling back the foil,

Eric gave the aging cork a casual, but expertly gentle, flick of the wrist. The characteristic and reassuring pop resounded in the room and Eric noted, "Sounds good, but it still could be poor; in fact, it's very likely."

"Oh, I hope not," said Maggie with true concern.

Eric poured a small amount into his tall rectangular obsidian glass, tested the bouquet and sipped. It was perfect, a true oenological delight. He filled their glasses. "To us."

Maggie seated herself on the low black couch that slid out of the wall. She crossed her long legs with the erotic slithering sound of silky cloth on cloth and said, "You know, Eric, that young Horvitz of yours?"

"What about him?" said Eric, sitting next to her, but on the edge of the couch with chin in hand, and elbow on knee.

"Well, something bothers me about him. Strange, he's so idealistic."

"He's so young."

"Yes, I know. But his dissertation back at Fischer's seminar. . .it's almost a precarious position. It's fine to have ideals about creativity, but there's a rub to his theory. The rub is that man is genuinely in danger of becoming subordinate to his own creations. . .that they may overcome and dominate him and he become strangled by the very inspirations of his own hand and mind. This must not happen and we of Oleandre must see that it does not. God knows, I've seen enough of that kind of hell!"

"Bravo, McMaster," cheered Eric mockingly. He bowed low, then snapped straight up, saluting "and good show Harvard!"

"WHAT," she replied in a tone of approaching indignity, "how can you say. . ."

"Oh Maggie, I *do* agree with you, but this is supposed to be a celebration. . .a fun time. I'm really sorry about that crack."

"It's all right. . .I'm sorry too. . .just need to relax I guess."

"Glad to oblige you."

Her hand went under his tunic and slid up his back as she took a deep sip of her champagne. The beams from his eyes touched her face. He leaned down and kissed her softly. He started to pull away, but her hand slipped warmly behind his neck and brought him back, her moist lips opening, her tongue entering his mouth. Their tongues fought for an instant and then established a rapport of mutual exploration.

Her almost empty glass clattered to the floor, the few remaining drops turned to foaming, bubbling spheres on the hard surface.

"Yes, oh yes," she whispered softly in his ear, and she bit gently on the lobe, then flicked her tongue over the depression her teeth had made in the skin.

Now standing, he kissed her deeply. Her thighs pressed hotly to his and he could feel her breasts rising with excitement even though they were crushed against his chest. In a fluid motion she reached behind her and pulled the long continuous seam; the flowing garment fell in a crumpled heap at her ankles. She undressed him slowly, caressing him, kissing him, finally leading him to his own bed.

Maggie lay back before him. In the dim light she was flawless. Her arms beckoned. Eric came down beside her, his mouth covering the deep-red pinnacle of one mountain of warm, eager flesh. He could feel her nipple stiffen and throb against his tongue and Maggie moaned softly, "It's been so long."

Her hands ran gently over his back and shoulders, while he explored her every crevice and erotic zone. He entered her swiftly and was lost in the warm and humid and undulating cavern. Their lovemaking was not expert; their bodies bucked together violently, her nails tracing long purple ribbons of fire down his back and over his buttocks. Finally, she brought her knees up over his hips and locked her ankles, her body rocking vengefully. He burst forth within her all the pentup desire and frustration he had carried for a decade. The universe whirled.

They lay together with the transparent black sheet covering hem. Maggie snuggled under his arm and rested her head in he hollow of his shoulder. . .her hair brushing silently against is neck. He felt a rivulet of perspiration run down his muscled ack; and Eric kissed the side of Maggie's head, his nostrils elighting in the hypnotizing odor of her damp hair.

"You're wonderful, darling," she murmured, "so-o-o ood."

Together several hours. Saying nothing. Touching the varmth. Contemplating the silence.

He knew she was at peace for the first time in ears. . .finally, at peace with nature and herself.

She arose, went to his toilet module, and emerged fully ressed. After forbidding him to take her back to her quarters, he turned to leave.

"Maggie," he said in a barely audible voice, "we could be narried tomorrow."

She merely nodded, the tears building in the corners of her uburn eyes, then spilling over onto hot red cheeks.

She was gone.

Eric lay for a few moments, his hands locked behind his ead; but he was not alone, for the wet image of Maggie's face ngered in his mind, the reverberations of her voice echoed in he room. Soon, he rolled over and the shroud of sleep vercame him.

On the partition over the entrance, the digital clock silently egistered the onset of the new day: 23:00:01.

These were the first, fleeting, never-to-return seconds of leandre Day twenty-three.

CHAPTER 4

It was over eighty days ago that Commander Se
Hayakawa performed the simple ceremony with an emotion
his voice that indicated his fondness for Maggie.

They were united.

There was no great amount of detail in the marria
preparations. Maggie and Eric merely registered with th
Reproductive Committee whose job it was to regulate th
population on Oleandre. The committee authorized only o
birth per death, and regulated the sex of the child in order
retain the proper male to female balance on board. Howeve
Elizabeth Roegten, the voluntary head of the Reproducti
Committee and an incurable romantic, had added a somewh
strange, yet appropriate touch to the marriage ceremony.

Decades ago, a certain nonsteroidal polypeptide-lithiu
complex was found to have perfect contraceptive effect c
females with no detectable hazards for males. There was als
no effect on female children until menstruation. Thus, th
ideal contraceptive was a permanent constituent of Oleandre
water supply. Elizabeth Roegten had inserted a rite into th

marriage ceremony in which the female partner drinks from a symbolic flacon of distilled water containing no contraceptive.

Eric and Maggie had not planned to have a child immediately, although their right to do so was reserved with the Reproductive Committee. There had, thus far, been one hundred ninety-two deaths and only thirty-six births on Oleandre, so there was certainly no objection to their having a baby right away if they wished.

Eric and Maggie had talked eagerly, but indefinitely, about having a child.

Late one afternoon, they were preparing for a quick zero-G tennis game before having an early supper, and then going to an art exhibition by Anura Jarvik. Maggie had moved into Eric's private quarters when they were married because it gave them the greatest amount of space.

On that afternoon, Maggie had stepped into her white body stocking and was lacing the hood. As Eric bent over to snap up the grippers on his magnetic sandals, he said, "Say, Babe, now that we're married, how are we to be collectively addressed? Certainly no Mr. and Mrs., nor Doctor and Mrs. Perhaps Dr. and Dr.? Or, the Doctors Senka. Maybe, Doctor squared."

"Your mind is squared," she giggled, then hollered as he came after her, "Oh no you don't. . .ERIC!" He slapped her on the rump with the back of his aluminum paddle.

The zero-G court was perfectly spherical once the entrance was sealed, so the ball could be played off any surface of the chamber. The game was played inside the surface of the sphere with points being automatically tallied by a computer outside. The score was announced by the machine's metallic voice.

On their way back from the tennis match, the question of the child arose. Maggie agreed that it would be better if they had a boy first. The appropriate genetic information was already on hand with the Reproductive Committee. Each of them received a vial, Maggie's filled with white capsules and Eric's with small and curiously dry orange discs, that contained a drug to destroy all his sperm with prefemale genomics. This would guarantee a male first-child.

"Oh Eric, I really can't wait. Could we? I mean, well. . .could we tonight?"

"Yes, darling, tonight."

"What name would you like Eric? Do you. . .I mean. . .are you partial to any in particular?" said Maggie, her eyes carefully avoiding his.

"Of course I am," Eric replied with a broad smile lighting up his face. "There's no question about it. None whatsoever. We'll name the young man Sean."

"OH!" She was almost shocked; but the look of thankfulness in her eyes was all the assurance he needed that the choice was a wise one.

"Have you been drinking from your bottle of pure water?"

"Yes, for three days now, the required time."

The meeting with Commander Hayakawa took place in an atmosphere of guarded optimism. Willoughby, McMaster and Eric Senka were all present when Seth Hayakawa announced the location of Jason Oleandre's second probe. Although it had been generally assumed that the second probe lay just outside the geoastro limits of the solar system, the instrument package had been landed on the surface of Titan, Saturn's sixth satellite. This had been a spectacular guidance achievement in a time when far-planetary exploration had only reached Jupiter. . .in the days just preceding the General Recall.

"Gentlemen, we are now approximately five-point-six billion miles from our destination: I have given the order for a slow, linear deceleration of Oleandre. We will approach Saturn at a rate of a thousand miles per second and slowing. Senka, you and Willoughby will again have the honor of the pickup, though it is not likely to be as straight-forward as the picking up of the first probe."

"Why the slowdown, Seth?" asked McMaster, who was in a sullen mood for some reason known only to himself.

"Well, I'll be very frank. I know it seems illogical after we expended so much energy in gaining the speed we have now, but I am not positive we are going to get the information we need from the second probe. If we cannot obtain the Powers Equation, it's no use streaking around the solar system, wasting nuclear fuel. Which reminds me, Eric."

"Yes, Seth."

"After you and Harlin leave Oleandre in the new Sub-Orbital Craft, I will slow to somewhere around a hundred thousand miles-per-hour in an elliptical orbit about nine million miles from Saturn. This is just outside its farthest satellite, Phoebe. This will give you plenty of time to locate and pick up the probe without having to worry about catching up with us. You will, by the way, be departing in about thirty-five hours. I've had a memory module prepared for each of you. . .to refresh your minds as to the conditions you may encounter. Harlin, you will have to give the Sub-Orbital Craft a shakedown flight right *now*. I'm sorry about the rush, but must realize the entire concept of the Mission is at stake. All questions should be answered for you on the tape. However, in the case of any last minute problems, we will meet again, here, in exactly twenty-five hours. See you then."

The Commander turned swiftly and disappeared through the vibrating air curtain. Eric looked over at McMaster, who was also leaving and saying, "Titan, Goddamn!"

"I'll talk with you later, Harlin," said Eric, picking up the black tube from the desk.

"All right, I'm going to start the prelaunch count-up for the Sub-Orbital Craft."

"What the hell is it, anyway? The 'Sub-Orbital Craft.' I wasn't aware we had anything but the Hovercraft fleet."

"It's very new, a prototype. . .so new it hasn't been tested very well I'm afraid. You can get a good technical review on it

by using the F-A-one setting on your computer's general
output circuits."

"Fine, Harlin, thanks."

Eric hurried back to his quarters with the memory module
under his arm and a knot tightening in his guts. He was getting
one of the feelings he always got when he was not absolutely
sure of something. The last time he had such intense, grinding
pain was just prior to the launching of the missiles that had
destroyed the Earth.

After eating with Maggie, he insisted upon being left alone
with the tape. Even though she protested vigorously, Maggie
left to hear a concert by the understaffed, though surprisingly
excellent, ship's orchestra. Pseudomonius brought a beaker of
hot green tea as Eric plugged the tape unit into the audio
center. ". . .and of course the sixth satellite of Saturn, called
Titan, has a diameter of approximately twenty-eight-hundred
and fifty miles as compared with the Jovian Ganymede's
thirty-one-hundred miles. Titan occupies a unique spot in this
planetary system since it is the only satellite to retain a
gaseous atmosphere. Composed mostly of methane and
molecular hydrogen, Titan keeps its atmosphere, it is
theorized, by virtue of its extremely low temperature. The
Titan surface is thought to be composed of frozen ammonia
and ice, covering a rocky mass; and it is further theorized. . ."

After about thirty minutes Eric turned off the machine,
thinking that there wasn't much new material here since he
had taken 'Survey of Planetary Science' back at Earth Free
University. He energized the F-A-one setting on his computer
system that connected him with Oleandre's Prime Computer
Banks.

The televisor screen before him pulsated in shimmering
chromatic splendor for several seconds, then snapped into the
image of a complex mathematical expression. The theory of
the Sub-Orbital Craft's design was abstracted and lasted only
about fifteen minutes. It was not necessarily a radical design,

although certain innovations made the SOC the most advanced of this prototype series. The design gave the SOC a great deal of versatility, with the capability of limited planetary flight at speeds up to three thousand miles-per-second on sustained power, with bursts up to much higher velocities. It was also extremely maneuverable in low planetary orbits at speeds down to five thousand miles-per-hour in thin atmosphere. Being powered by twin ion propulsion units for extreme velocities, the SOC was equipped with what could be considered ancient propulsion for low speeds. . .an old, asymmetrical benzidine-nitrogentetroxide hypergol engine.

The tape ended with a colorful representation of the Sub-Orbital Craft on which was painted the name DESIREE. The craft was gliding through deep space across the Orion Nebula, to the pounding rhythm of Wagner's Valkyries. This is a hitherto unseen side of Harlin Willoughby's personality, Eric thought.

The music faded out, as did the image, in a blaze of multicolored, computerized surrealism. The screen went black and the audio unit clicked off.

"We had a date, remember?"

Maggie's voice startled him, and Eric whirled around. He had been so engrossed in Willoughby's new ship that he did not even hear her enter.

"How was the concert? Mozart or Dylan tonight?"

"Never mind that!" Maggie's mouth was warm and wet on his.

They awoke at precisely six-hundred hours and were on their way by six-fifty. . .Maggie to the Astrophysics Computational Center, and Eric to his laboratory next door. Maggie was analyzing some new statistical data she had obtained from a heretofore unknown radio source at the edge of the galaxy.

Eric had time to kill until ten-hundred, when he would

meet Harlin Willoughby to make final arrangements for the
coming rendezvous. Since Jesse Horvitz had begun university
classes two days ago and was now only assisting him four
hours a day, Eric's laboratory seemed unwelcomingly cold and
empty. Partly for lack of something better to do and partly for
practice, he inserted a cerebrovascular telemetry package into
the Circle of Willis, deep in a rabbit's brain.

The Oleandre was now following a great arc across the
system of the Sun. Saturn was in conjunction with the Sun as
far as Oleandre's position was concerned. Sol's dull
luminescence hid the Saturnian disc, and the stars of the
constellation Canis Major blotted out Sirius, the canine's heart
of white fire.

The gleaming Sub-Orbital Craft stood as a reclining queen
bee in her nest, as literally hundreds of technicians swarmed
over the ship to make last minute adjustments and conduct the
seemingly endless number of minor countdowns and pulse
timings. Eric entered the hangar complex wearing the sealed
black body-stocking that was normally worn under the
high-risk flight suit. A white tapecase, strapped to his left
forearm harshly reflected the brilliant light of the
molybdenum-arc torches.

"Harlin!"

"Oh, Eric. . .yes, good to see you. Is it time for Hayakawa's
final briefing already?"

"How're things proceeding? And how was your checkout
flight last night?"

"Everything functioned well. . .a few minor mishaps but
nothing of major consequence."

Looking over the sleek craft Eric said, "She certainly is a
beauty. But I don't see the name."

"Name?. . .Oh, of course! No, no name yet. That was only
in my tape."

"Good show, too! What's this Wagner business, Harlin? It's

certainly not very scientific. And who is this Desiree? Come on Harlin, give! Who is she?" Eric gave Harlin Willoughby a truly lecherous smirk. "Someone you've got hot drawers for?"

"I'll never tell," Harlin replied and then laughed idiotically.

"Goddamn, Harlin, you're almost human!"

They both laughed and Harlin proceeded to give Eric a thorough tour of the Sub-Orbital Craft. The SOC was about fifty feet long and could accommodate six people including a normal crew of two. The two crew members sat at the command module where clusters of instrumentation danced and flashed on the indicator panels. Above the command module area were two large ports separated by a televisor screen about two feet square. The four passengers' chairs were grouped in pairs facing each other. In the center of the passenger area was a split-screen televisor which provided simultaneous fore and aft telemetry.

The next compartment was entered through a hatch that was in the center of the thin bulkhead. This was the only part of the SOC that could have artificial gravity if needed for experimentation. The circular room spun on the axis of the ship, and one could enter the spinning room only by climbing down a ladder on the axis. Of course, when the gravity situation was not in use one could enter through the regular hatch.

The rear compartment was just ahead of the propulsion system and the radiation shields. This area was filled with thin metallic sheets that folded in on one another. This, Eric was told, was the atmospheric airfoil for suborbital flight.

"Just one thing Harlin."

"Yes?"

"Does this thing have a crapper?"

"A what?"

"A head. . .you know. . .a toilet. That's the one short-coming of the standard Hovercraft you know?"

"Yes, there *is* one," said Harlin supressing a grin and clearing his throat. "It is under that hatch," he continued, pointing to the portside of the passenger section and just under the subquantum inertial guidance system.

"Good," said Eric matter-of-factly.

"Not very private I'm afraid. . .lack of space, you know. It's a standard excretion disintegrator."

A great panel was slid open in the bottom of the Sub-Orbital Craft between the command module and the passenger area. Several puffing technicians and their servomechanins were lifting a large transparent sphere through it.

"What in hell," Eric exclaimed.

"That is the Surface Descent Module."

"Of course," said Eric facetiously.

The sphere, about eight feet in diameter, was filled at one end with a propulsion package, two acceleration body forms and an instrument console. The rest of the spheroid was of completely transparent material, allowing a one-hundred-eighty by three-hundred-sixty degree visual field.

It was not known if Jason Oleandre's second probe was in orbit around Titan or really on the surface. It was just *there*. The SD-Module's capability permitted a surface landing, although it was expected that the probe would probably be in a tight Titian orbit. They wouldn't know until they were close enough for Hayakawa to activate the homing devices on the second probe if they were still functional.

With the sphere now in place, Willoughby detached a small instrument cluster from the command module and uncoiled a long bronzed wire. Depressing a red heat sensor activated a panel in the opaque portion of the sphere, and it slid open. Willoughby entered first; and before Eric had crawled to his seat, the panel slid shut. The only sounds were his labored grunting and the low hiss of the environmental control system.

Strapped into an adjustable body contour chair, Eric was given instruction in using the magnetic grappling devices. He fit his hands into a set of metal rings that covered the knuckle of each finger and thumb. Outside the sphere another panel slid open and two mechanical, robotoid arms emerged. The sensitive rings transmitted each delicate and precise move of his hands to the obedient slave hands outside in the hostile atmosphere. Eric would be able to lift a thin sheet of celucel or a thousand pound space probe.

It took very little time for Eric to become comfortable using the robot device, and they noticed that it was getting close to the meeting time. They stopped first to check out the pressure suits they would need. Meanwhile, the hangar area was depressurized and the Sub-Orbital Craft moved to its launching facility at the Hoverport.

The entire operation nearly ended in disaster as a hovercraft went slightly out of control while making a power-nil landing and narrowly escaped colliding with the SOC. This would have meant the abortion of the Mission because there was no backup vehicle and it would have taken over two months to construct another. The lack of a second ship also excluded the possibility of rescue should an emergency ensue. Eric knew this and accepted it stoically. Maggie, however, had worried for several days, and her mood was reflected in the intensity of her love-making.

Eric Senka and Harlin Willoughby spent about thirty minutes in the logistics division of the External Transport Unit getting final fittings for their high-risk pressure suits. These were not the ordinary Zelon-filled foil suits. "Risk" was a term to be taken seriously. The inner black tunic had built-in physiological monitoring and telemetry devices that kept the internal environment at nearly perfect equilibrium under a great range of temperature and pressure conditions. A cardiac monitor even sensed stress situations and could put gaseous isofluroadrenalin agents into the internal atmosphere to augment any emergency condition. Over the inner body stocking were two self-contained pressure suits of thin foil pressed onto a highly flexible silicon-octane backbone. The high-risk pressure suit withstood pressures of up to a million pounds-per-square-centimeter and resist temperatures of from fifty to five-hundred degrees on the Kelvin-Link scale; yet the material was as flexible as a second skin.

The helmet of the high-risk pressure suit was bubble-like, slightly asymmetrical, and opaque, except for a thin transparent viewing slit. Multiple filters automatically flipped down over the opening to adjust for light and other radiation conditions. Inside the helmet, besides the usual communications and environmental control devices, was a viewer attached to a small telescanner on the rear of the helmet. Eric merely had to glance down in the helmet to get a wide angle picture of what was going on behind him. After some time of wearing the helmet it became an unconscious process; Eric's physiology soon adapted to the unique stimuli of extra-peripheral vision.

Their suits fitted and gear stowed in lockers until just before departure, Eric and Harlin entered Commander Hayakawa's conference room. Harvey McMaster and the Commander were bent over a table pouring over piles of data. A starry background was projected on a televisor behind them. In one corner of the field, a small luminous disc seemed to grow in brightness with each passing hour. Hayakawa looked up.

"Yes, good evening, Gentlemen. I trust all is in readiness. McMaster, here, and I have just been going over last-minute preparations for the transmission of the code to activate the second probe."

"We are ready," replied Willoughby, "although I am not too pleased about using the Sub-Orbital Craft without further testing. I realize, however, the necessity."

"What's our distance from Saturn?" asked Eric.

"A hundred-and-three million miles and traveling tangentially at three-thousand miles-per-second. That puts you about nine hours pre-departure."

There were only a few questions, mostly of purely academic interest: had the grapplers of the Surface Descent Module been actually tested in chambers approximating the atmosphere of Titan? Did they work? What might the Titan surface be like if a landing should be required? The answers and discussion did not really matter since they were committed to the mission. The meeting was adjourned, but not without a toast to success with cognac.

Maggie awaited Eric's return. The illuminated numerals of the digital clock read twenty-fifty hours.

"Hello," he said softly, almost meekly upon entering, "I've just been with Hayakawa."

She turned to get up, poured some hot coffee and said, "What time do you leave?" Her voice was icy.

"In about six hours."

With her back to him, she exhaled deeply. Her shoulders began to shake. Her voice stammered, "Why does it have to be *you*, oh Eric!" She whirled and ran into his arms which encircled her, hands running lightly over her hair.

"I-It's just that I couldn't bear to lose you, too," she sobbed.

"You won't, Darling, you won't. Willoughby's a good pilot. . .the best we have as a matter of fact."

"But why you? Why not someone else?"

"I'm as qualified as anyone on Oleandre to be back-up pilot; and I was there at the first pick-up. I'm the logical choice. Hell, even Jonathan Fischer has had *some* flight experience and has a Class-7-Astrosoar rating."

"I guess so." Maggie's tone was beginning to stabilize.

"We'll be back in twelve hours, maybe even in less time if it's an easy pick-up."

"All right, Mister," she said, having regained her composure, "you get the devil to bed and sleep awhile."

"Sure, good idea. Join me?"

"Oh, no. . .too much coffee and besides, I want you to *sleep*. What time shall I wake you?"

"One." He *was* exhausted, but driven to wakefulness by the apprehension of the coming flight.

He crawled under a lightweight cover and put his hands characteristically behind his head. "You know, we really are going to be in bad shape if there's no clue to the third probe."

"I know." Her voice was very serious.

"I suppose it wouldn't be too bad if the Mission aborted and we returned to the Martian bases. We could survive very nicely in the underground complexes. But it wouldn't be the same. . .not like Earth."

"Yes, I, too, want to breathe fresh air and feel the warm wind blow again, although that's pretty romantic and idealistic, isn't it? The Earth had warm winds, all right. . .hot wind from atomic furnaces that polluted the air and whose thermal wastes killed almost all the aquatic life forms — except for that putrid algae that seemed to thrive in the polluted oceans, what was it called again?"

"*Thermopylae pyroformis,*" he yawned. "Oh yes, well, there was no fresh air and even far from the urban hubs, people died gasping for breath, their blackened lungs brittle and fibrous."

"The pollution was hideous, Maggie, I agree; but the worst thing was that we *could* have controlled and stopped it. And we didn't. Ironically, it wasn't the medical crisis that made pollution so dangerous — that was alleviated when everyone wore that damn antipollution mask: the Amolynsisator. The danger was in the social implications of world pollution. . .remember? When Pope Leo XXXV wouldn't give in to the young, nouveau-cardinal's demands: condemn national governments for not halting pollution when they had the technology to do it. And he refused to chastise the Zambian Common Market's campaign of genocide against the Ebos. Leo was finally assassinated on the crumbling balcony of his basilica by a sniper who had to use a holograph-coupled infrared scope to shoot him, the Roman smog was so thick. Then, Christ! All hell breaks loose — riots in the streets of world capitals, barricades, and a coup in Nor' Ire when it is discovered that the assassin is a Zodian.

"To cap it off, the new Pope, what was his name?. . .Regus, I believe. . .breaks all tradition: takes a papal name never used before, gets married and, of all things, decides to move the Vatican out of Rome because the city had become a virtual megaslum. So the married Pope sets up the Vatican in Denmark of the Scandanavian Commonwealth, and what does he announce? On top of all that has transpired, he and his new wife, Victorae, are using contraceptives!

"Jesus, that started it. Revolutions and more killings. It had to come; and in the end it did some good. Governments made some attempt to clean up the air; but it was too late — about three decades too late — as was the edict advocating artificial contraception. Too late. The Great Asian Wars were brewing.

"There wasn't much natural beauty left on Earth, but there could be again: the memory of unspoiled, multicolored canyons and green forests remains in our minds.

"In our minds maybe," he added, "but certainly not on Mars."

He had soon lapsed into a light sleep while Maggie watched over him, thumbing nervously through one pile of celucel sheets after another. She smiled slightly, thinking he looked like a sleeping infant; yet her heart was filled with the recurring sense and dread of impending loss. It was the same feeling of nauseating horror she had known in that awful time when her husband, Sean, was taken by Alliance MSD agents, interrogated and finally tortured to death. His eyeless, earless, nailless corpse was tossed into the polluted Thames, only to be dregged up days later, and delivered to her as a warning to others in the scientific community. When it came to instilling

terror, the MSD made Hitler's Gestapo, the Ton Ton Macoute
and the Minority Control Commission look like inept pre-
schoolers.

Nudged gently on the foot at precisely one-hundred hours,
Eric awoke and jumped quickly to his feet, feeling only
slightly rejuvenated. After a shower and defecation, he slipped
into his body-stocking, kissed Maggie, held her tightly for a
few seconds, then was off down the corridor to meet
Willoughby.

The express tram stopped at the area in which he and
Willoughby would be dressed. The rigging of the high-risk
pressure suits went smoothly enough, although Harlin had to
laugh out loud at Eric's expression when, without warning, a
technician grabbed Eric's penis to insert it into the flexible
catheter that ran down into a sealed reservoir in his left boot
where his excretions would be processed.

A gleaming white pressurized tram that moved on a
monorail track took them to the surface of Oleandre and over
to the launching area. They were moving at such high speed
that Eric could only see blurs of light and dark through the
small port. The tram rolled right up to the side of the
Sub-Orbital Craft, and a great hiss filled the vehicle as the
hatches were connected. The vacuum-sealed hatch opened
with a pop, and in stepped Seth Hayakawa dressed in ordinary
work-overhauls.

"Good morning, gentlemen."

"Seth?" They answered in unison.

"I just came out early to look over the SOC and to wish
you both good-mission."

"Thank you. . .I hope we won't *need* any luck," said Eric.

The Commander explained that after the Sub-Orbital Craft
departed Oleandre would arrive at its far-orbit station in two
hours. He would then activate the second probe's homing
devices on the Sub-Orbital Craft.

Once inside the ship, and with the final checkouts completed, the technicians left and the Commander bade them farewell. Eric secured the hatches manually and heard the tram break loose outside. Willoughby turned on the telescreen, it flickered for a few nanoseconds, then came on with sharp clarity. They could see the tram disappearing in the distance and the transparent dome of the observatory was partially visible on the screen, over the horizon. It contrasted sharply with the dark rocky curve of the horizon and the backdrop of profusely scattered stars, with the almost solid band of the Milky Way arcing over the crystal sphere.

All around the ship, the brilliant lights of the workmen's torches played in eerie glows and monstrous, everchanging shadows.

Sitting in their acceleration chairs in the command module, Willoughby announced their readiness to Oleandre Control.

The husky voice of Seth Hayakawa gave them permission to depart. Willoughby touched a series of sensors in a simple code, and the great cluster of instruments on the command module came flashing to life. The single word, GO, appeared on the telescreen. Then, inserting his right thumb and first finger into two golden metal loops on the arm of his contour chair, Harlin brought the thumb over to touch the tip of the finger, stretching the loops. Eric felt the craft give a slight lurch, and he could see the horizon move.

Because they were facing directly away from Oleandre's flight path, only a slight power thrust was needed. The surface of Oleandre fell away beneath them. Looking out the port, Eric could see the steady red and blue glow of their engines reflected in the observatory dome.

Oleandre Control confirmed their lift-off. A double row of digital indicators simultaneously read out distance from Oleandre and Titan in exponential miles.

"What's our ETA Harlin?"

Willoughby touched a scarlet heat sensor and the characters:

<pre>
         ****
</pre>
2.376hr*******END*READOUT
<pre>
         ****
</pre>

appeared on the black televisor screen in green numerals.

"Good, I'll put our helmets in the descent bubble."

Because there was no gravity, all decks, wall and ceiling space that wasn't filled with instrumentation had been covered with Interlochen Material. The bottoms of his boots too were layered with these little grippers, so Eric could walk up the wall or on the ceiling if he desired.

For more than an hour nothing exciting happened except for an occasional micrometeorite hit on the hull. The silver, needle-like craft sped toward its destination as Eric watched a ringed disc grow in the right side of the visual field. The singular beauty of the Saturnian ring system was indescribable. It was even more moving than the best chromagraphs he had seen.

At a distance of seven million miles, they passed through an unexpected region of unusually intense gamma radiation. Although this was not dangerous to them, the phenomenon was recorded verbally in the SOC-running-log and relayed to Oleandre Control.

When the distance to Titan read 4.9, Willoughby initiated a retrofire to slow the Sub-Orbital Craft. Thrust-invertors eliminated the need to swing around the ship.

The satellite, Titan, loomed ahead of them and was now a steadily glowing, finite disc, whereas it had previously been only a pinpoint of light overshadowed by the mother planet. Glowing in green-blue light, the disc appeared devoid of landmarks, because its thick methane atmosphere reflected most of the light.

Titan changed phases as they passed around the dark side. The Sub-Orbital Craft gently retrofired again and the computer inserted it into a loose elliptical orbit about Titan. . .with its apogee at five-thousand miles.

As the ship swung out from behind the satellite, the great eminence of Saturn came into view. Both Eric and Harlin were awed by the immensity of the banded, streaky sphere and delicacy of its ring systems. A huge white spot lay in the equatorial zone of the planet. Probably an atmospheric disturbance, like the giant red Jovian spot it seemed out of place, an invader and defiler of the sphere's symmetry.

It was six-forty-five hours and fifteen-point-three seconds when Oleandre Control crackled over the communications system. The Sub-Orbital Craft had been in Titan orbit an hour longer than planned because Willoughby wanted to make last minute checks of all internal circuits.

"Oleandre Control, we are receiving you loud but garbled," said Willoughby.

"Yes SOC, we are having the same situation. . .wait. . . Commander Hayakawa to speak. . .one moment. . .Harlin? Can you read me?"

"Just barely. Try shifting your transmission. . .plus two-point-one-two centimeters."

A static-like noise was heard, followed by a high-pitched whistle. Eric covered his ears. Then nothing. The Commander's voice suddenly came in loud and crystal clear.

"How's the transmission now?"

"Excellent, Seth, very clear."

"There is a belt of ionizing radiation out here. You must have passed through it."

"We did, and reported it to Oleandre Control."

"I see. . .I was away for an hour or so. It's of no matter now. We are ready to broadcast the code. Jason Oleandre took the day and year of his birth and made the day a whole number and the year a decimal. Thus, his birthday. . .twenty-two August, nineteen-sixty-one, reads: 22.1961. The number is raised as an exponent of ten, and the code is the antilogarithm of the decimal portion of the exponent. The transmission will be in four sets of numbers. . .five each. The probe should respond in three ways...first a radio signal, releasing an ion source which you should be able to detect with your IONAR tracking capability; third a visual laser source is activated. If you are ready, we will begin the transmission."

"Ready, Seth."

The transmission was made in about a micro-second. Eric and Harlin watched their telemetry. Nothing. The IONAR scanning screen was blank, the radio range-finder was uneffected, and, when Eric got up to scan the area visually with a small but powerful holographic monocular, he saw nothing.

"Seth, we're getting no receptions."

"I know, perhaps it's the radiation zone."

"No, your transmission got here all right, it registered on my sensors."

"GODDAMNIT," said Hayakawa, who was never known to raise his voice, much less use profanity.

"Still no reception...neither from an orbital position nor from the surface. Try the transmission again!"

The code was broadcast several more times with the same result. Nothing. The probe was either not there or it was not functioning.

Hoping for the latter to be true, Eric and Harlin scanned the space around Titan with heat- and metallic-seeking telemetry. Finding no targets, they turned their search to the frozen surface. As Eric was transversing an area in the satellite's northern quadrant, he registered a weak impulse that indicated a small metallic object. This *had* to be the probe, and they joyously broadcast the information to Oleandre Control. Actually, there was no decision involved, since descent to the surface was an obvious and necessary act.

Harlin swung the Sub-Orbital Craft out of orbit, pushing the ion engines to their blue line. Meanwhile, Eric told Oleandre Control not to expect any transmissions until they were back in Titan orbit.

As they approached the outer Titan atmosphere Willoughby cut the power and the ship buffeted slightly as the first molecules of methane hit its hull. Entering on a tangential approach, Willoughby slowly got the needle-nose down and then touched a series of computer studs. A slot began to open on the back of the Sub-Orbital Craft near the rear compartment. A great luminous ribbon of metal foil unreeled out of the slot until a huge bat-like set of wings were neatly in place. They grabbed the thin air creating lift for soaring. The huge metal pterodactyl slowed considerably as the howling cross winds of the upper atmosphere tossed it about.

Harlin had complete control since the wing and airfoil were very thin and flexible. The Sub-Orbital Craft sailed down in large arcs to a height of ten miles and Willoughby ignited the hypergol engine. While they descended to the surface the onboard computer would "fly" the ship, mostly soaring, but using the powerful hypergol engine in any unforeseen emergency. Harlin switched over the command module to the computer as Eric opened the hatch to the Surface Descent Module. He followed Harlin in and the hatch snapped shut. A mist filled the cabin of the Sub-Orbital Craft as depressurization took place; and quicker than he could blink, the SDM dropped from the belly of the ship.

They plummeted straight down through great clouds of blue vapor. A filter flicked down over Eric's stat-helmet to alleviate the almost painful brilliance of green light surrounding them. The noise of the descent was sickening.

"What keeps us upright?" yelled Eric, his whitened knuckles gripping the edge of his seat.

"There's a series of tubes, in levels, in the bottom of the SDM. The tubes are filled with mercury. The little computer here senses every change of air density and wind currents and compensates by pumping the mercury into different levels. Very simple."

"Simple? Goddamn!"

"Sure, even our own body movements in here are compensated for."

They suddenly broke out of the glare. Looking down, Eric could see a greenish cloud bank, and through occasional breaks, dark areas that must be the surface. The analogue altimeter read ten thousand feet and Willoughby began firing the two tiny engines to slow their descent. A voluminous orange and black flame erupted from the base of the dropping sphere, sending balls of dark vapor past the visual field. They reclined in the contour body seats as the retrofire increased. A small televisor screen rose from between them, and on it they watched the frozen ground rush up at them.

In a final surge of power, the SDM touched down on three flexible legs that absorbed a good deal of the impact. From the brilliant blue-green sky, fine ice crystals tinkled on the transparent bubble and a hideous wind could be heard raging outside. The seats rose to an upright position.

Outside, the bleak landscape was buffeted by swirling clouds of ultramarine vapor that evaporated, only to reappear again elsewhere. Howling gusts of crystalline material clattered against the ship in an unbearable din. What they could see of the surface was covered with a clear icy substance, while far in the distance, several thin rocky spires jutted out as lonely pinnacles against the bright sky. The blue light was so intense that Eric had to squint even with filters in place. It was like being inside a luminous frosted bulb, inside a glassy nucleus.

Willoughby started triangulation procedures with the metal-detection device. The source seemed to be about fifty meters behind them. He touched a stud that rotated their chairs to face the area from which the highest-intensity reading of metal originated. An ice-covered, dome hillocked, cut on one side by a shallow rill, obscured their view. Harlin noted with satisfaction that they had landed on the side of an incline, but the tripodal landing gear had adjusted to it.

The SDM depressurized with a whoosh of phlegmish-green

vapor that filled the cabin, striking claustrophobic terror into Eric's soul. Eric was first to crawl out. The ground was slippery, spongy in consistency. Harlin followed him, bringing two metal cannisters slung over his shoulder.

"You can carry these Eric. We'll get some geologic specimens. The cannister with the valve is for a sample of the atmosphere."

"All right."

Even though his boots were slightly weighted, Eric felt a strange sense of pressure. He had expected the gravity to be somewhat akin to the lunar situation, although he had no sound basis for this assumption. No planetary explorers had ever gotten near Jupiter, much less Saturn, and no interplanetary probes fired ever landed, although many informative fly-bys were made in the competitive days between the United States and the Soviet Union, in the time before the rise of the Alliance.

Willoughby opened a small, rectangular section in the lower part of the SDM and pulled out a thin, but very durable Trygon cable. This would unreel behind them as they walked.

Leaning against the pounding gale, Harlin Willoughby held the end of the cable and a small control and directional module, while Eric carried the cannisters, stopping occasionally to pick up any loose rocks and frozen material. He was amazed that whenever he touched any of the frozen substance it immediately evaporated into a bluish gas that was caught in the wind and dispersed.

The metallic sensor indicated the high-intensity source to be just over the rise ahead. They had expected to be presented with a good view of the surrounding landscape. When they reached the summit, instead, and to their disappointment, the extent of their visual range was only about a hundred meters. Even the craft in which they had descended was covered by the blowing vapor clouds, with only the cable protruding.

About half-way down the slope lay a twisted shape, alien to this cold world. Slowly working their way down to it, Eric and

Harlin saw that the Second Oleandre Probe lay encrusted with
a fused, crystalline material. Willoughby commented that it
probably entered the Titan atmosphere too fast and had begun
to burn up. This was merely an academic observation.
Willoughby made several loops about the jagged piece of metal
and tightened the cable around it. Then he pressed a panel on
the small module. The cable took up slack, then moved the
entire mass of wreckage several feet. The probe held together
and the cable did not break. Satisfied the Trygon cable could
withstand the strain, Harlin pressed the panel twice and the
cable began reeling in, dragging the probe with it.

Suggesting they return by going around the side of the
small hill to gather more geological specimens, Eric led the
way. He filled the cannister with the spongy undersoil that he
loosened with the edge of his boot. He secured the materials in
the cannisters before they blew away.

The wind blew the icy matter in all directions and it was
only by chance that something under the ice caught Eric's eye.
He leaned down and brushed away the loose material. Harlin
too bent down, and they cleared an area about three feet
square. Their eyes darted back and forth between them in
unspoken communication.

"It can't be possible," Eric finally muttered.

"It is *im*possible," gasped Willoughby.

Under the transparent layer of ice-like material that covered
the spongy gray rock lay a perfect set of footprints. . .
footprints about fifteen inches long and, apparently, with four
toes.

"Goddamn!" Eric's senses were primed and titilating.

"Whatever made these appears to be a biped."

"But what?"

"I don't have the foggiest idea and, dammit, all we have are
the cannisters, no camera. And we could never find this
landing spot again."

"Perhaps we can leave a metallic object from the SDM.

That way we might find this place again," Eric suggested.

"Good, but let's try to extricate a print with the soil still attached."

Try as they would, the rock merely crumbled into small pieces at their slightest touch.

"Let's get back." There was a sense of urgency in Willoughby's voice.

They covered the ground back to the SDM in three minutes, finding the probe lying neatly at the base of the tripodal landing gear. Eric got inside and operated the robot arms that locked with a death grip onto the probe's dangling pieces. It drew the probe gently into a hold in the side of the SDM. The hatch closed. Eric Senka was about to rejoin Harlin outside the craft with a spare cannister when he chanced to look up.

Across the small hill where they had just been came a whirling mass of brownish-green gases, throwing up great clots of ice, frozen methane and rock in all directions. Obviously a severe atmospheric disturbance, the gale moved toward the craft.

"Harlin, get the hell in here!"

Willoughby had already seen the danger, and was half-way in, when he remembered he had left the cannisters containing geological specimens outside. Willoughby turned and went back.

"Harlin! Harlin, damnit man, get in. . ."

The rush of Titan air struck Harlin Willoughby with unnatural violence. He was picked up and pitched against a protruding landing-spoke. His spine snapped, while one of the cannisters, traveling at fantastic speed, struck his helmet and shattered it.

The Surface Descent Module practically toppled over, but the onboard computer had sensed the wind's force and widened its stance in compensation. Gripping the arm of his contour chair, Eric was thrown against the curved wall of the sphere. Through breaks in the gusting wind, he could see

Harlin Willoughby. Eric screamed something; but his voice was lost in the roaring noise of the howling air currents.

The gaseous methane gale had rolled the body of Willoughby away from the ship and up against a pile of eroded black rocks. The shattered visor was caked with bright red, frozen blood. Harlin's eyes had exploded from his head. The mouth was contorted in a hideous, inanimate scream.

Eric almost hypnotically closed the SDM hatch, repressurized, and fired the main engines. Pushing the computer override, he touched the ascent panel and the SDM blasted off its landing gear, now serving as launching pad, in a flash of flames and white fumes. At ten-thousand five-hundred feet, he regained some degree of composure and switched control back over to the computer. The consciousless mechanical brain guided the SDM perfectly into the underside of the Sub-Orbital Craft which had been soaring in great, condor-like circles above them all the time.

He was only aware of the gaping emptiness in the seat next to him in the command module.

Goddamnit, he thought, I was just getting to know Harlin, I thought a friendship was in sight. . .I find it so hard to make meaningful relationships. . .Goddamnit to hell!

Looking over the power controls for a short time, he started the hypergol engine and ran the thruster stud up to plus-five, full power. The blast pushed him back in the acceleration chair which tilted on a spring-like mechanism. He pounded his fist in frustration on the arm of the empty contour seat next to him. The engine burned out at the predetermined time, inserting the Sub-Orbital Craft into a low circular orbit sixty miles above the Titan surface. Then he started the ion propulsion system, returning control to the onboard computer with a programmed course to Oleandre by the quickest astro-projection.

In a few minutes the speed was a thousand miles-per-second. It would take a full two hours to reach the mothership, Oleandre. Two lonely hours — hours for contemplation. Having put it off as long as he could, Eric took several deep breaths and finally opened a low frequency transmission cone to Oleandre.

"Oleandre Control. . .Oleandre Control. . .Sub-Orbital Craft calling. . .Oleandre Control, please acknowledge conic reception."

''SOC. . .SOC. . .Oleandre Control receiving you. . .up frequency five conic wave numbers."

"Five CWNs. . .energized."

"SOC. . .stand by. . .Commander Hayakawa coming on."

"Acknowledged."

"Yes, is that you Eric? Switch on your telescanner. . .did you get the probe?"

"I have the probe," he replied, his voice in a cracked, ominous tone.

"Eric, what's the. . ."

"Willoughby. . .Harlin is dead!"

It struck Seth Hayakawa like a hammerblow. He wanted all the details; but, after seeing Eric's ashen countenance on the televisor screen, he thought better of it.

The Sub-Orbital Craft made its gentle landing at fifteen hundred hours, and the grim news had already spread to all decks.

A tram bearing Commander Hayakawa, Maggie Senka, and several others was already pulling up as Eric shut down the propulsion system and all guidance went external. The launch-line crew was soon working to lower the SDM into a waiting tram equipped with magnetic grapplers. A hissing was heard as the airlock between tram and ship was established. The hatch broke open and Seth Hayakawa was the first through. His face was solemn. Eric whirled in his chair, his eyes meeting Maggie's who rushed past Seth and took Eric's arm. She squeezed it tightly. A team of four medical men brought in a stretchered automaton.

"Where is Harlin?" asked Seth softly.

"OH. . .oh God, Seth. There is no body. I couldn't get to it."

"I see," said the Commander. He turned to the medical personnel, "You people will not be needed. Thank you."

They led Eric into the tram while Harvey McMaster took charge of the recovered probe. A hot meal was waiting in the Commander's study (Willoughby's was hastily removed), and after several relaxing beakers of brandy, Eric's tongue began to loosen and he talked freely of the disaster. They listened in awe as he told of landing on the frozen spongy surface, the bizarre footprints, and the hideous storm that had killed Harlin Willoughby. He finally commented that since he could substantiate none of this — no camera, no cannisters, no Willoughby — the whole episode was like one horrible nightmare.

He was reassured by the Commander that he could have done nothing more and that Harlin's own rash judgment, though admirable in intention, had killed him.

"Seth? We *could* go back. I used the emergency ascent system so the tripodal landing gear is still on the surface of Titan. It would be easy to locate again."

"No, Eric, I will not risk any more people. The primary purpose of the mission, the recovery of the probe, has been accomplished. It is not worth the effort and danger. Is there any. . .just the slightest chance that Willoughby's alive?"

"No, none at all. His helmet visor was shattered, and the sensors showed a surface thermal profile of a hundred degrees Kelvin-Link."

"Yes, I see. Well, that covers it. Fitzgerald will give you a thorough medical debriefing. I trust you and Maggie will keep the details secret, for a while at least. . .footprints? Strange!" The Commander just shook his head.

The medical examination took only thirty-five minutes; Eric was given a light sedative. Even with the calming fluid flowing in his veins, Eric slept nervously, often dreaming — short sequences of dull depression coupled with insane fear.

The probe had been taken to Willoughby's old laboratory since it was already set up and prepared. Inside the twisted, fused metal was the tape package, still intact. In strict secrecy, the tape was played. Only McMaster and the Commander were present.

At first, the raspy metallic message was exciting. It gave locations of no less than ten stars within fifty light-years of the Sun's planetary system. Each of these stars was thought to have a multiple planetary system possibly containing a planet similar to earth. The celestial-real coordinates were given and all the known data pertaining to each star was presented. Hayakawa's computer listened and made a simultaneous printout. The dissertation lasted twenty minutes and the computer had printed about thirty celucel sheets of small letters. McMaster critically looked over each as it dropped from the printout carriage.

The situation looked even more promising as the voice began to discuss the Powers Equation; but their hopes were quickly extinguished when the voice suddenly said, "...THEREFORE, AS THE POWERS EQUATION AND SUPPORTING DATA PIECES ARE INCLUDED IN THE THIRD AND FINAL PROBE SENT OUT BY JASON OLEANDRE, AND SINCE ITS LOCATION HAS BEEN PREVIOUSLY TRANSMITTED, THIS RECORDING IS HEREBY ENDED.. *EBI NECRO PHAGE.*"

McMaster looked at the Commander in shocked disbelief. Even though they were prepared for this, it was still traumatic.

"Good Lord, that finishes it," muttered McMaster.

"I suppose. It would take a century to explore all the satellites and asteroids of this solar system. Even then, we may not find it."

"Not just yet. Let us consider it awhile. I already have a

thought: Who is on board Oleandre? The most diverse conglomeration of creative individuals ever assembled. Right?"

McMaster nodded, not quite grasping where the Commander was headed with this line of thought.

"Well then, let us put the problem directly into everyone's hands. If this group can't solve it, no one can. We will stop all research, stop all projects. Everyone of Oleandre must delve into this with all the fortitude available. Every possibility must be given careful consideration."

"I agree, Seth; besides, I hate that Goddamned Martian atmosphere." For possibly the first time in his life, Harvey McMaster's voice was edged with humility.

That evening, at exactly nineteen hundred, the Commander spoke to all advocates of the Mission. He told of Willoughby's fate, although omitting the exact circumstances and the episode of the mysterious footprints. He related the failure of this probe to disclose the location of the third. Then he gave them their task: Oleandreans were to devote all their collective energies toward the finding of the last probe. This would continue until the Counsel felt that all possibilities had been thoroughly explored. He wished them good hunting and Godspeed.

A wisp of smoke curled upward from the bowl of the silver pipe and evaporated. Eric Senka sat back, letting the stem of the pipe dangle in the corner of his mouth. He reached up and ran his forefinger around the neck band of the black turtleneck sweater. Maggie sat on one corner of the bed with two tiny buttons in her ears. . .listening to Mozart. She was oblivious to Eric's presence. She was two-months pregnant with their first child. Reaching over to the instrument rack next to his chair, he produced a wand-like mouthpiece. He twisted the bottom of the device, and the head suddenly glowed in amber solitude. Eric Senka dictated:

". . .This being the forty-fourth entry in this journal, Eric C. Senka transmitting. Oleandre Day one-four-seven has ended with no tangible results in the search for the last probe. . .not even a clue. The Oleandre is still in circular orbit about nine million miles from Saturn. We will stay here until no new ideas for locating the missing probe occur. Most efforts have been of a theoretical nature. Our only practical attempt is the production of a fleet of unmanned instrument packages. These are under construction and will be sent to scan various areas of the solar system, especially the satellites of Jupiter.

"Willoughby's tragic loss has resulted in the enactment of an isolationist policy. Commander Hayakawa has ordered that no manned craft will leave Oleandre for any reason. The thought of Harlin's death still haunts me and I sometimes think people believe I killed him. . .this is utter paranoia on my part. Still. . .I have never mentioned this lest they think me mad. . .but while that hideous storm was racking the SDM, I had the almost uncanny feeling that evil intelligence was lurking nearby. . .and those footprints. . .were they real? I almost begin to think we imagined them. Yet, Harlin saw them, too.

"There are too many loose ends, and I am an empirical man. It bothers me that events must go unexplained. Perhaps I am too sensitive; perhaps I attach too much significance to minor things. But some strange occurrences have taken place.

"Thus, I will record for my journal's completeness that in the PEPTIDE SYNTHESIS CHAMBER yesterday, two servo-mechanins overrode their programs, and seemed to go berserk. They destroyed several valuable and almost irreplaceable pieces of equipment. They were, of course, quickly nullified and reprogrammed; but I consider this a very unique occurrence. However, if I am in error, I have wasted only a few picometers of memory bank. But if there is significance, I have recorded it for my children and their generation. End transmission. . .code A. . .z. . .one. . .three. . .dash. . .seven."

THE DARKNESS

". . .driven by galactic winds
into the darkness of both
the crumbling intellect and
blackened temple of Thoth."

— *Collected Lyricisms of Nea
Abusen*, 2893, 4th year in
the reign of Jos-Ri of Photos,
Baron of Elephantine, Emperor
of Lights.

CHAPTER 5

It was not that Willoughby's violent and untimely end had
een forgotten; rather, the entire population was just too busy
ith the crisis at hand to spend precious time concocting
nartyrs. The construction of a series of deep planetary probes
as proceeding smoothly and the launch date was set.

The emergency seemed to have brought most of the people
loser together, and they worked more diligently than ever.
here was some dejection and a sense of frustration: this was
> be expected. However, spirited debates of how to solve the
ilemma overrode any tendency to defeatism. All but the
asic, life-sustaining services had been shut down or shifted
ver to working out The Solution. Of course, the food
roducing, environmental control, and medical services units
emained fully functional.

Most of the physics and engineering research programs had
een pressed into service to devise new and ingenious
istrumentation to be added to the planetary probes. The High
nergy Physics Group, headed by Lin Hsu Piao had developed
scanning system so sensitive that it could pick up the

asymmetric stretching frequencies of a metallic object
centimeter square at a distance of two hundred miles. Th
capability could be programmed to detect all of the know
metals and man-made alloys.

The basic problem, however, was excessive weight. Th
Extraterrestrial Engineering facility had been working t
eliminate all but the vital components. This problem had bee
recently solved by installing one large, but extremely compac
central computer system for all the sensors on a prob
Eliminating the need for each sensor system to have its ow
individual computer, this method drastically cut the probe
weight.

There were to be a total of twelve interplanetary probe
each with a different mission, although some overlap wa
deliberately planned. Each probe was housed in a shinin
chloromagnesium-carbide cone about fifteen feet high an
nine feet in base diameter. Behind the instrument cone wa
mounted a dual-ion propulsion unit. The entire package wa
mounted on a small booster engine that operated on the o
oxidizer principle.

The booster could lift the probe from Oleandre, and prop
it out of the Saturnian gravity field until its limited fuel suppl
expired. Then staging would occur and the ion engines woul
take over. The boosters were to orbit indefinitely aroun
Saturn, and they were equipped with homing devices so the
could be picked up to be used again if it became necessary.

On the one hundred and eighty-eighth day of the Mission
the entire sphere of Oleandre shook twelve times as th
powerful boosters were ignited. Each probe was launche
without mishap and all but one pulled free of Saturn
gravitational field. The probe destined to explore the are
around the small planet Mercury, and then as close to the Su
as safety would permit, had failed to achieve staging and ha
gone into orbit about the ringed planet at a perigeal distanc
of seven and three-quarters million miles. The booste

separation was carried out through a complicated set of telemetric exercises; and, finally, after only six hours delay, the Mercurial probe was on its way.

Through logical argument, it was thought that an obvious place for Jason Oleandre to store his last probe was in the asteroid belt between Mars and the giant planet Jupiter. Here, among the myriad fragments of some tenth planet long since pulverized by an unknown cataclysm, a space probe could have been hid from the skillful intelligence networks of the Alliance and K'uang Fong.

Five of the probes were now directed to that area. Two others were sent to scan the Martian and Venusian sectors, while another pair would investigate Jupiter and its satellites. The remaining duo would scout the trans-Uranian area. Oleandre itself, would check the rest of Saturn's moons.

It would take at least a month for most of the probes to complete their missions, although the five that scanned the asteroid belt would require eighty days.

Meanwhile, the intense investigations aboard Oleandre continued. Jonathan Fischer had put aside all his work and was drawing upon all the Receptacle's information about Jason Oleandre in hopes of finding even the tiniest clue as to the last probe's location. He had most of Oleandre's writings on hand and many hitherto unreleased personal interviews and correspondence. The Receptacle's computer maze would compile a complete profile of Jason Oleandre.

To make the study as complete as possible, all personnel were to send Fischer any information they had on Jason Oleandre. . .no matter how trivial it seemed. One of the most interesting pieces of data to come out of Fischer's request was a fairly complete copy of Oleandre's medical history which Fitzgerald had hidden away in his diagnostic memory coils. It was things like this that Fischer needed to make his study complete. It became almost a contest to see what piece of trivia someone could contribute, although the need for accuracy was stressed by Fischer's staff.

During a rather heated debate on whether there actually *was* a third probe, Harvey McMaster was taken suddenly ill. He presented a classic acute liver failure to Fitzgerald's diagnostic clinic, and it was only after a few hours of testing that the need for a complete liver transplant was established. McMaster was well into his sixties, although his slim wrinkleless body and the upsetting sharpness of his intellect made him seem two decades younger.

The liver transplant presented no particular problem since the surgical procedure involved standard technique, even for a person of his advanced age. (War, with its disastrous effect on medical research, and pollution had caused a regression in the average human life span, which had progressively creeped to a high of eighty-four years by 2003, but was now only sixty-nine due to the pollution-related genetic damage.)

It had been over a decade ago that the problem of tissue rejection had been solved. This occurred when a team of immunologists headed by V. E. Shlepanov at the Mendelyeev Institute had succeeded in isolating the so-called histocompatability antigens. Once done, it was a relatively simple matter to find natural and synthetic inhibitors to these antigens.

One of the few valuable things to come out of the Great Asian Land War was a goodly supply of antibodies to the various histocompatability antigens. The Slavic Alliance Partner, victorious in the hard-fought Battle of the Kosygin Steppe, took a million K'uang prisoners in three sweeping campaigns, although it sustained extremely heavy losses itself. Many hundreds of thousands of the wretched yellow creatures were injected with the specific histocompatability antigen by field representatives of the Human Factors Presidium, the political arm of the Mendelyeev Institute. When the serum titers were high enough, the prisoners' blood was drained, and the anti-bodies isolated from the blood serum. Despite their rather dubious origin, Oleandre was able to obtain a sizable quantity of these anti-bodies. The tissue rejection syndrome had been eliminated and there was really no need for tissue-typing anymore.

In the Organ Storage Bank, all the various organs that could possibly be needed for transplantation were kept perfusing in bubbling vats of isotonic saline. Vascular tubing ran in nutrients and removed the wastes of cellular metabolism. Hearts, kidneys, livers, and lungs were most plentiful due to the frequency of need. However, in the event of a rare case, several bladders, cornea, pituitaries, adrenals, bone marrow and thymus were kept on hand. Of course, there were no brains; and even the transplantation of eyes was not yet perfected since the delicate matching of the optic nerves had not yet been mastered.

The stored organs were replaced with fresh ones after a month of artificial maintenance. The supply of new organs posed no problem, since everyone on Oleandre had pledged his body as part of the recruitment vows. As each member died, his healthy organs were automatically placed in the bank if needed, while any other tissue was used for research as a committee saw fit.

There were no burials on Oleandre. There could be none, for if that mundane practice were followed, within a few generations, Oleandre would be nothing more than a giant interstellar mausoleum. What remained of a corpse was homogenized and used for fertilizer in the hydroponics section or as a food supplement. This was the fate of all dead animal matter on Oleandre; most fecal material, too, was put to this use. Whole and perfect corpses unnecessary to basic medical research were preserved for students of classical gross anatomy.

Renate Sontag, head of the Organ Storage Bank, had commented often on the irony that seemed inherent in cardiac transplantation. The heart transplant was common practice:

the constant supply of these organs eliminated the ethical problem involving the death of the donor. But in all these years, the contruction of a functionally perfect, artificial heart had met with dismal failure. The device, first crudely used in the late nineteen sixties, had never been perfected. There seemed to be some sort of divine curse on that area of research.

Harvey McMaster underwent a three-day desensitization to his new liver tissue before its insertion. This involved the use of antibodies to the six liver histocompatibility antigens. The surgical procedure required only forty-five minutes. A laser scapel made the thin opening and McMaster's swollen, cirrhotic liver was removed, lobe by lobe, and discarded as fertilizer. The transplant was completed and the closure accomplished with the ruby laser beam. The sutureless wound, running from under one arm to the groin was but a thin, red trough, the width of a penciled line. McMaster was removed from the surgical suite by two sterile automatons and placed in a Recovery Module where the function of his new liver was continually monitored.

The newly transplanted tissue functioned perfectly and the yellowish skin was already beginning to fade. His eyes were regaining their usual brightness.

Maggie Senka was completing the fourth month of her pregnancy. She had been assured by her physician that all was proceeding normally.

Eric was at odds with himself. Not only did the horror of Willoughby's death prey upon his mind, but a seeping gnawing sense of uselessness was slowly overcoming him. He had stopped his brain transplantation research according to Hayakawa's directive, but after days of pacing and thinking could not come up with any positive contribution to the problem of finding the last Jason Oleandre probe. After six weeks of frustrating idleness, Eric finally resolved to resume his project. He needed to work. It would take his mind off that haunting day on Titan.

After puttering about in his laboratory for two or three days, Eric was suddenly struck by the thought that the mysterious footprints on the Titan surface could be related to the last probe. Jesse Horvitz was on leave from Oleandre University, as were most of the students. He was working for Jonathan Fischer in the Receptacle.

Eric sat down to dictate all he could remember about the footprints under the ice. He also made many crude drawings and, when he was satisfied as to the size and shape, he went to see Alfonsis Nikto, Oleandre's leading and only taxonomist.

Maggie was putting in long hours refitting the radio-telescope so that it could be used to scan for signals just outside the solar system in areas not covered by the twelve probes. The stress of the work, coupled with her condition, resulted in her being extremely tired and irritable most of the time. Eric sensed this and tried to make her as comfortable as possible by making sure Pseudomonius had the meals ready on time. Eric read aloud to her. She was especially fond of certain late-twentieth century poets: Yevtushenko, Dobel, and particularly Robert Creeley. Maggie was also rehearing the classic, STRANGER IN A STRANGE LAND.

On OD-192, two days after McMaster's liver transplant, Maggie was scanning an area just outside the orbit of the minor planet Pluto. It was a routine sweep and had she not by chance glanced at the digital readout sheet the phenomenon would have been missed. The scanning area was blank, but the background-null tracing showed an intense and variable radio transmission.

She quickly fed the celestial coordinates into the Astrophysics Department's computer system which automatically

compensated for Oleandre's changing position as it orbited
Saturn. After a minute of whirling tapes and flashing sensors, a
single series appeared on the thin celucel readout strip:

****

°°°°°°°°°°°°°PKS 0237-23°°°°°°°°°°°°°°°°°°°°°°°
°°°°°°°°°°°°°°°   °°°°°°°°°°°°°°°°°°°°°°°

****

"I understand," said Eric, seeing that a simple, quick
answer was not likely to come out of all this.

"I will feed this information to my data-retrieval center for
preliminary screening. It will take about fifteen minutes. While
we are waiting, will you think abou this: it looks from your
sketches, that this creature, whatever it is or was, was a biped
and walked or moved upright, *but,* it would be very helpful if
you can remember if there were any differences in the depth
of the print. Any indication of an arch would prove a lot."

"Yes, I see, but remember, I saw the prints through a clear,
icy covering which could have interfered with my perception."

"Uh-huh," said Nikto walking toward his computer and
muttering. "This *is* bloody exciting!"

"I seem to remember that the depressions were deeper
away from the split end. Could that be evidence of an arch?"

"No, not necessarily, but perhaps a heel."

While awaiting the computer's preliminary verdict, Nikto
thumbed through several large and ancient texts in comparative vertebrate anatomy, whose leather bindings cracked when
he opened them, while Eric busied himself by wandering
around Nikto's chaotic laboratory. He had an especially
complete collection of seeds with psychotropic activity, and
there were several plastic sacks of brown and red pods from a
plant in the genus *Rivea* which was usually found in the area
once known as Mexico in earlier times. These specimens,
however, were collected by scientists attached to an Alliance

pacification team sent into the foothills of the Himalayas. The pods had never been extracted and tested for hallucinatory activity. It was important, not only from an aesthetic standpoint, but from a practical one, to test the active component of the seeds from *Rivea Hsia*. Since the complete failure of the orthomolecular concept of psychiatry at the end of the twentieth century, no new agents had been found for the treatment of mental illness. Most of this had been due to the complete indifference of the Alliance leaders and their fantastic war expenditures. One other fact made research in this area impractical: mental deficients were executed!

It was sickeningly ironic that in the fifty years since the rise of the Alliance, absolutely no progress had been made in eliminating diseases of the mind. Technological hardware, however, had made tremendous strides forward, only to end up driving civilization back to the primitive.

As he turned the dark-brown vials and yellow specimen bags to see their labels, they reflected the diversity of Nikto's collection. . .many species of octopii and squid, reptiles,and exotic insects, profusely colored, all in magnetized cases. But an unimportant-looking, vacusealed sack, bulging with preservative caught his eye. It couldn't be, he thought, but it sure as hell looks like it.

"Nikto?"

"Yes, Senka," said Nikto, looking up from behind a stack of worn volumes.

"What the devil is this?"

"Is what?"

"The. . .eh. . .material, the specimen in this bag," he said, pointing to the place on the magnetic wall.

"Oh, those," replied Nikto supressing a laugh, "those are a very prized possession of mine. . .both historically as well as anatomically. The vacubag contains a human penis and testicles."

"Oh, Jesus, I was right!"

"But a very special penis and testicles, I might add."

"Oh, I'll bet, your own?"

"Certainly not, you rotter! Eric, my evilminded, lecherous friend, those are the genitals of Napoleon Bonaparte!"

"You're putting me on, really? I mean, how do you know and why would you want to. . ."

Nikto interrupted, "They are genuine all right. I have the antiquity-pedigree tapes to prove that, but they have a most interesting, grantedly grisly history. Would you be interested?"

"Don't stop now."

"As you probably know from your elementary study of historiography, when the Emperor died, the autopsy, which was, by the way, performed on a billiard table, revealed cancer, venereal disease, etc. But the dissector, clever fellow, retained certain parts of the cadaver, a femur, perhaps the heart, *and* the genitals. These organs passed from collector to collector, fetching high prices when sold at auction in the late twentieth century by a rather famous auction house, purchased by persons who, for obvious reasons, remained anonymous."

"Fascinating, go on!"

"Well, as far as I can tell, the genitalia came into the hands, you'll pardon the expression, of a Grecian hydrofoil tycoon, whose fast cargo ships were used by the Oleandre Foundation. I was aboard one of the vessels, called the *Adonis*, making the run from Baja to the Peruvian Base during the General Recall."

"You were on Earth during the General Recall?"

"Yes, I was one of the last to get out. But, as I was saying, I was to join the Mission on Mars. Anyhow, the hold of the *Adonis* was filled with art treasures, I don't know why, but among them were these specimens of Bonaparte, validity papers and all. So, what can I say, I took them. The ship was to be scuttled anyway, since it was the last hydro-foil going to the Andean launching facility. That is how I acquired them," said Nikto holding up the sack and examining them closely.

The blackened phallus floated freely while the oval testes lay in the bottom, still bulging in their scrotum with whorls of dark, pubic hair clinging to it and a flap of fatty groin tissue cut by the careless dissector's razor.

This designation was that of a known quasistellar radio source. Touching another sensor, the quasar's spectrum appeared and it showed a red shift indicating the object to be receding from them at more than eighty-five percent of the speed of light. There were also some rather puzzling absorption lines in the specturm, so she obtained a complete profile on the object. It seemed that not much was known, although it was theorized that a "dead" galaxy was superimposed between the quasar and Oleandre.

The amazing thing was that Maggie was observing and recording a variable radio emission from this object. The variable pattern ran about three minutes, then began over again. Each series matched exactly with the last one. She recorded it several times. Then, holding the readout tape in her hand, she sat back and stared at the illuminated ceiling. She thought, could this be a communication effort? Her thought was interrupted by the waves of nausea that periodically racked her body. It soon passed and Maggie noted that she had ten minutes to get to her appointment with her physician. Today was to be an important day. Today, Dr. Steinman would confirm the sex of their baby and give it its first *in utero* innoculations.

Using a thermoholograph-scanner to locate the fetus without the damaging use of X-rays, the servomechanin painlessly placed a small, hollow catheter in her side and removed a sample of the amniotic fluid, the fetus' warm liquid crib. Through this same sampling needle, a solution was introduced containing all the blood-group antigens and all the histocompatability antigens. Since the fetus was not able to recognize foreign material, having no immunological

competence itself, it would incorporate these substances into
its immunologic memory when it developed. These antigens
would be part of its "self." In adult life then, the being would
be able to take any kind of blood in transfusion and accept
any organ in transplant without the danger of rejection.

The treatment was over in about twenty minutes and by
the time Maggie had dressed, Immanuel Steinman had
confirmed that indeed, the baby would be a boy.

The amniotic fluid sample contained a few cells, sloughed
off by the fetus when it moved in the womb. A single cell was
selected, its nucleus isolated and carefully opened with
microprobes. The chromosomes were spread on a depression
on a glass tube, which was scanned by a computer and the
cell's karyotype deduced. It picked out the X and Y
chromosomes, indicative of a male.

Maggie left the clinic assured that there would soon be a
little Sean Senka.

Nikto's area was located in the Delta Sector of J-Deck, next
to the wedge that was the Museum of Extraterrestrial
Geomorphology, containing specimens from definitive space
exploration. On display behind ozmyglass panels were the
Tranquility Base basalts from the first human landing on
Lunare, the Ehrentite silicates from a later American Apollo
mission to the lunar dark-side, the Zernov nuggets of pure gold
from the first manned landing on Mars, the massive, yet
delicately beautiful Freedom by the Kenney Expedition's first
trip to the asteroid Toro. There were many others, and the
name-plaques under the rocks and needles of magenta crystal
read like a classic text in early astroexploration. The specimens
were here, not because of any intrinsic value, but as a reminder
of the heritage they bore: that of the unhampered pioneer
spirit before the rise of the totalitarians.

The working-living quarters of Alfonsis Nikto were
cluttered with old herbals, and stacks of ancient, yellowing

manuscripts sat atop row upon row of cabinets housing biological specimens. Nikto was an expert in the classification of both plants and animals. As there was not room for a complete museum of specimens, he kept a huge color, micropoint library of all of the Earth's flora and fauna, and of the few known Martian life forms. Eric had come to show him the drawings of the Titan footprints and ask Nikto for help in classifying them. Alfonsis was truly amazed when he saw the sketches. He leaned back in his chair and crinkled up his nose.

"My God, Senka, I didn't really believe this story. I'd heard rumors, but thought that's all they were, just rumors."

"The prints are real all right. But whether you can help is another question."

"I'll certainly try. . .Senka? Uhh, your first name again?"

"Eric."

"Oh, yes, of course. You'll have to excuse me. It's a strange thing about me, I can remember and recite the species and subspecies names of the most insignificant plants or fungi or PPLOs, but can't recall the names of people I meet."

"Forget it. You *do* realize why I came to you? These prints could have a bearing on the last Oleandre probe, since we found them not too far from the wreckage of the second probe. Perhaps it's coincidence, perhaps not."

"Yes, by all means. Even if there is no connection, it is a tremendous discovery. You're sure of these dimensions and the split area at one end?"

"At one end? You sound as if you're not assuming they're toes. I surely thought they were."

"Not necessarily. In an Earth animal yes, but we must not forget this is likely to be an alien creature. The digitation could be on the rear part, who knows, it may not be digitation at all. We must explore all possibilities."

"That *is* amazing! I've never heard anything so wild in my entire life, the Emperor's cock! Christ!"

"Rather silly I suppose, I could have brought out an oil, a

Monet or a Klitz, but this attracted me. Besides, I was high on
amphetamines at the time, we all were. . .seventy-five hours
without sleep trying to dodge the Alliance Thermoseekers. We
were to have picked up Chiodi on that trip."

"Chiodi! T. H. Chiodi, the dialectician?"

"Yes, and this is the unfortunate thing. . .you remember his
famous work in interpreting the various dialects of the
elephant seal, actually communicating with them? Chiodi
would have been of great value to the Mission. He had been
recruited and cleared too! That's the tragedy. The *Adonis* was
to pick him up at the Linus Pauling Laboratory of Marine
Acoustics on San Miguel Island, then a smog shrouded
aquasuburb of the City of California."

"And?"

"He decided to stay. No amount of persuasion could
convince him to change his mind. He wished to die on his own
planet. There was no time for much argument, because, by
that time, the hydrofoil was under attack by a squadron of
Thermoseekers, but we repelled them and escaped with
towering splashes of steam erupting all around us from their
laser blasts. We were lucky to get out of that. I'll not forget
that last Pacific sunset, darkening shades of blue sky, streaked
with wispy orange and purple clouds."

"You're right about Chiodi though. If we ever encounter
aliens, his future work would have been invaluable. Too bad.
Not to change the subject, but your collection certainly is
fascinating."

"But, alas, they are all dead. It's a necrotorium. Oh, to have
zoos again! It is the living species that are important, for they
are the terminal products of long anatomical history. Of
course, evolution still goes on. We shall see this on Oleandre."

"Do you think so? After all, Oleandre is a closed
environment. Wouldn't that be enough to slow down — or
altogether halt — evolution?"

"Perhaps. But remember, Eric, all species are kind of anatomical mosaics; that is, they have general and specialized functions, primitive and advanced systems. . .probably all adaptive. So why should the evolutionary process here on Oleandre be hindered? None of us has reached the Vislov Genetic Nullpoint."

"Yes," said Eric, running his finger under the fold of skin at the corner of one eye to remove a piece of lint. "I believe I see what you mean. I was just correlating what you said with my neurological experiences. You know, the brain has primitive or, as I would call them, ancestral areas where the primeval instincts lie, as well as areas for more advanced traits such as reasoning. I believe that these. . ."

A high-pitched whistling noise interrupted them and announced that the computer was on a printout cycle. Nikto went to the machine and looked over the tape as it spewed from its slot. He frowned. A little man, perhaps five-feet-two, and completely bald, his entire head when he frowned seemed to erupt into a mass of fat wrinkles with beads of perspiration dotting the smooth areas that remained.

"Anything?"

"I don't know exactly. . .computer says there is no analogy from Earthly data. . .no comparison on any reference scale. However, if your data on the spacing of the individual prints and the variable depth of the depressions are correct, computer says we have an upright creature."

"It would be fairly large then, judging from the size of the print."

"Not necessarily, you have no samples of Titan soil, so we can't use the depth of the print and the soil density as a parameter for size. Besides, gravity would play a big factor."

"No real clues then?"

"No, not really. We could make a lot of speculations, but they would be *only* that. . .speculations."

"I see."

"Sorry. . .may I keep your sketches?"

"Sure, but make me a copy and send it to me."

"I'll make it right now. I've enjoyed talking with you, Senka. I'm sort of a loner you know. Do drop in again. . .any time."

Jesse Horvitz walked slowly through what seemed an endless corridor lined with micropoint files. In effect, this section of the Receptacle was endless for the passageway wound in a perfect helix. It was thirty feet in height and lined from the deck to its translucent ceiling with tiny numbered openings about two by three centimeters. The entire area was brightly illuminated by indirect lighting.

He looked at the illuminated guide that sat at the base of each column. It read: 14717:000-199.

The celucel card in his palm read: 14717-177.

This is the column, he thought. Stepping onto a plate about two feet square, he touched a panel with his foot and the platform began to rise. The numbers flashed by his eyes and he stopped the ascent when 14717-177 was at eye level. Touching another panel on the platform, a televisor screen rose up to his waist. He tilted it to make reading easier. The two magnetic leads from the televisor were then attached to a tiny metal plate next to the number he was looking for. Instantly, the first page of what seemed to be an old book came into view:

ALLIANCE MILITARY ECONOMICS

-An Assessment-
by
Jason Oleandre

He touched a small heat sensor on the screen and the micropoint pages began to slowly pass. Jesse Horvitz read rapidly. He had the capacity of two thousand words-a-minute with eighty percent retention. . .not a spectacular rate, but adequate. He was on assignment from Jonathan Fischer to read certain works of Jason Oleandre published by the Foundation in order to glean any possible clues of value.

Listening to the verbal version, his thoughts wandered as he sat in the "reading room." He decided to examine the cracking and brittle pages of the original work. The typesetting was atrocious, with many errors of transposition. He toyed with the idea of a code being set within the scope of the printing errors but later dismissed the idea as impractical. Fischer had agreed.

He made a few notes on a small celucel pad, then detached the telemetry leads, and the platform descended. Standing steadily, he remembered the gripping terror that welled within him the first time he had mounted a platform to check something filed high above the floor. However, he quickly gained finesse at rising thirty feet on a metal plate two feet square with no railings.

The platform stopped at floor level and he stepped off backward, his mind oblivious to his surroundings. He did not see the girl with an armload of tapes behind him. He stepped on her instep and knocked her to the opposite wall. The pile of tapes clattered to the floor, reverberating again and again down the corridor.

"HADEM! What the devil are. . ."

"Oh, I'm terribly sorry miss. . .h-how clumsy of me."

"You're damn right. . .clumsy oaf!"

"Here, let me help you with these tapes," said Jesse sheepishly.

"Go to Hadem! *I'll* get them. I don't need any help. . *yours* especially."

Her flowing white sari was open at the top and she

presented his eyes with a quick glimpse of her large, firm breasts as she bent over to pick up the tapes.

"Take a holograph," she muttered to him, then continued down the corridor and disappeared around the gentle curve.

Didn't have to be *that* nasty, he thought; but he shrugged his shoulders and went back to writing a memo.

He did not chance to see her again until three days later and even then he did not know she was Iridani Beshiva. While taking his midday meal, he spied her sitting alone at a short table. Her curtness had intrigued him. Her black glistening hair fell over both shoulders to frame an oval face and compliment her dark flawless skin and intense black eyes. Jesse thought she may have been of Moorish extraction. He walked over to her. He could see that she *had* seen him, but was trying to ignore him.

"Anyone sitting here?" he asked, referring to the empty seat and knowing full well that no one was occupying it.

"No." Her voice was neutral, emotionless.

"May I?"

"If you wish. . .it is not my concern."

"I do hope you're still not offended by my knocking you down. I *am* sorry."

"I'd forgotten about it a second after I walked away. Now, if you please, I am trying to read."

"Do you have to be so surly? I didn't bump into you on purpose you know."

"Oh, I know. . .it's just, well, I'm very busy," she said, this time in a softer tone.

"Of course, we all are. What do you do?"

"I am a poet or poet*ress*, whatever you like."

"OH. . .oh, you're *the* poet."

"Yes, *the* poet," she mocked.

It was not that the Oleandre concept precluded poets, quite on the contrary, but Iridani Beshiva was the only established poet that could be recruited. As it was, there were few true poets during the time of the Alliance.

Iridani's fluid poems of love and violent revolution had been supressed; she had taken refuge in the stronghold of the El Fetah in the High Atlas Mountains where she continued to write. Her works were circulated by underground presses and widely read throughout the world. She had things of value to say to both sides and this was reflected in translations of her poems in both English and Mandarin. Her best known work was the epic *Proudhon Upanishad.*

El Fetah was an offshoot of the ancient panArab organization that swept the Middle East in bloody holy wars that all but destroyed the Zion Imperial State. It had been outlawed by both the Alliance and K'uang Fong who then controlled most of the north African buffer zone. El Fetah ultimately retreated into the High Atlas Mountains of Morocco, with headquarters not far from Ouarzazate, where it continued to carry out fanatic guerrilla raids even up to the Earth's last day.

Her poetry had one very influential and powerful admirer, Jason Oleandre. His small fleet of Recopters, in a lightning attack on the El Fetah fortress, succeeded in repatriating Iridani Beshiva. El Fetah took heavy losses while Oleandre lost two Recopters and their crews; however, Iridani was soon safe in the Foundation's Andean base. She was nineteen then and was quickly processed to the Martian exile, disguised as an astrocommunications technician.

Jason Oleandre, though, had made one vital mistake in assuming she would *want* to be part of the Mission. She was, in fact, a pure humanist although she had slight anarchist tendencies. She was, in fact, kidnapped. But seeing the Earth's predicament, she eventually volunteered for the Mission.

"I've always enjoyed poetry, although I must admit that I don't know much about it. I have never read any of yours. Could I see some of your work?"

"What? A technocrat like you? I am amazed. . .surely you'll want a sterilized, computerized, iodized and vaporized synopsis of my poems along with the complete syntaxial analysis!"

"Christ! I would just like to *read* one, that's all!"

"You are truly serious, are you not?"

"Yes."

"May Hadem twirl in his musty crypt! Fine, I have a recent poem with me," she said, reaching under the table and pulling out a small case brimming with amber papers. "It is on paper, so you won't be able to put it into a 'reader.' Is that all right?"

"Of course. Anyhow, I miss the feel of real manuscript paper."

"You amaze me! Here is the poem I mentioned. It is called *The Programmed Man.* Read it if you wish, and perhaps we could discuss it at a later date. . .I must go now!"

She abruptly stood up, whirled to walk away, then turned to him, a quizzical look on her face.

"Don't worry," he said. "I'll get this back to you."

She almost smiled. Then, brushing the dark hair from her face, she was gone.

Maggie Senka had been in the sixth month of her pregnancy when the announcement was made by Commander Hayakawa. The probes launched from Oleandre had completed their missions. There were no positive findings. It was as simple as that. Of course the four probes combing the asteroid belt had not yet reported in. Five probes were launched; one, however, had been destroyed in a collision with a small asteroid. The Commander's voice was firm, but one could not help but detect a hint of disappointment.

The news of the failure to gain any clues as to the whereabouts of the last Oleandre probe had hit Eric extremely hard. His nervousness increased and the nightmares of Willoughby became more frequent. He would often awake, soaked in his own perspiration, shaking uncontrollably. He could not work. He paced the curved corridor talking to himself under his breath. Everyone seemed hard at work; no one seemed despondent. . .only him. Trying to fight off the sweeping paranoia, he pestered people incessantly, convinced that his brain research could make no positive contribution to the Mission.

Eric hounded Alfonsis Nikto about the Titan footprints to the point where Nikto refused to open the entrance to his suite.

One morning, while talking with Seth Hayakawa, he had been able to get the Commander to admit that if no one was successful, and the remaining unreported probes did not provide any worthwhile information, the Oleandre would return to its Martian ancestry. This furthered Eric's depression.

At nineteen-hundred-ten hours on OD-227, Harvey McMaster took a huge gasp of air, clutched his chest with a shaking fist, clenched his teeth hideously and keeled over dead. It was thirty-six days after his liver transplant and he had been progressing perfectly, resting a lot, but still able to work in his private study. There had been no hint as to any cardiac problems; autopsy showed the classical myocradial infraction.

. A public memorial service, with Seth Hayakawa giving the eulogy, was attended by all of fourteen people. . .a tribute to McMaster's popularity.

A week later, the telecon console sounded in the reading room of the Receptacle. An anonymous and somewhat voluptuous female voice answered, "Yes."

"I wish to speak with Mister Horvitz, Jesse Horvitz. Is he there? Eric Senka calling."

"I believe he is in the micropoint stacks. I shall transfer the call."

"Thank you."

A pause, and Eric heard several electronic beeps.

"Horvitz."

"Jesse? Eric here. How're things going?"

"Uh, fine, I suppose."

"Good, listen my boy, can you come to the lab? I've something to talk over with you."

"Well, I. . .guess I can."

"Listen, it's extremely important."

"I'll be down in a fusion."

CHAPTER 6

The birth of Sean Eric Senka occurred without complica-
tion. He burst forth from the womb's warm security into a
world never before faced by humans. The time of the event
was precisely three-hundred hours, OD-309.

Maggie felt the first contractions at dinner the previous
evening. Dr. Fitzgerald, summoned from a concert of Mason
William's works, came to begin the delivery. Fitzgerald's nurse,
Genevieve Ribald, readied the incubator that sat next to the
Senkas' bed, and adjusted the bacteroicidal unit. Eric paced
nervously. Maggie, covered by sheets and the delivery devices,
smiled up at him in anesthetized stupor. Her labor was not too
difficult, but Eric could not stand the occasional cries of pain,
although Fitzgerald assured him everything was proceeding as
usual. Finally, he left their quarters, went next door, and
furiously smoked one pipe after another.

Miss Ribald popped her head in and said, very matter-of-
factly, that the baby was born. Eric rushed into the room just
as Fitzgerald carried the red and screaming little creature to
the warm, plastic pseudowomb. Its wrinkled body quivered

and then assumed a fetal position. Maggie lay glassy-eyed and breathing heavily; but she managed a slight smile and Eric took her hand. Fitzgerald eventually took the afterbirth, and they got Maggie into her own bed. Nurse Ribald would stay five days to care for the new mother and child.

Eric's head was spinning with the presence of the new arrival and the assault on his sacrosanct privacy. However, he soon looked at and held his son with pride.

Maggie had been given a sedative and Nurse Ribald was to give little Sean his first feedings. Eric, restless and irritable from the first trauma of fatherhood, had volunteered to sleep on a pull-out cot in his laboratory. For a while he lay in the dark, eyes wide. The clicking of automated biochemical apparatus echoed in the night and amplified the thunder in his head. With the first waves of sleep his mind whirled in an eternal mist. . .

. . .*the cold transparent block closed over him and his body was spun out of its bed and through the silver wall. As if Oleandre were a molecular sieve, his corpse was strained until it finally broke out of its spherical tomb, the Malovium sarcophagus of Oleandre. He was propelled faster and faster toward the Saturnian ring system that glowed ahead. As he passed through the rings he could feel the tinkling of icy dust hitting his shoulders, encrusting his whitened hair with glitter. Out into deep space now, faster yet. . .at incredible speed the stars rushed at him and passed him by. Behind, every pinpoint glowed as red as the fire in his heart. Faster. . .through choking gaseous nebulae. . .through a spiraling pinwheel of blazing light. Past multiple sun systems. . .partners of red and green, spinning 'round a common center. . .rocky, lifeless giants in gaseous shells so vast that companion stars are immersed within. . .out into the receding clusters of galaxies. . .passing them by. . .out into the void. . .as an astrofoil bouncing in the universal ether. . .out into nothing.*

He was drawn eternally through the claustrophobic vacuum at the edge of the universe. . .to the end of the universe. And at the physical limit of the unending entity, before the universe and time turn back upon themselves, he came to a solid brick wall of ancient orange cubes, set by crumbling mortar. Glass vines, purple clematis grew from chinks in the masonry. Set within this infinite barricade was a rusting iron door with one broken hinge, so that it sat off balance, at an angle.

Approaching the wall, his ankles swathed in a swirling white vapor, he tugged at the Door-of-the-Ages and it creaked open. Instantly, he was buffeted by a blast of cold, heavy air and great panels of flashing lights appeared ahead of him. The icy, clear coffin of Oleandre closed around him again, and moved him through the gate and out of the universe. Crimson lights came in on him and he could feel their warmth through his transparent tomb.

Suddenly, all was dark again. . .just as suddenly, he was bathed in fierce white light. He tried to shield his eyes against the painful photons, but could not will his arms to rise even though they were not physically restrained. Squinting, he could make out a mist in front of him that moved in off-sync waves.

Gradually he became accustomed to the intense brightness and visualized a figure ahead. The mist cleared and it became apparent that he was in a laboratory of some kind. A naked, male figure stood with his back to him. The figure turned. . . his eyes widened. . .his heart pounded, and a sweeping feeling of disbelief surged through his paralyzed body.

It was Willoughby; and the torn yellow face with its jagged brown gash across the forehead was frozen in a perpetual sneer. Slowly, very slowly, the figure raised a stiffened arm. Its finger pointed directly at Eric. Then it whirled around again. Through the mist came a self-propelled gleaming cart containing a small red squealing infant. Many wires and electrodes protruded from Sean Senka's skull. Eric tried to *scream out but his vocal cords were paralyzed. Terror welled up within him. The spectre of Willoughby staggered over to the table, dragging its shattered leg behind, and lay down beside the infant. It lapsed into a coma.*

A blade appeared, held by an invisible hand and made great cuts on the Willoughbian skull. The baby's brain was removed and Willoughby's brain hung suspended while blue stroboscopic light irradiated it. The brain shrunk to infant size and inserted itself into Sean's empty head. Willoughby would, in revenge, take Eric's son's body as immortal casing for his own brain.

Eric was filled with loss and shaking revulsion. The scene dimmed and Willoughby's broken cadaver was removed. The infant lay, outlined in dim purple hue. Then a gurgling ochre foam erupted from its mouth and spread over the small body. The baby lay encased in a transluscent cocoon. Eric was aware of shadowed activity inside the crusty chamber as the metamorphosis took place. Soon a crack appeared in the wall.

A bristled leg stuck through, and on the end of the appendage was a foot with two great Titan toes. The beast burst forth dripping with sticky fluid. It came toward Eric, fierce eyes burning and talons extended. Eric's frozen crypt began spinning and he knew the creature was inside, for he could feel its hot, urgent breath. The abraded walls of the chamber bled in great, viscous droplets. The throbbing pain in Eric's head grew unbearable and huge fissures cracked the sides of his glass prison. . .blackness came over him in hot, sickening fury. . .

He awoke, crying out, his chest heaving spasmodically.

Eric staggered to the basin in the laboratory and activated the cold water dispensor. It spattered for a second, then came out of the coiled bronze outlet in a steady stream. He vomited again and again until his retching brought up nothing. Cupping his hands, he filled them with water and splashed the stimulating liquid over his face, letting it run down his neck and back in cool, wet rivulets.

This tops it, he thought, I'm losing control. . .I must find that last probe and redeem myself. . .but it's crazy, no one blames me for Harlin's death. . .me. . .only me. . .it must be done. . .I'll be healed if I can find it.

Punching a series of digits on the telecon, he waited. No answer. He tried again.

After a few seconds, a musty voice said, "Y-y-yes?"

"Jesse?"

"Yes, wh-who. . ."

"It's Eric. Did I wake you?"

"No," replied Jesse in a somewhat steadier voice.

"Are you alone?"

"No!"

"OH. . .oh, I see. I beg your pardon, clumsy of me. Will you call me when you finish — I mean, when you have a chance?"

"Yes, of course, Eric. Is it about what we discussed in the lab?"

"Yes."

"Are we ready?"

"Definitely."

"Oh, Eric? How is Maggie?"

"The baby was born earlier this morning," said Eric very matter-of-factly.

"Wonderful. . .a boy?"

"Yes, Sean Eric."

"Congratulations, and your wife?"

"She's fine. . .very tired, though. That's normal. There's a nurse with her and the baby. I'm sleeping here in the lab."

"Listen, since that's the case, I'll meet you there at about seven-hundred. Is that all right?"

"That's fine. . .uh, and I'm sorry about disturbing you."

The harsh metal was cold where his elbows rested on the oval desk, yet he did not feel it. With head buried in palms and fingers rubbing rhythmically at his temples, Eric began a dialogue with himself that was mostly contained within his mind, with only occasional verbal mutterings. My God, he thought, so this is insanity. But it's hard to say exactly what madness is. The aberrations begin so subtly, usually going undetected; and even when they are first consciously noticed, the weather or gastric distress or a malfunctioning of the carbon dioxide recycler and all sorts of other demons are inevitably blamed. . .anything but the truth.

But then, what madman ever knows he's deranged? Or does he? And how do they begin, these mental disturbances? With unfounded premonitions of impending doom? Or the slow deterioration, leading to complete renunciation of ideals once sacred? A disaster, the blame of which is fixed upon one's self? With the surfacing of once-suppressed neural circuits comes the staggering reality of madness — then the rejection, the endless bargaining and, finally, acceptance. Ah, normalcy, one has regained it. Then, without warning, the misty, fuzzy, vaporous crypt rushes up and encloses its victim. . .a man warm with internal friction, yet a man apart.

"Oh Jesus," he cried out, pounding the desk heavily with a clenched fist and thought, I must purge myself, and it must come soon.

Feeling somewhat soothed and less agitated, he cut off the conversation with himself, and fixed himself some strong, black coffee. Then Eric stuck his head into his own quarters. Everyone was sleeping, Maggie in their big bed, the nurse on pnuemocot next to the pseudowomb. He smiled approvingly at the peacefulness. Even Pseudomonius was still.

Sitting on his swivel chair next to the metal desk in his laboratory, Eric rocked and pivoted. He stared blankly across the room. He sat, seeing nothing, his mind spinning.

Then he had a thought. Looking in next door again, he whispered, "Pseudomonius!" No reaction. Again. No response. "Damnit," he grumbled softly. Eric went to the computer console and touched a single panel. In about ten seconds the door slid open and the blinking metallic wizard entered silently, the airscreen closing behind it.

"YES DOCTOR SENKA," it said in its usual monotone.

"Goddamnit, I called you twice!"

"I RECEIVED BUT ONE ELECTRONIC TRANS-MISSION."

"No, no, damn you, I *called* you verbally."

"OBVIOUSLY YOU DID NOT EXCEED MY AUDIO THRESHOLD. YOU KNOW THAT IT IS. . ."

"Oh, Christ — it doesn't matter. Just bring me some breakfast; but get it down at the dispensary so you do not disturb the baby."

"YES DOCTOR SENKA," replied Pseudomonius, pivoting on its track and starting toward the airscreen.

"And be damn quick about it!"

"MY MAXIMUM ALLOWABLE VELOCITY IN AN A-LEVEL CORRIDOR IS PRECISELY FIVE-POINT-THREE KILOMETERS PER HOUR AND. . ."

It disappeared around the corner, and Eric almost had to laugh out loud. He loved to insult Pseudomonius, but mostly he liked the servomechanin's calm, matter-of-fact replies. Eric sometimes thought he detected a note of subtle sarcasm in Pseudomonius' remarks, although he knew this was emotion and therefore impossible. Servomechanins based their decisions on an infallible logical process, not on intuition nor emotion. Its fourth-generation analogue mind had not even the slightest conception of the word emotion.

Jesse Horvitz sat on the edge of his bed, shivered, and pulled a sheet up around his bare chest. He rubbed the corded

muscles of his shoulder and looked down. She lay face down
on the bed and Iridani's dark, lithe body contrasted sharply
with the white sheet. Her eyes were closed. He looked away
and out into the darkness of his tiny room. In the blackness,
Jesse relived the previous hours' adventure.

He had met her for a late dinner, with the expressed
purpose of discussing her poetry. Over the steaming meal of
hot thymus stew, they talked seriously about lyrical
mechanisms and the construction of imagery. Iridani was very
intense and he learned much from her. During the discourse on
imagery, Jesse proclaimed that, though he liked all of her
poem, *The Programmed Man,* there was one line that
especially appealed to him.

"What one is that?" she had queried.

"Oh, the line that makes reference, or rather, analogy in
relating the human intestines to computer tapes."

"Yes of course. . .

> *twisting, turning intestinal readout*
> *tapes,*
> *full of fecal feedout from neural*
> *memory banks*

. . .is that the one?"

"Yes, I like that one."

"Why?"

"Well, from precisely what we've been talking about, it has
imagery."

"I am flattered, but don't you think you like it because you
understand it?"

"Perhaps, but shouldn't I understand it?"

"That is debatable. It has always been almost the duty of a
poet to be as inscrutable as possible."

"I don't think your poetry is totally indecipherable,
although I admit I don't know much about it. *You* are what is
inscrutable."

"What?"

"What?" He mocked her. "Yes, you are almost schizophrenic, in that you present two entirely different personalities."

"DO I!"

"Yes, you do. Look, the other times we've met you have been cold to say the least. . .a bitch even."

The beer was giving him courage; she knew it and almost laughed at him. He continued, "But tonight, you're instructive, happy and really pleasant to be with."

Iridani looked down and straightened the folds of her white sari; then she looked up and said, "Thank you, Jesse. I'm not really a cold person, but I guess I am defensive. . .being the only poet aboard."

"It's an honor. It should make you feel good."

"Are you sure it is an honor?"

"What do you mean by *that*?"

"Well, could it not merely be cultural tokenism? After all, the Oleandre Mission *is* the great cultural and civilizing expedition."

"I don't think so: your work is excellent."

"I am a good poet, Jesse, only if my verse is able to make you feel that the day has suddenly turned to darkness or the night has erupted in brilliant, white light. The words on the paper should transmit the images in my brain and reproduce them, with all their delicacy or intensity, inside your head. If the lines cannot do this, I am not to be called poet, because I have failed in my purpose."

"It does for me. . .not exactly when actually reading the words; but when I have finished, and sit back, eyes closed, your verse has stimulated pictures and color and deep feelings within me. So you see, you *are* a good poet, one of the finest. Admit it! Why would Jason Oleandre in fact, kidnap you for the Mission? I know, because I'm researching his records and I found several passages showing his admiration for your early work."

"Really?" Her dark eyes brightened.

"Yes, I could show you. He especially liked your poem. . .I think it was called *Illusions.*"

"That is correct."

"Could I see it sometime?"

"Of course Jesse. I'll write you a copy and send it to you."

"I'd like that," he said, trying to look seductively into her eyes and spilling his beer on the table. They laughed. He regained some semblance of composure.

"From our brief talks, I have detected a kind of mistrust for technology, Iridani."

"I suppose that is true," she replied, "after all, look what technology did to my beloved Earth, destroyed it. *You* actually destroyed it, but had you not, it would have done so itself."

"It wasn't technology, itself, that destroyed the Earth. It was the misuse of technology by a degenerate people."

"Merely semantics — had the technology not been there it could not have been misused."

"That's not a good argument. If you say that then you say the Neanderthals misused fire, which they probably did. Their relatives forged weapons by its light: but they also formed tools. Humanity has always been that way."

"True, but even here, your GREAT scientific advances are being perverted. For example, look at your damned Reproductive Committee, Hadem! They dictate who can and cannot have children and even designate the sex of any *approved* child. Soon you'll be growing fetuses in Goddamned metallic wombs. Hadem!"

"That is precisely what we must guard against. Yes, this is definitely possible: In fact, it's been done on an animal level for years; but it must not be applied to humans!"

"Why Jesse, I would have never believed it!"

"Really Iridani, I'm serious. The gentleman I work for, Dr. Senka? He and I have discussed things like this as we work. We both agree that it is things of this nature we must prevent from becoming established. There is one ethical problem, however."

"And that is?"

"What if the capability eventually exists for growing humans in 'Orwellian' tanks, *and,* what if a pregnant mother dies or something? Should the fetus be implanted to save it?"

"That *is* a dilemma isn't it? I would say no."

"Why?"

"Because once you start, it is very easy to make that event a common occurrence. . .'just one more time'. . .something like that."

"You're probably correct," said Jesse, taking the last sip of the now-warm beer and letting the foam slide down the tall purple glass until it tickled his upper lip.

"It comes to this," she continued, "it is the sworn duty of the Mission to promote the advance of creative technology; but to prevent the process of dehumanization."

"In theory, yes."

"But it will be a difficult task because history has shown that technological advancement and the alienation of humanity are directly related. . .they are almost synonymous."

"Perhaps, then we all have a personal mission, that is: to prevent dehumanizing. Maybe that's *your* function. Maybe you are here to offset any reduction of the human condition. If that is so, yours is the most challenging task!"

"Yes. . .yes," she said softly, her mind elsewhere, "Jesse, you may be right. It would seem that you have given me a new outlook. . .a horizon. I'm grateful."

He was infatuated with her and all the erotic fantasies that had dwelt within him for days. Since she was six years older, Jesse was afraid she would look upon him as a child. . .a pupil. But sitting across from him in that flowing cloth, with intense upswept eyes and a dark skin that seemed to emit a black light of its own, she stirred him. Thinking he might as well throw all chance to the galactic winds, "I hope you won't take offense, but I have some brandy back at my room and. . .well. . .I mean. . ."

"I would be delighted."

As they walked into his orderly quarters, he dared to touch her shoulder and she did not reproach him. Swallowing the constriction in his throat, he kissed her soundly.

"That was nice Jesse."

He bid her to sit at his small writing table, since he had no couch.

"You want me, do you not?"

"Y. . .y. . .yes," he stammered embarrassingly, surprised at her frankness.

"Well, then?"

"I'm. . .I'm not very. . .experienced."

"I'll teach you."

"I th-think I-I love you," he stuttered.

"You do *not*. . .you just want me and I am fond of-you. . .I do not love you. . .I cannot. . .but we have a thin bond and this will strengthen it. I am fond of you and want you to be happy."

"But. . ."

"No buts. Come, I will show you Hadem's Way."

And she did. Standing there, with bodies touching, her limber hands went around his head and caressed the engorged cords of his neck and back. Her lips brushed lightly over his, then proceeded to lay their warm tribute on the altars of his eyelids and ears. Then her head moved to his neck. Jesse felt her lips part on his throat and her moist tongue dart on to his skin. Just for an instant her body pressed tightly to his and her mouth opened and her sharp, hot tongue burst into the cavern of his mouth. She released him and went to the unmade bed. She bade him to follow, and he was as a mindless slave is to the mistress.

In a twirling motion, she emerged from the sari revealing her magnificent olive body. The twin mountains of dark flesh were capped by rigid, red peaks and her hips swung like a pendulum. Her legs were slender, but well-muscled. As he undressed, her fingers were running over him. She was sometimes gentle, sometimes a violent, primitive beast, attacking him in a fever of arousal and a tangle of nerves. She bit him. . .biting with hatred in her eyes. Her tongue probed all the furrows and crevices of his aroused and tingling body.

He cried for her. She sat astride his chest and his hands moved over her and explored the writhing creature above him. Sliding down she let him enter and, in a swift continuous move, rolled over and locked her legs in a violent grip of death's dance. She rocked back and forth and the bones of her hips ground into his skin. There was a low moaning growl deep in her throat as he thrust into the hot wetness.

He was lost in her, awash in her, and the entire finite universe exploded into one permanent expanding erotic supernova.

He lay expired and limp within her, breathing shallowly. Iridani's thumb rubbed a muscle of his back, but her eyes were half closed and water-filled.

Later, an eternity later, she warned him again not to love her as they clung to each other. After a long silence she said, "Do not be so afraid of dying, my young lover. It is only a fear of the unknown, and the unknown is all we have. There is no permanency. . .nothing is permanent except death. Accept this with me."

He kissed her forehead, and they began again.

Late in the early morning hours the telecon sounded.
"Damn," he muttered.
Iridani rolled over asleep. It sounded again, and Jesse Horvitz stumbled toward the receiver in the darkness.

Iridani slept, but not peacefully. Her breathing was strained and erratic. Occasionally, little sounds came from deep within her throat. The recurring dreams accosted her once more.

. . .Running, running. . .out of breath, chest heaving. . .the
bright full moon gives off its brilliant light creating great dark
shadows. . .shadows. . .and in the shadow of the shadows lay
low buildings of crumbling masonry. Running. . .running in
slow motion. . .running in bounding leaps that cover thirty
paces in one stride. . .running through the streets and market
places of Marakesh, yet getting nowhere. Still they gained on
her. . .two hatless men. . .in white tropical suits with armpits
wet with perspiration. . .each carrying an instrument of
death. . .

"IRIDANI," they cry, "WE ARE FRIENDS, THE
ALLIANCE IS YOUR SAVIOR." Their hollow words echo
and re-echo down the empty streets. . .running. . .puffing. . .up
a dusty path, swirls of ancient soil dancing 'round her fleeting
sandals. Running. . .around a corner, body leaning in defiance
of gravity. . .up a brick covered street. . .knock down a
peasant, drunk on Algerian wine. Running. . .slowly. . .
pain. . .hideous pain in the side under her rib cage. . .slowly
. . .cannot run any longer.

Over the din of pulsing cranial blood, she hears the steady
puunding of the footsteps behind her. . .growing louder. . .
closer. Iridani falls to her knees, the dry taste of the century's
dust in her mouth. Tears turn to dirty stains on reddened
cheeks. The footsteps stop. . .she can hear their forced
breathing above her. She cannot face the vile ones.

Then, a loud staccato thunderclap sends the two pursuers
sprawling to her level, faces in the street, red vicious liquid
spurting from their bodies to blacken and grow crusted on the
parched bricks. She is aware of a figure standing over her.
"COME." Her body rises as if by levitation. The hooded, black
figure is amorphous save for two slanted yellow eyes peering
from behind the shroud. "COME, THE ALTAR OF K'UANG
FONG AWAITS YE!" Run. . .cannot. . .paralyzed. . .she
follows the apparition. . .wind blowing against her
face. . .black hair streaming behind her. . .wind. . .dust in

eyes. . .cool wind blowing off the desert in the night. . .
growing hot from the buildings that baked all day. . .heat
rising in shimmering waves, making the Market Place of the
Devil dance and pulsate in the moonlight. . .altar. . .blocks of
stone stripped eons ago from the Pharaonic monuments at
Gizeh. . .how are they here. . .at Jemaa El Fna. . .standing on
the altar now overlooking the square?

Now run. . .no. . .unable. The unseen hand rips the flowing
white manteau from her. . .dark lithe body shaking. . .alone in
the light. "KNEEL." Her head bowed. . .ankles tied to
pyramidal stones still under her. . .body pulled back. . .Heels
under trembling buttocks. . .back of the head touches
stone. . .cool. . .hard. . .comforting. . .thong around neck. . .
tied to the stones of time. A clear crystal beaker appears
suspended above her, filled with glowing stones, each giving
off its own atomic light. . .face bathed in blue heat. . .hilt of a
Han dagger protruding. . .the hooded spectre is here. He
removes the dagger with cloaked hand. . .blade glowing white
with fire. . .helpless knees lay wide apart. . .dagger ruthlessly
shoved up between them. . .pungent odor of seared
pubis. . .pain of indescribable degree. . .please. . .death. . .now
. . .

It is not to be. . .not yet. Her once perfect body, now
unbound, is laid flat. . .wide eyes upward still. . .blade between
thighs. . .drapped in black flag. . .hilt straight up like a
transphallus. "IRIDANI," says the unseen voice that
permeated everything, yet, came from everything. "THE
K'UANG FONG LIVES IN THE HEARTS OF
ALL. . .K'UANG FONG IS ALL. . .ALL PRESENT. . .ALL
FUTURE. . .ALL ILLUSTRIOUS ANCESTORS. THE
ESSENCE IS K'UANG FONG. . .DOWN WITH ALL
ALLIANCES. . .DOWN WITH CONTRACEPTION."

Death. . .a silver flask hung over her. . .valve opening. . .
drop of liquid. . .crashes into forehead. . .through brain
. . .death. . .not so quickly. . .death.

*"K'UANG FONG DOES NOT KILL. . .DEATH ONLY BY
ONE'S OWN SELF."*

*Dropping. . .pain again. . .O Hadem! . . .Death. . .dripping
. . .slowly. . .drop by drop. . .threshold decreasing. . .dripping.
Each drop producing misery's throb. . .death. . .*

*"NOT BY K'UANG FONG'S IMPERIAL YELLOW HAND,
BUT YOUR OWN WORDS, IRIDANI."*

*·Dripping. . .each drop burning into her poetry as it struck
h e r   b r o w .   .   . d r i p p i n g .   . . l y r i c a l
revenge. . .autopoeticide. . .dagger words, and poisonous
phrases. . .death?. . .yes. . .now. . .*

Her eyes blinked, then closed again, and then opened. Iridani
lay wet with perspiration in a strange bed whose sheets were
soaked from the night's horror, the night's ecstasy. There was
a dull, aching pain in her left hand and she saw that it was
clutched tightly to the pillow. She looked at the gripping
fingers a moment. They seemed almost alien to her body,
detached. She released them. After she was aware of Jesse's
room and after the paralysis of the nightmare eased, Iridani
wondered where he had gone, why he had left her alone in his
bed:

Presently, the entrance module sounded. He has returned,
she thought.

"Are you sure we can get the Commander's approval for
this, Eric?" Jesse asked in a concerned voice.

"I am confident; but it doesn't really matter."

"You. . .I mean, you would do it without permission?"

"Would I? If it came to that, and I believe it will not, are
you still with me?"

"I suppose," said Jesse, his eyes rolling in disapproval.
"Yes, but I must admit some skepticism of doing it against
orders."

"Let's not discuss *that* situation until it is a reality, if it ever is. Coffee?"

"Please. . .black."

"I know, damnit. You used to work here. Remember?"

Jesse began to laugh at Eric's sarcasm, but suppressed it when he saw that Eric was deadly serious. Jesse Horvitz had certainly admired him — it was even hero worship of a sort, since it was Eric Senka who had instilled in him the love of exploration and gathering of knowledge. It was this respect and admiration that had led Jesse to agree to this pact.

Days ago, Eric had called him in almost a state of hysteria and panic. Eric presented a wild and fantastic plan that seemed more logical and plausible the more he talked. Eric had talked sensibly about the growing paranoia and the ways to cure it. In order to find the last Oleandre probe, Eric would, with Jesse's help and Hayakawa's permission, take a two-man expedition through the solar system. They would slightly modify the Sub-Orbital Craft for this longer mission. Eric was obsessed with the plan. Jesse mentally noted another obsession: the Titan footprints.

Understanding Eric's psychic need for this mission and the benefit that could accrue to Oleandre, Jesse had agreed to the partnership. Even though he was dubious of its success, it would be exciting and informative.

Eric brought Jesse a beaker of hot, steaming, dark brown brew, and he sipped it slowly.

"Well, Jesse, today we will approach Hayakawa."

"Really. . .today?"

"Yes, I scheduled us on his appointment tape just now. It's the first appointment. . .in exactly thirty-five minutes."

"You want me there, too?"

"Yes, if you wish."

"Fine, I will meet you there."

Jesse made his way back to his own room on a lower level. As he rounded the corridor and turned into the short antechamber hall, he was almost run over by a girl running up the hall. Sue Rafferty looked up at him, burst into tears, and ran past him and out of sight. He saw Iridani just shutting the airscreen ahead. She was wrapped in a sheet.

"Oh Jesus and Mother Fletcher," he muttered, "Iridani, wait!"

He ran up to the entrance.

"What the devil was *that* all about," he cried.

"O, Jesse, I am glad to see you. You were gone when I awoke, so I waited. The airscreen sounded, and I thought it was you; but this little red-headed girl was there. I am afraid she had the wrong idea."

"Oh?"

"I do hope she was no one very special."

"I'm not in love with her if that's what you mean."

"I fear she is with you."

"Balls!" He muttered again and ran his hand over the top of his head. "Damnit, I don't have to account to her!"

"Of course you don't. One should be held responsible only to one's self."

"Listen," he said placing his hands on her hips, "I've got to go to a meeting with Dr. Senka. May I see you later?"

"Yes, I shall be in my room writing. I shall await you in my bed."

She kissed him lightly on the mouth, and he left.

They appeared in the antechamber of Commander Hayakawa's suite at precisely eight hundred hours. The Commander was giving some instructions to an aid when they entered. Commander Hayakawa looked up and then glanced at the digital clock that was suspended over the large televisor screen.

"Oh, Eric. . .is it that time? I will be with you shortly.

Now, Simmonds, I want you to run a linear transligation pattern of zero-point-zero-five degrees and. . ."

He soon finished and dismissed his assistant who left promptly via the entrance to Oleandre Control. The Commander walked to them holding a small antianalogue tube in his left hand.

"Well, Eric, I see you have brought your assistant. Nice to see you again, Mr. Horvitz."

"Yes sir," said Jesse, not knowing exactly what to say.

"Please, sit down and tell me what is on your minds at this early hour. *You* look very serious Eric; anything wrong?"

"Yes and no Seth. . .oh, by the way, the baby was born this morning."

"REALLY! Congratulations," exclaimed Hayakawa, jumping to his feet. Then his expression changed, "There's nothing wrong with Maggie or the child is there?"

"Oh no, they're doing fine."

"I see. Then tell me, what *is* the problem?"

Eric told Seth of the creeping paranoia involving Willoughby's death and the plan for finding the last Oleandre probe. Jesse sat and said nothing. At first, the idea was completely repugnant to the Commander and he suggested that Eric see a psychosomatician. However, when Eric argued eloquently, as a man possessed, for the double value. . .that of saving his sanity and finding the probe, Seth Hayakawa began to weaken. The argument became even more valid when Eric mentioned the conversations with several of the engineers who built the planetary probes recently sent out. Carlyle of Astronautical Engineering had admitted that the sensitivity of these instrument packages had been greatly over-rated. Seth agreed and said he knew all about it but could do nothing now, since all the probes had been launched and most had returned with no data of significance.

Eric brought a thick sheaf of drawings for the modifications of the Sub-Orbital Craft. Hayakawa was impressed, but still a bit wary.

"I am not in the least bit pleased with your idea, although it is a logical one. You are not that experienced in piloting the Sub-Orbital Craft."

"I've a Level-Four classification."

"I realize that, but. . .well, if your mind is made up, I will agree with one exception."

"And that is?" Eric asked dubiously.

"That you take along a back-up pilot of my own choosing."

"Sounds reasonable. Who would it be?"

"My First Bridge Officer. . .Jemma."

"Who?"

"Ahab ben Jemma."

"I don't believe I've ever met him, although I may have seen him about."

"I will arrange a meeting, but I must remind you that I will make it *his* choice. . .strictly voluntary. If he refuses, then you will dispose of your plans. Agreed?"

"Yes Seth. . .agreed."

Ahab ben Jemma was the blackest man Eric had ever seen. Standing about six-feet-six and with a powerful build, his face was like polished obsidian, inset with two, alert ivory globes that darted about continuously. Born in Khartoum, the son of Ubandan diplomats, Ahab was schooled in Extraterrestrial Engineering at The Hague with emphasis on guidance systems. Although a brilliant student, Jemma was also a reckless adventurer and soldier of fortune who had flown in support of the proAlliance rebels in Djakarta. Seeing the world orders approaching their nadir, he had joined the Oleandre Mission and became, after extensive orientation, Hayakawa's protegee. Ahab ben Jemma was quick to volunteer for Eric's expedition. Eric did not speak more than fifty words to him before he agreed.

The time of departure was set by the Commander. They would leave in two weeks, on OD-323. It would take that long for the Sub-Orbital Craft to be modified according to Eric's specifications, which included the addition of a small food-producing system, more hypergol boosters, and a pulsed, nobelium laser coupled to the onboard guidance, to be used in situations when the microRAM was impractical. The work was handled in a superlative manner and was completed nearly two days ahead of schedule.

As plans neared completion, Maggie's disapproval and dejection grew. Having begun the mandatory two month leave due to the baby, time lingered for her. She paced their quarters all day with little Sean on one arm. She smoked furiously, even though she had to make her own cigarettes. Her terror increased. Eric had narrowly escaped the last time, when Willoughby was killed, and Maggie could not help having that nagging sense of impending doom. "Damnit Eric," she would say, "think of your son if you won't think of me." Other times she would use more subtle tactics such as bursting into uncontrollable tears as they lay together. However, her protestations were to no avail.

It was definite; he and young Horvitz and the towering Afrocaner would leave for only-God-knew-where the next morning.

The launching had been promoted as a pilgrimage with almost religious connotations. The three Oleandreans were leaving on a dangerous voyage for the sake of the entire population. In reality, it was for the stability of *one* psyche, the reinforcement of *one* admiration, and the satisfaction of *one* wanton urge for adventure. The ascent of the sleek, silver Sub-Orbital Craft was monitored anxiously on all televisors throughout Oleandre.

As the needle-like embodiment of all of Oleandre's deep-seated hopes and wildest dreams lifted from the surface, Maggie Senka sat in front of her glowing televisor. Tears streamed in clear salty rivers down the reddened ridges of her high cheekbones. Her heart pounded and her lower lip quivered. Behind her, in his tiny gold pneumocrib, Sean Eric Senka slept peacefully, unaware of his mother's private hell.

The fading flicker of the Sub-Orbital Craft's booster finally vanished from the field of the tracking telescope. Electronic surveillance would continue and communications were intact; but the ship was visually gone.

Ahab ben Jemma sat at the controls. He was flying the Sub-Orbital Craft manually now, just to get the feel of her. Eric and Jesse were poring over large, celucel sheets that were projected overhead. They were looking at the most recent version of the Catalogue of Minor Planets, the EPHERMERIS ASTROPANDIAD COLOQUI. It was the forty-fourth edition, printed in 2008 — old, but still the most up-to-date. The sheets, speckled with black dots, gave positions, orbits and eccentricities for more than eighty-three thousand planetoids . . .remnants of Nimrrah, the tenth planet.

Since the planet was thought to have broken up many eons ago, Earth scientists used to believe that the asteroids represented an intermediate state of planetary evolution. They thought that to explore these asteroids would be extremely fruitful because they would show the condition of ancient Earth before its contamination with living molecules. In 1977, a joint American-Soviet expedition landed on the asteroid Geographos and set up a small sampling laboratory. But tests of rock specimens did not uphold the theorized time of the planetary explosion.

The mystery was solved in 1981, when a team of archeologists from the University of Chicago excavated an ancient Sumerian astronomical 'observatory.' Clay records were found of a hitherto unrecorded planet, with its orbit charted. It was called Nimrrah, God of Tribulations. Etched into the baked clay, the cuneiform inscriptions of a particular section of the Cohen Palate gave the date of a gigantic explosion that was visible even during the brightness of daylight. Later records never spoke of Nimrrah as a celestial entity, rather, as a God returned to the place of its birth in the womb of Narth, God of Gods, creator of the Universe.

The Sub-Orbital Craft cruised effortlessly in the void at a relative velocity of ten miles-per-second. Jupiter's disc loomed ahead, a banded-sphere attended by several sparkling moons. A tiny black dot moved over its surface as one of the satellites moved in front, projecting its shadow on the Jovian surface.

The Trojan Minor Planets were in two groups. They revolved about the Sun in Jupiter's orbit, about one-sixth of the circumference ahead and to the rear. There were six major and forty-four minor Pre-Trojans, and eleven major and thirty-nine minor Post-Trojans. It had been theorized that the Jovian moons, themselves, had once been in the same condition; but they had moved too close to the giant planet and were captured as satellites. This had remained only a theory.

Soon, a rocky shape loomed ahead. Trojan planetoid Z-18 was irregular in shape, about five by eight miles in size. It hadn't the gravitational attraction to pull itself into a spherical shape. As Jemma slowed the Sub-Orbital Craft, Eric ran a scanning program designed to detect visual and radio signals. These proving negative, he then ran a metallic profile. Nothing. Jemma accelerated to the next asteroid, lying about fifty thousand miles ahead on the program. It took two days to survey all the Trojan asteroids.

The Sub-Orbital Craft planned to move slowly into the area of dense asteroid population, between Mars and Jupiter. The crew would scan twenty hours, freeze their position and sleep for six hours, then resume tracking.

It became wearisome to accelerate, decelerate, scan, then accelerate again, over and over, finding nothing. The myriad of planetoids gave no positive findings, showing only the slightest variations in composition.

They were almost in a hypnotic trance from the endless

starry pattern on the color televisor screen that hung between
the two large forward ports. The screen, about three by five
feet and only half an inch thick, was a marvel of technology,
mostly due to the Charkov Principle and the great advances
made in amorphous glass semiconductors.

Early one day, a rather beautiful sight appeared on the
televisor screen. Jesse called Ahab and Eric, who were eating
the first meal of that particular working day. The Sub-Orbital
Craft had swung around according to the program and the Sun
had come into view. Between them could be seen the dark disc
of Mars. The Sun, however, surrounded by irradiating halos,
was not its usual painful brilliance. It was dulled. Beyond
Mars, the projection showed a broad band of glowing nebulous
material where the Earth had been. A strange and totally alien
sensation came over them.

During a routine navigational calibration, Eric noticed a
new phenomenon. The usual orbit of Mars contained a slight
perturbation, probably due to the Earth's vaporization. He
duly recorded this for transmission to Oleandre Control.

Late on the eighth day of their journey, when Horvitz was
at the command module, the Sub-Orbital Craft found itself in
a bind. Jesse had maneuvered it between two small planetoids
where a third blocked its way. Rather than waste both time
and power to reverse the craft, Eric decided this was the time
to test the laser. Activating a series of levers and heat-sensitive
spots, a panel opened on the underside of the Sub-Orbital
Craft's needle nose. Its computers locked onto the small piece
of rock which was about fifty yards across and half-a-mile in
the distance. Touching the power-surge stud, a pulse of blue,
glowing light emanated from the opening. It streaked
instantaneously to the miniature asteroid. The rocky mass
absorbed the energy, glowed white, then red for a moment,
and finally vanished, leaving nothing but a patch of greyish
dust.

Just after Eric had scanned the thousandth asteroid and found it barren, Jesse, who had been preparing the last meal of the day, announced that the carbohydrate synthesis unit was malfunctioning and that he had shut it down. Eric muttered something totally unintelligible and proceeded to take the tool satchel into the aft compartment.

The entire rear area had been converted into a total environmental control unit. The carbohydrate synthesizer was only one part. A side of the compartment was covered with clear flexible tubing in which the Oleandre photosynthetic algae grew in continuous culture. The carbon dioxide from the ship's personnel was collected and bubbled into nutrient broth where the algae produced sugars and oxygen. Tubing filled with the bluish-green organisms came over to the carbohydrate synthesizer. In a continuous process, the algae were killed, stripped of their protein and sugars which fed into two hoppers. The powdery protein and sugars were used to make bread or cereals. A water and waste recovery unit stood next to the synthesizer. All urine and fecal material was fed into this device which extracted the water, purified it, and fed it to a central reservoir that stood in the center of the room covered by a clear dome. A fountain aerated the water and also gave an aesthetically pleasing appearance to the aft compartment.

As Eric entered with the satchel slung over his shoulder, grumbling under his breath, he was greeted by a squawk from the rear of the room. Just under the water purification coils were housed two chickens in an aluminum cage. Eric had named them collectively as "Morgul-and-Inez" since he could never tell them apart. Fed on a hormone enriched diet, the pair presented six eggs every morning.

Observing the carbohydrate synthesis module standing solemn and quiet, Eric went to work. He tested the electrical and transistor circuitry and found them intact. After testing most of the mechanical components, he soon found the trouble. A bushing from an input valve leading from the algal culture to the prime breakdown unit had misaligned, causing a pressure rise that broke a membrane in the oligosaccharide molecular rearrangement chamber, causing it to collapse upon itself. There was no recourse other than to tear down the machine.

Getting down on the deck, Eric slid under the module and loosened a few snaps on the underside. As the plate started to come off, he noticed an ooze beginning to creep out around the edges. He tried to push it up again. Too late! The mass of homogenized algae flooded down on his face almost drowning him in greenish slime.

"Mother of Rasputin," he howled, choking and almost gagging to death.

Ahab ben Jemma, hearing the commotion, ran in, saw the situation and began laughing heartily.

"Don't just stand there, get me the hell out of here! Sure, go ahead, laugh, you obsidian cock!"

It took all of four hours to repair the carbohydrate synthesizer, but it was soon functioning again. Jesse, who was crowned unofficial chef, finished preparing the last meal.

Ahab put the Sub-Orbital Craft in orbit-freeze about ninety million miles from Mars. They ate, sitting in the area just behind the command module. Jesse made some notes in a journal he was keeping. Taking the last chunk of fresh algal bread and dipping it into the warm broth, Eric began a light conversation with Jemma. Somehow the discourse turned to Harvey McMaster.

"You know, Eric," said Ahab ben Jemma, "it is a pity that he died. I am never glad to see the loss of a colleague. Nevertheless, that does not change the fact that he was a gnu's ass."

"Good Lord, why do *you* say that?"

"I never *could* get along with him. I suppose he was prejudiced. No, no. . .not because of my race or anything like that. Really, I think he envied my adventurous longings for excitement. I believe he was jealous that *he* led such a dull life."

"Dull? Dull is a relative thing," replied Eric and then belched softly.

"True! Absolutely! But he questioned everything I did. Went right to the Commander. Honestly Eric, when the Alliance was busy executing the plan to put metal plates in the heads of degenerates, I shall never for the life of me, understand how Harvey McMaster escaped unscathed."

Jesse coughed slightly and grinned. They all chuckled. Then Jesse said, "Say Ahab, I understand you've had some fairly exciting missions in your lifetime. . .something about an expedition down in South Asia?"

"Oh yes," he laughed, "the Djakarta Affair. It *was* exciting. If you won't be bored, I'll tell you about it, just to kill some time."

He did. The Federal Liberation Alliance, a guerrilla group, had landed at the port of Djakarta which was then part of the South Asia Coalition. The rebels gained a firm foothold at the port, but were driven back by Coalition "volunteers" flown in by the K'uang Fong from the Asian mainland. With their backs to the Java Sea, and after taking horrible losses, the rebels radioed for Alliance assistance. Ahab ben Jemma headed an aerial attack group that was based in a stronghold on K-2, high in the Himalayas. He personally led a fleet of seven Jet-Conqueror helicopters over the Bay of Bengal, then down on the deck along the Indian Ocean side of Sumatra, through the Sunda Straights, and attacked the port area of Djakarta driving back the Asians who suffered extremely heavy casualties.

"What then?" asked Jesse who was enthralled by the whole thing.

"Well, once the Asians were dispersed we attacked the Presidential Palace which was then operating as the biggest bordello on the Java Sea. It was fantastic. We just strafed the building, didn't hurt anyone," and he started to laugh almost hysterically.

"What's so funny?"

"Jesus! After the first flyby, you could see all these naked women sprinting around the grounds and out of the building. It was hilarious. . .we lost three gunships in that escapade. . .but it was great fun."

"How did you get back?"

"After strafing Djakarta, what was left of the fleet flew north, under the Coalition radar, through the Gaspar Straights and landed at the secret Alliance redoubt on Karimata Island. We eventually returned to North America Alliance under the sea. That was really a good show and K'uang Fong lost not only a goodly number of her crack commandos that day, but a hell of a lot of prestige. Looking back, the whole thing was a farce anyhow."

For over sixty days, they cruised the area of the asteroids. The end of the first year since the Earth's destruction had come and gone with no celebration. The endless scanning and tracking of the lifeless, barren outposts of celestial flotsam had become an obsession. Even the mercenary Jemma had become a repeater of coordinates and quoter of statistics. Had it not been for Eric's insight into himself, the ceaseless hours of watching sensors and changing course could have stretched into eternity.

As they awoke on OD-396, Eric opened a channel to Oleandre Control. They were promptly notified that they were using an improper dating sequence: it was OD-2:31.

The sight of his wife and baby on the flickering televisor screen brought tears to Eric's eyes. Maggie's eyes and his spoke the unsaid words that are always exchanged by parted lovers. Seth Hayakawa appeared behind Maggie and Eric told him of the low fuel supply. There had been miscalculations as to the amount of fuel expended with the numerous stops and starts. Could the Commander send more hypergol boosters? Yes, it

ould be done. Wasn't there enough fuel for the return to
Oleandre? No, Eric would use the extra fuel for another
mission. He and the crew of the Sub-Orbital Craft would
return to the area of their birth; they would go to see what
was left of the Earth.

The package of gleaming booster units, ten in all, took two
days to make the journey from Oleandre to the area of the
Sub-Orbital Craft. Eric guided the space-train the last ten
million miles. The sunlight reflecting off the silver hulls of the
boosters, which were collectively over five hundred feet long,
gave the appearance of an intruding comet. Once they were
coupled to the rear, the sleek Sub-Orbital Craft looked as if it
had suddenly acquired a tubular malignancy.

As each hypergol unit ignited and, in turn, dropped off, the
crew was pushed back into their conforming contour chairs.
At a hundred miles a second, it would take several days to
reach their destination.

In the space ahead an eerie eminence grew. It blotted out
the starry background and dulled the Sun itself. The region of
the universe that had once been taken up by a water-covered
sphere teeming with occasionally intelligent life was now filled
with a cloud of radioactive dust and debris. Even the Earth's
one natural satellite, Lunare, had crumbled into large jagged
pieces. The dust glowed with a mysterious fluctuating light.
This great amount of pulverized and atomized matter was
already beginning to spread in an arc. . .the Earth's former
orbit.

They could not take their eyes from the televisor screen.
The glowing cloud seemed to have hypnotic powers and a
sentient life form seemed to live within it. . .the collective evil
of a hundred billion vaporized psyches.

Sensors indicated the total radiation emission at the center
of the cloud to be twelve on the Hemholtz scale. Hemholtz

radiation was a theoretical integration involving all know
types of emitters. Outside the Sub-Orbital Craft, the reading
varied between two- and three-point-seven. They were still
million miles from its center, and the ship's shielding had a
upper threshold of five-point-five. Jesse made a complet
photographic and spectrophotometric record of the
pilgrimage.

Eric decided they would launch a scout-probe into th
cloud, collect samples of the gases and dust, then have th
probe proceed to Oleandre which could handle the intens
radiation. The little, dumbbell shaped missile sped toward th
Earth-Cloud, its tiny engine burning cobalt-blue defiance i
the darkness. As it entered the cloud's interior the prob
exploded in a not-too-brilliant fireball.

They could not contact Oleandre Control due to th
interference of the radiation. Eric started up the main io
engines. Their subatomic pulsation increased the ship
velocity linearly. Returning to Oleandre in a great arc, the
would pass the Sun at a distance of thirty-five million mile
Bypassing what had once been a green and poetic land, th
silver needle swung toward the Sun. As the white, painfu
brilliance of the Sun came into view, Eric touched a panel, an
polarizing shields slipped into place over the ports; the visua
telemetry automatically switched on filters. Through th
brownish filters the Sun's several great dark spots could b
seen, each with a colorless core fading at the edges. The yello
sphere seemed disturbed and angry. . .angry because of th
murder of its child, a child gone berserk.

Eric sat in the command module with the powers o
creation at his fingertips, with indicators flashing an
computer banks whirling; and he could feel the shroud of guil
being lifted from him in a flood of release. He knew it now. H
had tried. And he had failed. But it didn't matter. Eric Senk
had cleansed the sickness from his mind. He switched to th
rear scanner, and the image of the new asteroid belt filled th
televisor screen.

The Sub-Orbital Craft moved past the Sun like an electron around its fiery nucleus. The number of sunspots increased and with the proper filters in place, great solar flares could be seen erupting from the surface in huge arcs, only to fall back again into the boiling holocaust. The crew was bombarded by intense solar radiation, but the shielding held. Sensors indicated that the hull withstood fifteen hundred Solar Neutrino Units.

On the opposite side of the Sun, where their course was charted, Venus and Mercury were in conjunction. Rocky and lifeless Mercury changed phases as they passed.

One could not describe the look of joy on Jesse's face as he shouted up to the command module, "HEY. . .hey, there's a target. . .reading metallic true."

"What?" Eric spun in his chair so fast he almost got whiplash.

"Yes, yes. . .in orbit about Venus. Come see for yourself!"

On the small viewing screen of the Analogue Base Metal and Alloy Detector was the dull back disc of Venus. Around it, moving in an obviously tight orbit, was a bright pinpoint of light. They were still too far away to run a coupled atomic absorption spectrum. They were also in the wrong position to contact Oleandre Control. Ahab ben Jemma touched the deceleration programmer stud and computed the precise power removal necessary to put them in Venusian orbit just behind the contact.

Viewed from Jemma's port, the bright planet grew larger. It was covered with swirling green and blue clouds and an occasional fleeting dark area. The Sun was now sixty-two million miles behind and its light, reflected from the dense Venusian atmosphere, prompted Jemma to place another type of filter across his port. He touched the accelerator and increased their speed to twenty-two miles-per-second, then the deceleration programmer took over and slowed them to five miles-per-second, inserting them into a perfectly circular orbit. Jemma cut the power.

Ahead of them, just out Eric's port, was suspended a perfect sphere covered with a kind of silver foil, which gave an erroneously large neo-radar target. The sphere was only about three feet in diameter, and there were several foil streamers extended from its surface.

Jesse announced that the spectral analysis showed no unknown metals or alloys and that the sphere was of common Earth material: aluminum silconate, magnesium, etc. Sensors also showed the absence of any radiation or explosive devices.

"Bring it in," ordered Eric. "Oleandre sent a probe out here; how could it have missed this?"

The Sub-Orbital Craft moved ahead slowly under computer guidance and a small hatch opened on its underside near the aft compartment. Once the sphere was inside and the area repressurized, Eric, Jesse and Ahab went in to inspect it.

The silver ball lay in the center of the gravity room of the Sub-Orbital Craft. They walked about it quizzically. Eric bent down to touch it. . .solid. They rolled it over to find a small panel through which the foil streamers protruded. A look of disgust and disappointment came over their faces, for on the panel was printed:

狂風

This roughly translated: K'uang Fong. . .the enemy. . .the Furious Winds.

Jemma was most surprised. "When I was with Alliance Intelligence, just before I joined the Mission, it was thought the K'uang Fong would not have this capability for many years. This was launched as a complete secret. Thusly, although it is not the Oleandre probe, it could be extremely important."

Quickly overcoming their disappointment, the panel was cautiously removed to reveal a rack lined with magnetic memory cores from a rather primitive computer.

Eric pulled one out. It was a cartridge about four-by-ten centimeters and two centimeters thick.

It was attached to the onboard computer by several wire leads. The first audio transmissions were in a language Eric thought to be Mandarin, the official language of the Asian scientific community. The second was a section in Mundanlingua, and the last in English. This package was a celestial Rosetta Stone for another civilization. It recorded a plea for peace by the K'uang Fong scientists. It also recorded the Alliance's complete rejection.

"If the tapes are what I believe they are," said Jemma, "then this is a depository of Asian knowledge, thought and achievement. They must have foreseen losing the War. Perhaps they even visualized the Earth's end. In any event, this will be invaluable to Fischer's work in historiography." He turned to smile at Eric, then to Jesse, and said, "Congratulations, young Horvitz, you have made a permanent contribution to the Mission."

Eric increased the thrust to full exchange as Jemma calculated the course back to Oleandre. It would be a six-day voyage.

Something was definitely amiss. Oleandre Control could not be reached. Before passing beyond the former Earth orbital area, this could be attributed to intense radiation causing a communications blackout. But the Sub-Orbital Craft was streaking, with ion engines at full power, past the Martian orbit, and Oleandre Control was still silent.

Eric dismissed it as a malfunction of their own transmitter although all internal sensors were normal. As they got within a hundred-million miles of Saturn, however, the spacewaves came alive with a crackling transmission from Oleandre Control.

"S. . .O. . .C. . .THIS IS OLEANDRE CONTROL. . .YOU ARE CLEARED FOR APPROACH PATTERN. . .DELTA FIVE. . ."

That was all. Try as he would, they would not respond to any other messages. So he let Oleandre's computer guidance take over the Sub-Orbital Craft's flight pattern. The approach pattern took them over the surface at low speed, and Eric could look down. He saw no activity. All the Hovercraft were in their berths and he could detect no movement at the landing site.

The touchdown was gentle, and the Sub-Orbital Craft was drawn onto a part of the landing area that was a long conveyor belt. They were moved into the surface hangar area and the large airlock was closed behind them. As they opened the hatch on the side of the Sub-Orbital Craft, Jesse Horvitz jumped out quickly carrying his personal case. Then Eric and Ahab emerged. There was one solitary figure on the long inclined ramp. . .Lee Fields. Eric walked faster, past Jesse, and up to Fields.

"Lee, good to see you!"

Fields' face was solemn.

"What is it, Lee? Where is the Commander?"

"I want you three to come directly to Oleandre Control. Immediately!"

"What? I mean, why? Wait a minute, Lee, where *is* the Commander?"

"Seth Hayakawa has resigned and is being held in his quarters. You and Ahab ben Jemma will command. It has been decreed so by the Council."

CHAPTER 7

The two years that followed on Oleandre were as intellectually dark as the days of the Alliance. Although there was no police state, nor hint of totalitarianism, suspicion and dejection swept the population of Oleandre.

Upon the return of Eric Senka, Jesse Horvitz and Ahab ben Jemma from their unsuccessful voyage to recover the last Jason Oleandre probe, they found that Seth Hayakawa had indeed resigned as Commander.

During their absence, he had come under extreme criticism from the Council, and there had been a scene of emotional accusations in the Council Chambers. Lee Fields had shouted that Hayakawa acted in haste by launching the Mission so soon, and others joined in merely to relieve their psychic tension, accusing Seth of bungling incompetence and bad planning. In a burst of disgust, Seth Hayakawa relinquished his command on the spot and went into self-imposed exile in his private suite. Seth Hayakawa warned his accusers that they would regret their actions, and when they did so, not to come to him for guidance nor sympathy.

The question of the vacant Commandership then faced the Council. They considered an interim government made up of Council members, but Lee Fields argued eloquently for the election of two specific people. Since Harvey McMaster was dead, the Council unanimously voted to appoint Ahab ben Jemma and Eric Senka as co-Commanders. Fields had convinced the Council that this would provide a balance between spirit and scientific logic and practicality. . .the perfect attributes for a Commander. Without even so much as a formal ceremony, Ahab and Eric were swept into a virtual whirlwind of duties. At the advice of the Council, plans were quickly made to return Oleandre to Martian orbit. It was to be kept in mind that work to discover the location of the last Oleandre probe would still have the utmost priority.

As Oleandre was in such a distant orbit around the ringed planet, it did not take much of a power thrust to slowly move the vehicle out of Saturn's gravitational attraction. There was no great or pressing need to hurry back. The return to Mars would take twelve days.

In the distance a reddish disc could be observed to enlarge with each passing day. The steadily glowing ruby hung against the stars of Gemini. . .the God of Wars welcoming them home. Oleandre was scheduled to arrive in Martian orbit on OD-4:51. It would not go back to the orbit it had once occupied before being called Oleandre, when it was known as Phobos: should the Mission ever venture out again (and that *was* a question in many minds), too much energy and structural stress would have to be expended. So Oleandre went into a rather loose elliptical orbit, three hundred fifty-eight thousand miles out at the apogee.

It was not that the population of Oleandre would be cramped in the facility of the old Alliance metallurgical complex on the surface. If anything, there would be more room. However, living in something built by an enemy destroyed was repugnant. So, to save very valuable research time, only half the groups were to move permanently to the surface. Most production and engineering would go, where the expanded working area could be put to good use. The theoretical research and medical facilities were to stay on Oleandre.

As the orbital insertion occurred, a let's-get-it-over-with attitude abounded. Commander Jemma took the first hovercraft to the Martian surface to survey the situation and renew the environmental regulation systems in the sprawling underground complex. Eric Senka stayed behind. With his chief aid Jesse Horvitz, he supervised the teams preparing for the trip to the surface.

The polar caps were swollen and ragged on the edges, and the entire northern latitudes of Mars seemed to be covered with one swirling dust storm. Jemma made a power stall in the area of the old landing strip near the entrance to the metallurgical complex. The foil runway, about a hundred yards long, sat beside the large and very ancient Mobius crater. The runway had long been covered by the loose, sandy Martian soil. As the Hovercraft touched down, great clouds of yellow and violet dust flew up around it, only to be caught in the crosswinds and turned into ochre dervishes that twirled above and behind the ship.

Commander Jemma was accompanied by Flight Officer Youngman, Environmental Engineer Haywood, and Security Officer Fields, a title Lee Fields had bestowed upon himself, much to the Council's disdain. Haywood immediately went deep into the complex, down a thousand foot shaft under the Martian surface, to a huge cavern carved out of solid bedrock. In this chamber were housed the dozen nuclear turbines that created the power for the mining and ore smelting procedures. The atomic reactors were still functioning, although at minimum fission. It was not particularly difficult for Haywood to start up the turbines. Soon lights flickered and then burned steadily throughout the multileveled complex.

Meanwhile, by the light of laser torches, the rest of the party had made their way to the personnel-living sections, which had once held over ten thousand "volunteers" from the Alliance's political camps and memory control centers. It could easily accommodate seven thousand Oleandreans.

As the lights came on, signaling Haywood's success in starting up the turbines, the cool and slightly stale smell of new air accosted their senses. Artificial air was being pumped through giant ducts all over the complex. Now they removed their clumsy respirators. As the group moved toward the massive nerve-center of the metallurgical complex, they felt lilliputian. They walked through great caverns, filled with the giant ore smelting apparatuses and continuous fabricating systems with huge metal arms that looked as though they were the appendages of a sinister and monstrous orange insect.

In the control room, Youngman established contact with Oleandre Control and made a status report. Commander Jemma activated the environmental control systems, checked them over, and made contact with Haywood far below them. Lee Fields had wandered off to who-knew-where.

Self-appointed Security Officer, Lee Fields had gone exploring. He originally planned to make his way through the complex, winding down to where Haywood was working on the nuclear turbines and return with him. He never finished this grand tour.

While strolling through the seemingly endless corridor of the third level, he came upon a debris-filled side passage that looked even more deserted than the rest of the complex. It led to a series of antechambers and small empty rooms that reminded him of the tombs of the ancient Egyptian Pharoahs in the Valley of the Kings. At the end of the small passageway was a stout metal door with a round handle in the center. Vaultlike, he thought. Unable to resist, Fields tried twisting the device, but as it had not been lubricated for a long period it took a good deal of brute force and mental effort to move it. Finally, the door opened with a metallic rending sound. Fields' eyes widened slightly, he frowned and then showed the tiniest hint of a smirk.

Before him was a small, square room about ten feet on a side. It was lined from floor to ceiling with weapons. He surmised that this area had once been used as an armory by the Alliance garrison in the days before the General Recall. When the complex came into the hands of Jason Oleandre's group, this section was never used since it was too far from the main caverns. He made a quick survey of the arsenal.

There were over a hundred rapid-fire rifles made of some plastic material, and the same number of hand weapons looking as if they fired the rocketyne type of bullet; that is, a cartridge that is self-contained so as to be fired in a vacuum or underwater. There were plastic crates of ammunition for the rifles and hand weapons of the heat-seeking variety. . .enough to outfit a small army. A high rack of dull, black metal brimmed to overflowing with all types of tiny gas pellets. . .death gases (quick and slow), pleasure gases, sphincter-restrictor gases, vaginal irritation gases, and a hundred others. . .gases to make one cringe in terror, copulate frantically or merely die lethargically.

Lee's smirk widened to a grin and his hands were trembling so much with anticipation and excitement that he found it difficult to turn the metal wheel and reseal the vault.

"FIELDS!" The voice crackled over the communicon.

Lee Fields went to an opposite wall out in the hall where a small reply cartridge hung on a coiled cord. He depressed the green button and spoke, "Yes? Is that you Jemma?"

"Of course! Who did you expect, Harvey McMaster? Where the devil are you? We are ready to return."

"I'll be right up. I have found a radiation leak, but have managed to seal it. I will send down some of my boys to decontaminate the area."

"Fine, but please get up here. I have many details to attend to back on Oleandre."

"As you wish, Commander Jemma."

His boys, as Fields so fatherly called them, rose to become the most singularly dangerous threat to the Mission since its inception. . .dangerous because they were an enemy within.

About a week after the first laboratories were reinstalled in the metallurgical complex, Lee Fields called Commander Jemma and asked to see both he and Commander Senka on a matter of some urgency. Both Eric and Ahab ben Jemma had stayed aboard Oleandre, although Jemma made the trip to the Martian surface at least once a day. Eric came to Jemma's suite at Oleandre Control.

"What's this all about?"

"I haven't any idea," replied Ahab. "Fields sounded serious enough though."

"Christ, what devil is he exorcizing now?"

A hum sounded, indicating a visitor. Jemma touched the "ENTER" signal, while Eric was getting a drink of water from the little gold dispensor that sat under Jemma's reading machine.

The airscreen parted and Lee Fields entered. Commander Jemma said nothing, his frown indicating his surprised displeasure. When Eric turned around, he almost spit out the water he was swallowing, "Jesus, what in bloody hell are *you* made up as?"

Fields stood before them dressed in a silver tunic and high black boots. There was a gold braid over his left shoulder and the tunic had a black collar. Strapped to the back of his right hip was a sinister hand weapon in a shiny black holster. Behind him stood two similarly dressed men with high gold collars on their tunics. They had automatic rifles slung over their shoulders, and they stood with legs wide apart, their faces expressionless.

"Gentlemen," he began, "I believe there is reason to doubt the loyalty and competence of certain members of the Mission. As Security Officer, my boys and I will undertake the necessary investigations. Of course, you are still co-commanders, and we will not in any way interfere with your administration."

"But. . ."

Leaving no time for questions, the edict having been presented, Lee Fields whirled on his heel and left, his boys falling into step on either side. All that remained in the room with them was shocked silence. Eric spoke first.

"I don't believe it. I didn't think something like this was possible. We're being taken over, that bloody mongrel is. . ."

"No. . .I do not think so. I've seen Fields' psychoprofile. He *is* a fanatic, but completely loyal. . .overly loyal as we saw."

"But where did the weapons come from? There were to be none. It was part of the Oleandre Directive!"

"It's only an academic question now. The fact is, they have them, *that* is what matters."

"Is there going to be a purge?"

"I don't know. I'm not at all sure how far he will go with this, but his gonads are really in an uproar!"

Having no other comment, Eric merely rubbed at the ever-increasing muscular ache at the back of his neck and shook his head in disbelief.

It was not long before Lee Fields made his position very well known.

Disloyalty charges were lodged against Benedict Fu. When seven of Fields' boys went to serve notice, Fu panicked, pushed through them and rushed out of his room.

The young blond man named Gigantopithecus Smithe reached to his hip and, in a liquid motion, drew and squeezed the priming device. The weapon bucked violently in his hand,

leaving it covered with white slinging vapors and the metallic
bee streaked angrily down the hall leaving a minute vapor-trail
that was quickly distorted by the air currents in the corridor.
It looked as though Fu was being pursued by a smoky-grey,
ethereal snake.

Benedict Fu, his mind spinning with dredged up
antidiluvian fears, had rounded a corner, but the device's
thermoseeker had locked in on him. It crashed into the back
of Fu's head, penetrated, and, in white searing pain, exploded
within his skull sending tattered bone fragments and soft, red
and grey neural material flying in all directions. The impact
sent Fu's corpse to the ground with such a force that it slid
along the slick surface of the deck leaving a grisly, red smear
behind it. By the time other members of the Security Force
reached him, Fu's body was crumpled up against a wall, right
foot still twitching, unaware of its brain's death.

"Your men killed him!"
Eric's voice was high-pitched with indignation and rage.
Had it not been for Jemma's firm grip on his arm, Eric Senka
quite probably would have seized Security Officer Fields
soundly by the throat and throttled him on the spot. Finally,
after taking several deep breaths, Eric spoke more calmly,
"How could you *allow* this to happen?"
"He resisted," said Fields matter-of-factly.
"He resisted," mocked Eric. "He resisted what? Arrest?
You haven't that authority."
"Of course not. Listen, Fu was under suspicion. It is a well
documented fact that a cousin of his was a high-ranking
official in the K'uang Fong's Peoples Truth Tribunal. I sent
some of my boys to talk with him about this, not even
interrogate him, just talk. But what does the fool do? He
runs!"
"Christ, certainly he ran. Your thugs — and shit, there were
seven of them — show up armed to the teeth and eager for

some action. You knew Fu. He was a strange and nervous little fellow. And you know why, don't you. . .God, ten years in an Alliance maximum security camp! Anyone would be edgy."

"He resisted!"

"Of course he resisted. But where was he going to run to? Off the Oleandre? How? Back to Earth?"

At that moment an ashen look came into Eric's eyes and his face burned fiery red at the cheeks. His eyes radiated the sickening, contemptuous opposition he felt. He hissed, "If you try that with me, you anal-mouthed bastard, YOU WILL REGRET IT!"

Ahab ben Jemma got between them and said calmly, "Of course Lee, you'll admit that a mistake has been made, and, in the future, you will keep your men. . .I'm sorry, your *boys,* under more strict control. We will manufacture a cover story, perhaps that Fu went completely berserk and tried to kill someone."

"Good, Commander Jemma, very good indeed. I'm happy to see *some* of us still have our wits about us," said Fields, giving Eric a particularly disgusted look.

Security Officer Fields turned and left. His mouth hanging agape, Eric stared unbelievingly at Jemma. Finally, he spoke, "Are you in with them too?"

"Hagganah! Certainly not. . .how, how could you ever think that? Thanks a lot."

"Well, it sure sounded like you are."

"I am not sure if Fields is mad or not, but make no mistake, no matter what his condition, he *must* be done away with. . .and quickly."

"Whew!" sighed Eric. "For a second I thought I'd have to do it alone. But why the cover story about poor Benedict?"

"Two-fold reason! First, let Fields think we have given in. Second, to pacify the people. If they knew the real circumstances, there could be a real bloodbath. After all, Fields has almost all the arms."

"Almost? I thought he had all of them."
"Not exactly."

Throughout the first years of his command of the Oleandre, Ahab ben Jemma had obtained, what was for him, the most trustworthy counsel in his universe. At least twice a week, and sometimes daily, Jemma clandestinely conferred with Seth Hayakawa whom he still called "The Commander." Hayakawa had repeatedly warned him of the possibility of this kind of situation. He said it was a predictable reaction to failure and frustration.

Lee Fields adjusted the gold braid on his shoulder and muttered to himself. Great men are always misunderstood until history accepts their deeds, he thought. The green lushness, perverted by man's ineptitude, is gone. Gone. O Earth, gone to the fiery cataclysm of re-creation in energy's fusion. Am I never to lie in the deep grass, spotted with the velvet yellow, dandelion carpet, nor have my senses bombarded with the sweet salty sea air, nor feel winds buffet my face and tousle my hair? Is it not to be again? We have pulverized your lands and vaporized the pounding seas and for what? WHAT? To form the new world? If it is to be, if the fresh and virtuous world is to be found, then the Mission must not fail. It must not be jeopardized by a few mindless, immoral and disloyal fools. They must be rooted out as ants before the sloth and destroyed. It is my calling. . .my Mission.

"Have you any concrete suggestions, Eric?" Seth Hayakawa asked.

"Practical? No! But they *must* be stopped!"

"Yes, we are agreed on that point, but *how* is it to be done? Assassination? Imprisonment?" Jemma spoke softly.

"No, no," said Hayakawa. "We cannot lower ourselves to

their level. Furthermore, I do not believe his men are really at fault. Look at them. Who are they? Young men, probably frightened by the uncertainty of these times."

"Ahab," said Eric, "you spoke before — and very mysteriously too — inferring that Fields doesn't have all the weapons."

"That is correct. The Commander will explain."

Seth Hayakawa reminded them that in the data obtained from the first Oleandre Probe, was a section of futuristic weaponry. Specifically, there were plans for a small laser, many times more powerful than any they had now. It would be a scaled down version of the nobelium laser device Jemma and Eric had used on the Sub-Orbital Craft.

"Yes, but Seth," said Eric. "How long would it take to develop it? The work would have to be done in the strictest secrecy, and Christ. . ."

"It *has* been done, my boy!"

Touching a panel on his control console, a portion of the deck slid away. In the small compartment hung five weapons of dull black metal. . .four obviously to be hand-held and the other large enough to require supporting apparatus.

Eric picked one up. It was light and perfectly balanced. The grip was molded to fit any hand and the short black barrel was suspended within a coil of gold-colored alloy. The tip of the barrel housed a violet crystal which seemed to contain a light of its own.

It had taken Seth Hayakawa over six months in exile, working almost eight hours a day, to develop these destructors from Jason Oleandre's meager plans.

"Care to try it, Eric?"

"Yes, I suppose I must."

"All right, you aim as though it is a conventional weapon. Activate the destructor by pressing the small lever under your thumb. It is fired by just squeezing the grip, there is no trigger as such. You do not even have to brace yourself as there will be no kickback."

"Fine, what shall I aim at?"

"I'll get you a target," said Jemma.

He opened a small closet that sat under the dark televisor screen. From a cage in the closet, he produced a small, brown gerbil.

"Now wait," cried Eric. "Just a Goddamned minute! I'm not going to fry that bloody little beast."

"Eric," said Hayakawa, "you must test this weapon on the system on which it was designed to be used. Weapons are not designed to be maimers of metal cans, nor attackers and destroyers of paper bull's eyes."

Ahab had placed the little fellow on a short metal table and laid a seed at its tiny feet. It sat upright, nibbling unsuspectingly, its fuzzy, long tail coiled behind it. Eric sighted down the concentric circles on the barrel. When the gerbil was perfect centered, his thumb depressed the arming lever and he tightened his fist. His guts tightened concurrently. A pulse of blue light erupted from the laser and the little animal was bathed in it. Instantly, the furry beast exploded into a smoky heap of submolecular particles.

"It's painless, Eric. I have tested it with neural electrodes in a gerbil's brain. Unfortunately, it is an all-or-none phenomenon. If you miss, it lives. There is no wounding. If you are just the slightest bit on target, the subject dies. It is ironic that out of the Mission of peace and creativity comes the most potent dealer of death ever devised."

"I'm not so sure about the irony, Seth. I've been thinking, do you suppose Jason Oleandre could have foreseen this possibility?" Eric's tone was very serious.

"Yes, Eric, I believe so. I have been awake nights for a long time now thinking of just that very possibility."

"How will we use these?" said Eric handing the laser back.

"I have the plan," replied the Commander.

There were six conspirators. . .six against Fields and his hundred dupes. Seth Hayakawa, Eric Senka and Ahab ben

Jemma were joined by Jesse Horvitz, Maggie Senka and Alfonsis Nikto. Jonathan Fischer was morally included but not armed; and he, perhaps, had the most important role. The confrontation would occur when Jemma and Eric were to relinquish command to Fields and his men. Jemma and Seth Hayakawa had gone to Fields and played upon his paranoia. They admitted they were wrong and unanimously agreed that Fields was the most enlightened man on Oleandre. Thus, he should command. The ceremony to commemorate this auspicious event would take place in the Receptacle's small auditorium. Fields agreed and said he would have all his compatriots present.

This was more than they could have hoped for.

Fields' "boys" filed in in small groups talking excitedly with one another. The members of the Council were more restrained since they knew nothing of the events to come. The weapons of the Security Force were slung carelessly over shoulders or lay in the seat next to the owners. Some, however, held the piece like a sceptre. The low murmur grew louder as Jonathan Fischer entered, followed by Eric Senka and Ahab ben Jemma. Eric and Ahab wore their usual Commander's tunics. Fischer, however, presided in black academic robes.

Lee Fields sat in the very first row, his legs crossed. His face bore the sneer of confidence and just victory.

"Gentlemen and colleagues," Fischer began, "will you please be seated and give me your undivided attention."

He was speaking from the podium that had risen from the floor of the auditorium. Eric and ben Jemma immediately took seats to his right. Fischer spoke again, "It is my duty, if not my privilege, to preside over this, the change of command ceremony. Joint-Commanders Senka and ben Jemma are pleased to relinquish their posts to a person so competent and objective-minded as Security Officer Leland Fields. His diligence and foresight are traits to be emulated by. . ."

As Jonathan Fischer went on, his eloquence practically mesmerized the audience. No one noticed the three figures, in black, hooded cloaks glide silently onto the service ramp near the ceiling in the rear of the auditorium. A day earlier, they had cut a slot on the railing in the center of the platform, into which Alfonsis Nikto was cautiously sliding the bracket of the large destructor. He looked down the shiny coils and moved the sights over the backs of the unsuspecting crowd, carefully noting the positions of the Council members so as to not mistakenly hit one of them.

Maggie Senka and Jesse Horvitz took up positions on the edges of the platform. They stayed crouched out of sight until Fischer's signal. Nikto depressed the activator and a crimson glow appeared on the side of the flash-pulse chamber. He nodded to Eric far below, who cleared his throat to signal Fischer, who couldn't "feel" past the blinding lights. ". . .so it is our esteemed. . .NOW, I WOULD MOST URGENTLY ADVISE YOU GENTLEMEN TO LAY DOWN YOUR MOST VILE WEAPONS!"

The effect was like violently rousing someone from a sound sleep. Fields jumped up and screamed, "What do you mean, drop our weapons, you sightless fool?"

"It would be extremely advisable. Otherwise, I will order Doctor Nikto to open fire on you. Turn around, gentlemen!"

As if robotoid, the audience turned in unison. Maggie and Jesse had risen holding their hand destructors. Meanwhile, Eric and ben Jemma took their weapons from under Fischer's robe. They trained them on Fields who whirled around shouting, "What treachery is this? Darest thou use mock weapons against us?"

"Permit a demonstration before making such a rash judgment," said Fischer.

Eric released a large, white rabbit onto the stage from its cage hidden in the podium. Frightened by the lights and all the noise, the creature was sitting perfectly still, paralyzed. Fischer nodded, and Jesse Horvitz, his wrist resting lightly on the palm of his right hand, sent a pulse of blue death over the heads of the crowd. The rabbit was reduced to a scattering of ashes. There were a few cries of terror from the audience and several distinct Goddamns.

"Put down your weapons," ordered ben Jemma in an authoritarian tone, "and no one will be injured!"

Several did so instantly.

"Do not be fooled, my comrades. . .my boys," pleaded Fields. "O the Gods are truly foul. . .the great men, how they must suffer! Do you not realize, blind one, that I have saved the Mission? Yes, saved it, by exposing the incompetent. Why, it is possible that there are Alliance agents aboard. O Caesar, I dost now know thy torment! The Mission, God, how I have sacrificed for thee! And for WHAT? To be throttled by peasant assassins. . .operatives of the unholy Alliance? Vile perpetrators of sabotage. Bolsheviks in the rafters, ye shall not prevail, Albategnius, thou shalt be avenged!"

Fields reached for the weapon on his hip, his silvered eyes glistening in the bright lights. The six were frozen. It was one thing to vaporize an animal, quite another to kill a fellow human. But as the weapon left its holster, a series of waxy, ultramarine blobs erupted from the wing to the left of the auditorium. Lee Fields was bathed in brilliant, pure energy and the final, silent scream was etched upon his face as the corpse pulsated an instant, then crumbled to ashes. A pungent, nauseating vapor began to disseminate throughout the room.

From the wing, Seth Hayakawa walked to the center of the speaker's platform, the destructor in his hand dangling loosely at his side. He spoke in a broken voice, "G. . .gentlemen, y-you will file out through the front of this room, leaving your weapons on the stage. If you do not comply within ten seconds, you will be similarly eliminated. It is as simple as that."

Fields' Security Force filed out quickly, dropping their

arms as though afflicted with the plague. Not one glanced at the remains of their leader, whose white and gray ashes were strewn across several black-upholstered chairs and into the aisle.

Maggie's hands trembled and the tops of her thighs shook. She breathed a sigh of relief as the last of Fields' men deposited their weapons and walked meekly from the room; and her eyes met Jesse Horvitz's and there were unspoken words between them. Alfonsis dismantled the large destructor while Maggie and Jesse came down to the front of the auditorium.

"Well done," said Hayakawa, "certainly a difficult situation. I take full responsibility for the death of Fields, and I believe history will bear us out."

"Seth," asked Eric, "will you take back the Commandership?"

"Only if the Council approves!"

The members of the Council, most of them riveted in their chairs, realized the gravity of the situation which they themselves had allowed to arise. To the man, the vote was affirmative.

All the old Alliance weapons were taken to the Martian surface and destroyed in the ovens of the nuclear smelting devices. The destructors became the property of the Commander; and Seth Hayakawa had a vault built in Oleandre Control to which only he and his computer had the opening sequence.

The overthrow and death of Lee Fields and the disbanding of his security force had not given any new hope to the people of Oleandre. While the immediate danger of an armed coup was no longer present, the collective dejection still floated in a foggy, paralyzing cloud through their minds. It was a fact that most Oleandreans did not even know how close they came to being ruled by a police state again. They knew nothing of the twisted mind that operated under the guise of ultrapatriotism.

It seemed to be the general consensus that the Mission had been launched a little prematurely. The Oleandre *was* way ahead of its time. All the planets hadn't even been explored yet. Only Mars and Lunare had ever had permanent human bases, and Venus had only been approached by a manned Soviet expedition in the late nineteen seventies. Perhaps it was premature to launch a human settlement outside the solar system. These were the very charges leveled by the Council that had resulted in the resignation of Seth Hayakawa.

Perhaps it had been presumptuous to start the Mission before finding the three Jason Oleandre probes; but who could have foreseen that the location of the last probe would not be contained within the second? It was so illogical. Jason Oleandre had always been so precise. Seth Hayakawa thought it so illogical as to *be* logical. Perhaps events were meant to happen as they did. To test them? If so, he thought, it smacked of playing God. And he didn't like that. So far, they had not passed the test; however, they had certainly not failed. The Oleandre was learning.

If only the last probe could be found. And what if it could not? Was that such a terrible defeat? It would certainly be possible to survive on Mars and establish the creative society there. They could live in and expand the facilities of the old metallurgical complex. In a generation or so, the people might even adjust to the rarefied Martian atmosphere and become accustomed to breathing it without a respirator. For unknown reasons, some had always been able to naturally breathe it. Of course, underground living would be required, due to the frequency of meteor strikes and the great variations in temperature during the light and dark periods.

It would just not be like Earth. There would be no trees, nor oceans, nor rivers to swim in. The few Martian streams that filled during the seasonal melting of the polar caps were so shallow and so acidic as to discourage the immersion of one's body. Except for a few species of hardy lichens that grew in certain areas — particularly west of Tithonius Lacus and down the northern rim of Lorand's Fissure — and some primitive bacteria, Mars was devoid of life.

No, it was not Earth. Another planetary system must be found; and in order to do that, the last Oleandre probe was needed.

In the months that followed, the population seemed to settle into a rather dull routine. General apathy abounded. Basic research *was* being done with the vague aim of finding the last probe; but most people didn't believe nor had any hope for success. Attendance at Oleandre University classes was low by both faculty and students.

On the morning of OD-4:130, Ahab ben Jemma, now at his old post as Hayakawa's first officer, brought some rather alarming news to the Commander. There had been over the last weeks, he reported, a great number of cases of public drunkenness. This, however, was not the most distressing fact. In the last month, there had been thirty-five deaths attributable to suicide and fourteen more possibles — a total of forty-nine.

Jonathan Fischer had predicted only ten suicides in a whole year, based on the pooled psychological profiles of Oleandreans. At the beginning there had been several suicides; but this was at the time of the Earth's destruction. Since then, there had been only two. . .two in a period of over three years. This was well below Fischer's projection. And now, almost fifty in one month! Seth Hayakawa was understandably distressed.

Strangely, there were none of the usual notes left by suicidal people, nothing to trace the causes of their ultimate deed. They merely killed themselves. Most took the peaceful way — an overdose of drugs — while others were more violent. One woman, a dentist, stepped into an airlock at the surface of Oleandre without a pressure suit. She opened the valves and literally exploded from the pressure drop.

The only slim clue as to reason for the suicides, was a comment by one victim shortly before he died. This fellow, a servomechanin programmer, said that he wished to see just one green bush or tree again. He walked out of the west end of the metallurgical complex and into the Martian day. He kept walking. . .walking until he dropped over dead from lack of oxygen and water. A search party later found his body.

Several attempted suicides failed. A man called Roth, from the Applied Kinematics Laboratory tried to jump into the positron stream of a waste disintegrator — a painless death if carried out properly. However, in his frenzy, he miscalculated the size of the opening in the deck, so that when he dropped in, his shoulders and arms wedged in the orifice, leaving his legs dangling in the searing, greenish energy that severed them like a bandsaw. As the blood pumped from the open femoral arteries, it too was vaporized and a putrid stench began to permeate the room along with his gurgling screams. He was rescued by a colleague with his servomechanin, and rushed to medical facilities on a medstat-tram. His body was saved; but Roth's mind was irreversibly damaged.

Little Sean Senka was walking now and even had a vocabulary, though much of it was indecipherable to almost everyone except Maggie. Eric had some difficulty translating his son; but he swore Sean spoke fluent Sanskrit. Maggie and Eric spent hours on end just watching the little fellow play. Maggie worked in the astrophysics section only a few days a week and while she was there, Sean was cared for in the public nursery on D-Deck.

Eric spent much time in his laboratory now. He worked on the brain transplanting experiments with renewed vigor and sense of hope. His attitude was not shared by many others. However, Jesse Horvitz had finished up his small project for Jonathan Fischer and had returned to Eric's laboratory. The young man had acquired a new drive and excitement. Much of Jesse's new awareness had resulted from his liaison with Iridani. He had even gone so far as to write some crude poetry in his spare time. Iridani ruthlessly criticized it; but she was secretly pleased at his interest and persistence.

Jesse worked tirelessly under Eric's supervision. Together, they had done several more transplants. These experiments were designed to perfect the new cryogenic needle Eric had constructed. Coupled with the low-pulse microlaser beam, he was able to sever and reform nerve attachments with a minimum of tissue necrosis.

Since many of the people who had occupied the suites on Oleandre had moved to the Martian surface, Eric was able to expand his facilities in two directions. First, he outfitted an annex to his laboratory to house the growing orangutan colony. Then he took the large room next to the living suite and divided it in two; one part for their own bedroom and the other for Sean.

Maggie had admitted her growing concern about the rising suicide rate, and said that people she talked with were indeed abnormally depressed. She, too, was prone to periods of apathy, but never contemplated doing away with herself. Maggie once laughingly told Eric that all Oleandreans should be required to have babies. This would improve the mental situation as far as Maggie Senka was concerned.

Commander Seth Hayakawa continued to hold Eric and Ahab in the highest esteem, due mostly to their levelheadedness during the time when *they* were Commanders. He kept them informed of all developments.

Late in the afternoon of OD-4:139, Eric and Jesse were just finishing up a cisternal-ventricular perfusion on the brain of an orangutan that had just been transplanted the previous day. The communicator sounded. Jesse put down his vascular-suturing device and slowly went over to the control console.

"Yes?"

"PRIORITY CHANNEL THREE," said the loud mechanical voice.

"Eric? For you. . .priority three. . .I'll go down the hall for coffee. . .call me when you're finished."

After stripping off his transparent gloves, Eric stepped to the console and touched THREE. The voice of the Commander came on.

"Eric. . .you *are* alone?"

"Of course Seth. What is it? Trouble?"

"I am not sure, probably not; but *do* come up here as soon as you can."

"All right, in about thirty minutes."

"Fine. . .end priority call."

"PRIORITY CHANNEL THREE CLOSED. . . RECORDING INTERNAL ALPHA," responded the raspy, sexless, computerized voice.

Seth Hayakawa sat at a small semicircular table in the annex to Oleandre Control. Eric stepped through the airscreen, unannounced.

"Hello, Eric. . .sorry to spoil your evening."

The Commander projected a puzzled and concerned image.

"What's the trouble, Seth?"

"Well, as I told you before, I am not sure there is anything to be alarmed about. It comes down to this: some servomechanins down on the surface, in the structural metals processing plant, have malfunctioned. Two of them. Malfunction is not exactly the word for it — they went berserk!"

"What? Not again!"

"Exactly," Seth fumed. "The damn metallic bastards destroyed some equipment before the men down there could override their programs. They were inspected. . ."

"And?"

"Nothing. . .everything seemed to be in perfect order. I had the prime program checked up here and it, too, was perfect."

"Christ!" Eric said. "That's all we need now. . .psychotic
Goddamned robots. Jesus, there was a play written in the early
twentieth century about just such a situation. It was a satire
on totalitarianism."

"Did the robots win?" Seth asked.

"I really don't remember. I read it in a classics class about
ten years ago and can't even remember the name of it. Does it
really matter?"

"No."

"Are you having some sort of investigation?"

"Yes, unofficial of course. There is certainly no reason for
public concern. . .not now at least."

"There *could* be some reason for alarm?"

"Don't know, but I have a strange feeling. . .can't explain
it, Eric."

"You want me to look into it?"

"Yes, I have asked the Schmidts to make a formal report;
but I want you to do some snooping, too. You and young
Horvitz go to the surface under the pretense of setting up
some new animal facilitieses. I'll clear it and notify Ahab of
the situation."

The entrance to the metallurgical complex lay on the
western edge of the northern tip of Syrtis Major. The foil
landing strip glittered like a silver ribbon as Eric and Jesse
made their approach in a Hovercraft. As they landed, they
noticed the ever-present orange and yellow sandstorms
blowing on the horizon. The ground near the entrance was
covered with gray and steel-green lichen-like plants. Eric
pointed out a fresh meteor crater about ten feet in diameter
that had chewed up the ground to reveal the dark red
undersoil.

The only things on the surface that revealed the presence of
humans were two transparent bubbles for observation, several

exhaust stacks and four mirrors for harvesting solar energy. The rest of the Martian soil was untouched, unspoiled.

Upon checking in at the control center, Eric and Jesse pinned on combination identification badges and radiation dosimeters. The radiation detectors on their tunics were in continuous telemetric contact with the central computer and would sound several alarms if an overdose occurred.

The elevator whisked them rapidly into the bowels of the complex. Sometimes the shaft passed through solid rock; sometimes the transparent tube penetrated great caverns. Eric and Jesse could look out on the monstrous processing and ore smelting works where the humans present looked like ants swarming about a megalithic idol.

On the third "subterranean" level, where the major fabricating production line was located, Eric and Jesse walked up to a small office, commenting on how quickly they had gotten used to the continually curved corridors of Oleandre and how strange it felt to be walking down a straight passage. They could see the Schmidts through the ozmyglass window of the office talking with the head of this division, Roger Ringdoc. Margaret Li-Chi Schmidt and Rheinhardt Schmidt had designed the servomechanin series of robotoids, and they were the logical choice to investigate a malfunction. The Schimdts were on their way out and Eric pretended to be looking into several empty rooms adjacent to the main passage.

"Hello, Eric," said Rheinhardt.

" 'Lo Rheinhardt. And how are you, Margaret?"

"Very well, Dr. Senka," she replied. "And what brings you down to the depths?"

"Oh," Eric said casually, "we're thinking of moving our Orangutan colony down here."

"I see. . .well, we must be going. Nice to see you."

The couple went down the hall to the waiting elevator while Eric and Jesse introduced themselves to Roger Ringdoc.

The Commander had notified Ringdoc of their coming and he would cooperate to the fullest. Ringdoc's office held only the most spartan of necessities. . .an old metal desk, a chair and a communicator. In an even barer corner stood two deactivated servomechanins.

"Those the culprits?" Jesse suggested

"Yep, they are. And ah'm keeping them on remote shutdown, but there's really no sound reason for it. They've been thoroughly checked ovah."

"These are servomechanins of the Type III series aren't they?"

"That's right, designed for heavy duty work. They're compact, but able to lift and move two tons — fairly agile, too. Well, look fer yerself," said Ringdoc pointing out the wide panoramic window that was over his desk. "There are several working under program out there now."

On the floor of the long narrow cavern below, several servomechanins were busy moving the massive tungsten-carbide beams that came out of the automated production line. The huge, but very light beams were to be used as structural supports in another part of the complex where more living quarters were being constructed. A smaller servomechanin stood at a control console which regulated the great hoppers-full of crude ore. The hoppers were moved from the mining area and dumped into the gigantic smelting apparatus that sat like an omnipotent, orange mechanical locust.

"Is he the boss?" asked Jesse, half-joking.

"In a way, yes. It controls the production line," replied Ringdoc.

"Christ, even in the robotoid world brain controls brawn. Upanishad! A mechanical cybernetical, inhumanical, hierarchy!"

Eric suggested that even though the servomechanins checked out perfectly, they should not be allowed in an area where they could do some damage until the problem of their malfunctioning was solved. His plan was to locate these two servomechanins in one of the empty storage rooms to stack beams. Their activity would be rated priority. In fact, it would be a mock priority, just to see what happened. The robotoids would be monitored constantly. Ringdoc agreed and said he would initiate the plan that very day.

It was not until three days later that anything out of the ordinary occurred. Eric was reading line after line of micropoint cards that held the servomechanin telemetry record. Toward the end of the tape, a segment of high intensity electromagnetic waves distorted the normal pattern. This lasted only about a minute. Good, thought Eric. He switched over to the visual record and matched up the telemetry record with it. At precisely the time that coincided with the beginning of the strange transmission, the servomechanin on the screen picked up a tungsten beam and swung it into the wall. It went to get another; but before it could do so, its partner ran into it. The interference stopped and the two robotoids returned to their stacking as though nothing happened. Here's a fantastic clue, Eric thought. Now I'll have to track down the source of that interfering transmission.

Eric timed the transmission. It occurred every two days at precisely fifteen-hundred hours. After he had related his findings to Seth Hayakawa, it was agreed that the situation was more serious now. There were several questions to be answered. First, what or who was the source of the interference? Secondly, from where was it being transmitted? Why? And why did it effect only these two servomechanins?

The last of these inquiries was settled very quickly. Two servomechanins were *not* the only ones to be affected.

Jesse Horvitz had gone to the Martian surface to fake the setting up of some animal cages. He decided, just by chance, to check the telemetry and scanning devices that watched the suspect servomechanins. As he came down the corridor, he noticed that the door to Ringdoc's office was open. Not only was it open, it was torn entirely off its base!

Jesse ran in. The sight he beheld welled up nausea within him. Ringdoc's body, or what was left of it, lay next to the desk. Its arms and legs had been ripped from the torso and tossed aimlessly about the room. Dry, white splintered bones protruded from dark red tissue. The man's head was severed at the neck and sat face down on the chair, with pulled-out shoulder muscles and several cracked vertebrae from the spinal column dangling over the edge. A thin trail of already drying blood ran down the green, plastic upholstery and formed a small, clotty pool on the floor. The liver and gall bladder, ripped from the body, had been thrown with tremendous force against the wide window, leaving a hideous green and brownish smear. The entire deck was covered with great puddles of dark blood that had spurted from cleaved arteries. There were tread marks in the blood. In one corner sat a silent and still servomechanin. Its treads and driving device were dripping with gore. . .blood and bile and crushed tissue.

Horvitz, holding his mouth to keep from retching, circled it cautiously and pulled the circuit-breaker on the rear of the robotoid, then immediately called Eric, who called Hayakawa. In a matter of twenty minutes, they arrived together at the scene. Jesse was out in the hall pacing nervously.

One look at the grisly scene, and the Commander put the entire area on Black Alert.

The remnants of Ringdoc's body were removed in a transparent sack. The Commander ordered all servomechanins to be shut down. They returned quickly to Eric's laboratory on Oleandre to view the tapes of the servomechanins under surveillance. Several sets of triangulation equipment were hurriedly set up to locate the source of the mysterious transmission.

When Maggie Senka heard the order to nullify all robotoids, she hurried from the astrophysics lab to their living suite. When she entered, Pseudomonius was standing in the center of the main room. It said something extremely strange, almost frightening.

"GOOD AFTERNOON MADAM. . .I HAVE DETECTED
THE NULLIFICATION ORDER BUT CANNOT REACH MY
NULLER. . .IF YOU SHOULD BE SO KIND, MADAM, I
WOULD BE ETERNALLY IN YOUR DEBT. . .I BELIEVE,
MADAM, THAT. . ."

She pulled the circuit-breaker, which sparked and sent up a
small cloud of pinkish smoke, and thought, what does a
robotoid know of concepts like 'debt' and 'eternal'?

At the next transmission of the rogue electromagnetism,
the four detection teams computed the source of the
emanation and agreed that it originated in, of all places, the
memory banks of the prime analogue computer on board
Oleandre. All on the detection squad except for Rheinhardt
Schmidt were using signal averaging detectors, while he used
an integrator-coupled ataxial randomizer. Thus, Rheinhardt
Schmidt detected a shorter wavelength transmission, superimposed upon the unknown signal coming from the prime
computer. They calculated that the low strength signal
originated below the Martian surface, in the area of the eastern
rim of the Margaritifer Sinus and very near the Great
Leonovsky Crater.

The Commander noted that there were no installations in
that area now, nor had there ever been a record of one in the
past. It was very rugged terrain, he said, and, to his knowledge,
no human had ever set foot there.

As the drone Hovercraft swooped down to the area of the
low intensity signal's origin, a rocky piece of soil opened.
Through the slit, a fast heat-seeking missile was discharged. It
streaked at the Hovercraft, turning it into a red and yellow,
waxy fireball. There was a great deal of shock and confusion in
Oleandre Control. Seth Hayakawa readied a decoy Hovercraft.

He, Jesse, Eric and Ahab ben Jemma flew close to the
surface while the decoy sailed high over the area discharging
streamers of magnesium ribbons and inflated false, neoradar

blips. Several missiles were fired, but the streamers put ther
off target and they exploded harmlessly. Telemetry showe
the missiles to be armed with conventional, low-yield thermc
nuclear warheads. Jemma activated the dune-skis and th
group landed roughly on a sandy hillock just south of th
supposed launching site. They wore silver-leaf radiation suit:
They walked cautiously.

It was merely good-fortune that a small metal hatch wa
found, cleverly covered with imitation topsoil. Hayakawa ha
understandably issued destructors to each member of th
expedition. Jesse slid the hatch back while Eric and Aha
stood with weapons armed. Darkness. . .a black hole in whicl
nothing could be visualized greeted them. Ahab attached th
TRYGON ladder to the ground with explosive spikes. Eri
readied the arc-torch and went in first. He dangled in air, th
torch cutting great swatches in the blackness. Upon reachin
the end of the ladder, he saw by torchlight that the bottom o
the shaft was only a few feet below. He jumped. The floor wa
hewn out of solid rock and showed much the same kind o
blasting marks seen in the caverns of the metallurgica
complex. He shouted for the others to come down. As the
descended, Eric pulled the respirator away from his face for
second and took a deep breath. A fiery tightness gripped hi
chest. There was obviously no environmental control dow
here!

There was only one passageway, and it too was carved ou
of the solid, yet extremely light and porous, red rock. A larg
metal door blocked their way. Hayakawa remarked that al
evidence indicated an Alliance installation, and that the
should be very wary. The entrance was opened with som
trouble because the bushings of the massive hinges wer
severely oxidized.

Ahab and Eric crouched down, their destructors prime
and ready. As the door swung open, a bright light accoste
their eyes. Inside was a fully lit cavern. It was covered fron

floor to ceiling with literally millions of clear panels set end-to-end and side-by-side. Each was about forty by two hundred feet and a quarter-inch thick, separated by only a few centimeters. Each panel was attached to the next by multitudes of colored strands. Banks of lights flashed everywhere and great, pungent arcs of static electricity flew from several gold spheres suspended near the ceiling of the grotto. There was not a living thing on the premises.

They soon saw, however, that this was not exactly the case. They were actually standing *within* a living vibrant thing. Housed within this labyrinth of stone was the legacy of a hundred years of computer technology. Seth Hayakawa had heard rumors of its existence, but they had remained only rumors up to now. The Ultimatron, epitome of Alliance information science, stood pulsating and breathing before them in all its interwoven, microtransistorized, memoriocentric glory. Originally built to serve all extraterrestial Alliance outposts at the time of the General Recall, the computer was somehow left operating; and, since it was entirely self-contained, it continued to function undetected all these years. The Ultimatron had its own nuclear power plant which it maintained, and its own defense system which the Oleandreans had so recently seen demonstrated. Obviously having the ability to tie into the prime computer on Oleandre, its transmitting signal had been responsible for the misbehavior of the servomechanins and indirectly responsible for the death of Roger Ringdoc.

Seth Hayakawa was not convinced. He believed the computer to be *directly* accountable for the death. . .it had murdered! He felt the Ultimatron had completely overcome its ties with the Alliance. It was now a self-sufficient entity capable of conceiving its own actions. It was using the Oleandre computer and Seth thought it a menace. The Ultimatron had to be dismantled, and many of its components would be valuable to the Mission. If dismantling could not be accomplished, perhaps due to some internal defense devices, then the Ultimatron would have to be destroyed.

The Ultimatron, powerful as it was, had several serious inperfections. Even though its upper memory matrices had evolved cerebral capabilities, it had not yet acquired the ability to actually construct material things. Oh, it had plans all right, but at the present, it could only use the instrumentation left by the Alliance — and this did not include any protection against dismantling.

A tactical unit from the metallurgical complex succeeded in disarming the thing by cutting the circuitry to its missile modules. Dismantling began at the lower levels as routine memory banks, signal transfer coils, and impulse mixers were separated and taken away by heavy duty, Type III, servo-mechanins. While this was proceeding, Seth Hayakawa and Eric Senka listened to signals coming from the upper memory levels. The Ultimatron was going wild; but in effect, its digitalized spinal column had been severed. It even contemplated suicide by turning its missiles on itself.

Eric was literally frightened white and everyone involved could not help but be awed. They were witnessing the death of an alien, sentient, intelligent life form, ironically created by humans, but which had evolved of its own volition. Now it was being destroyed by its creators.

The instrumentation salvaged from the Ultimatron was incorporated into the prime Oleandre computer, almost increasing its memory volume a million fold. Entirely new concepts of information storage had been introduced by the builders of the Ultimatron. Memory data bits were stored on a conic matrix, allowing retrieval on many levels: circular, elliptical, parabolic and hyperbolic. This allowed practically unlimited memory reference frames. Coupled with Oleandre's electronic typesetting machines, the computer could provide over a hundred-thousand characters-per-second on a cathodic tube. What a boon this would be for the printed word in the new civilization!

The upper memory banks of the Ultimatron were not of much use as they had been irreversibly imprinted during the evolution process. Only these and the small nuclear power plant were left behind. As the last technicians departed, Eric and Seth looked up into the cavern. Suspended from the ceiling were several hundred vertical plates. Sparks arced between them and a glowing seemed to emanate from the core. It still lived. . .lived within itself. Ahab ben Jemma, himself, removed the Malovium damping rods so that the primitive reactor would soon exceed critical mass.

The small nuclear blast fused the cavern into crystals of glassy material. A red and black, non-radioactive dust cloud spread out over the Martian landscape occasionally blotting out the Sun or turning it to a dull tangerine disc.

The next several months brought the further decline of the Oleandreans. Choking fear and frustration continually increased both apathy and the suicide rate. Births continued at a flat rate; but all applications for children had ceased, so that when all the fetuses now in the womb were born, there would be no more. Perhaps even more distressing than the suicides was the fact that over fifty Oleandreans, some of them brilliant scientists, were being confined to their quarters. They were held for acts of murder and treason!

Seth Hayakawa had a gnawing sensation deep in his gut that Lee Fields may have been right. He refused to give this thought more than infinitesimal consideration. The core of the Mission was becoming rotten and could easily collapse upon itself, as did the Alliance. Unless a breakthrough was soon found, the Mission would indeed destroy itself, or the rise of a military regime was inevitable.

Iridani, always able to comfortably breathe the thin Martian atmosphere with no distress, had become completely disgusted with living in the underground complex. She built a

crude metal hut on the surface. An electrical line ran from it
to the complex. Her new home sat on a small rolling grey and
brown knoll overlooking a rugged valley pockmarked with
large and small meteor craters. The danger of a meteor striking
her hut did not greatly concern her.

She could be seen daily sitting on a small rock in front of
the door.

She wrote constantly.

She wrote of the pale blue Martian sky and the rising of
twin moons. She wrote of the bleak, windswept Martian
landscape, tormented by violent, dust-filled storms. She wrote
of the bleak minds of Oleandre. . .minds tormented by
sweeping, energy-sapping fear.

PROGRESSIUM

THE SEQUENCE

"Progress? Progress at what
cost? Certainly not in sacrifice
of all that is of the human."

— Rheinhardt Schmidt, in
conversation.

CHAPTER 8

"By Jesus, it works!"

Eric could not believe he said these words. There were
times, when his body was so racked by fatigue, his mind so
paralyzed with failure, that he was sure he would never be able
to utter this victorious phrase.

He had achieved the complete brain transplant, and the
orangutan had been able to repeat the multiple-task phase of
the experiment. Two weeks after the gross implantation, all
reflexes were intact and all tests of neural circuitry were
positive. But most important, the animal still responded to the
unreinforced color tests that had been learned before its old
brain had been removed and the new one put in place. The
wispy-haired monkey, which Jesse Horvitz had given the
remarkably unlikely name of Quanta D. Somata-II, was in near
perfect health. Jesse's monitoring devices kept constant watch
over the animal's metabolic functions. In making his entries
into the log of experiments, Eric noted: OD-4:305, QDS-II,
NORMAL METABOLISM, BABINSKI AND RIEGEL
REFLEX LACKING, CARTERONE REFLEX NORMAL
NOW: REF. ECS-I-33.

The next series of experiments were to test an orangutan's ability to remember series of characters and, upon recognition of these characters, to carry out a specific motor reaction. Q.D. Somata-II would not be used again because Eric thought the stress would be too great. A successor which Jesse named Dichtysomal, was procured from the orangutan colony, and Jesse noted in passing that, for whatever it was worth (probably nothing), Dichtysomal was the son of Pedyrast-IV.

The anthropoid Dichtysomal was a surly little fellow covered with hair unusually sparse for his species. Jesse brought him from the colony chamber and the orangutan clung warily to him, looking around with the eyes of a High Llama. The initial testing would begin that very day. Eric strapped the beast in the appropriate chair and moved the cathodic simulator up close to Dichtysomal's face, who seemed irritated and tried to bite Eric's ear. Electrodes were attached to its scalp and, after Jesse said that good neural recordings were going into the computer, Eric began flashing various characters on the screen. At first, only geometrics were used: squares, circles and triangles and occasionally an irregular polygon. Soon a pattern of geometrics appeared, a food pellet appeared to drop across the room, and, simultaneously, the restraining straps were released. Dichtysomal soon realized that whenever that series of figures appeared, so would food, and he would leap out of the chair. Very soon, no food had to appear to make the orangutan leave his seat at the visual cue of four triangles and a circle.

Training of this nature went on for several weeks. The characters to be remembered increased in difficulty. The familiar geometrics only appeared occasionally. Now other groupings showed: AAB, ZXZ or CAT or MAN.

The ape soon mastered the series; and a new series made its debut. The appearance of MAN on the cathodic was immediately followed by a light illuminating Jesse as he stood in the darkened room. The orangutan — or rather, the creature named Dichtysomal — was learning to read and form the most rudimentary concepts of the written word.

And it was entered in Eric's log that this strangely humanoid beast with the knowing eyes and saddened face learned much more than it was ever thought possible. Eric duly noted that the creature, of course, could only be a mutant. Still, the orangutan knew, actually *knew* the meanings of some words. He was not able to speak them nor write them, but he associated the word with an abstract concept as well as a material thing. For example, Dichtysomal knew that FOOD *meant* a food pellet. He also knew that Eric was represented by MAN. There was no distinction of sexuality, so Jesse and Maggie were also MAN. In this manner, he grasped the abstract.

Partly due to his eagerness to get on with the experiment and a sense of not pressing one's luck too far, Eric proceeded into the next critical phase. The complete neural profile was entered onto the memory lattice of Eric's computer.

The orangutan lay on the gleaming surgical table. It was a mindless thing, kept alive only through the efforts of Eric's Essenstainer system. The essence of the thing called Dichtysomal was dispersed among the moving electrons and multiple quantum levels of the Tholium-oxide matrix. It was imprisoned there.

The thing's useless tissue, that in the functional state was known as a brain, was removed. Jesse had prepared a new brain from a younger orangutan named Itis. The cadaver of Itis was destroyed and the essense of Itis, which was very little, stripped from its brain. Through the use of the cryogenic needle and microlaser beam, Eric and Jesse worked furiously to connect and renew the vital neuron junctions that finally attached the new brain to the waiting body. The pulsed-laser electrodes were put in the appropriate stereotaxic coordinates and the whole of the Dichtysomal being came swirling out of the computer in an orgasmic rush, filling the new brain with life. Dichtysomal lived. Only several recording electrodes remained as the skull was replaced and sutured with the laser beam.

They would wait a week. Jesse would go to the Martian surface. Eric would spend time with Maggie and his long-neglected Sean.

Eric was bursting with excitement *and* apprehension when he finally came to her. He kissed Maggie on the cheek, Sean squealing with enthusiasm between them.

Jesse procured a ride in a transport Hovercraft and, of course, went directly to Iridani. She had become an obsession with him. Jesse did not know, however, that he was being closely watched. . .watched by eyes blurred by tears and passion. . .

"I have been writing a poem for you, Jesse," said Iridani. She sat cross-legged on the cool ground. Jesse wore his respirator for the walk to her hut, but removed it when he sat down next to her. He could not very well kiss her while wearing it. He kissed her ear, but she was unfeeling as the pen flew over the page that flapped occasionally in the dipping winds.

"A poem for me? That's very nice of you."

"Not only is it for *you*, Jesse, but it is on *real* paper. I have only a limited supply you know. Soon I'll have to begin making my own and God only knows how I will do it. Hadem! Now you have me saying 'God'; you are perverting me!"

He looked over her shoulder and could make out the words:

> . . .the soft flowing Phobian light
> floods the mind and flays it
> upon the red alien sands. . .

Her tanned hand covered the rest, and Iridani said, "You'll not see it until it is complete! Now, let us retire to the business at hand. Inside with you!"

During the orangutan's recovery period, Eric went to see onathan Fischer, one of the few Oleandreans who still had a riving, passionate faith in the Mission. Fischer had once told ric that if the Mission failed, he might as well be dead. 'ischer had shifted the emphasis of his work. Instead of ataloging and filing all the works of the written word, he had aken the great computer of the Receptacle and, with the ddition of the cannibalized banks from the Ultimatron, had rogrammed the prime computer to glean all possible eferences on Jason Oleandre.

The electronic typesetter was coupled with the readout and 'ischer had already obtained a file of microdot information onsisting of a hundred million words. Examination of this ata gave no particular hint, so Fischer struck upon the idea of aving the computer scan all the acquired data bits and pick ut key words. Discarding all the obvious things like preposilons, articles and simple pronouns, the final readout ontained only several hundred key words. And many of these ould be eliminated as unimportant: Oleandre, Jason, Alliance, Cuang Fong, Anti-Intellectual League, Phobic Ministry of 'erosidation, etc.

There was one word, however, that struck him as being trange. It had really no particular significance, but was resent in an abnormally high statistical percentage.

The word was: Persimmion.

He checked for error. The word was not "persimmon" as in he fruit. This was a clue! What was Persimmion, with a capital 'P" and an "*i*on"?

Jonathan Fischer thought more of a hint could be gleaned y inspecting the word in context. Upon reprogramming, all he lines containing Persimmion were printed out for him. 'here were a hundred-and-three lines and phrases. He quickly nspected them and found that most were in the context of ither poetry, agriculture or botany. This was strange. He rowned, and thought that it was almost as if the word

Persimmion had been *deliberately* misspelled. Once again h
checked the computer and the reference for accuracy. One lin
of poetry especially struck him as being familiar:

> . . .*under the Persimmion white, with delicate*
> *petals and ethereal mist filled with*
> *fragrance of the night*. . .

Jonathan Fischer *knew* this line but couldn't exactly plac
it. He ran a quick retrieval and found it to be part of an epi
love poem by the brilliant Japanese poet, Yasuo Hieronamoto
This gentle and frail little man had won the Nobel Prize i
Literature at the end of the twentieth century, but had refuse
it on the grounds that for him, it was worthless in this life. Th
line of interest came from the 15th Canto of the epic entitled
Time's Reflecting Pool, a criticism of the powerfu
military-industrial complex in Japan, and a plea for the retur
of the sublime life of an earlier period. Fortunately
Hieronamoto died naturally of old age before he could b
martyred by the Alliance. It was ironic that Hieronamot
became one of the most popular poets among the masse
during the time of the Alliance. His posthumous works wer
not censored since the satire and criticism were much to
subtle for the ordinary man to grasp, and much too gentle fo
any intellectual revolutionary who *did* understand it.

But here it was, a line from Hieronamoto, quoted by Jaso
Oleandre at the beginning of an address to his colleagues. Bu
there was a rub: the line from Oleandre read: ". . .under th
Persimmion white," while the line taken directly from th
Collected Works of Y. Hieronamoto, read: ". . .under th
persimmion white."

It was obviously a deliberate misspelling. Jonathan Fische
checked several other lines and indeed, everytime the wor
persimmion was to appear, Persimmion was inserted. By Zeus
he thought, this is the key; but what does it mean? It canno
be mere coincidence.

At this time, Eric Senka appeared at Fischer's suite in the Receptacle. He found Jonathan brooding over coffee.

"Any clues, Jonathan?"

"Yes, I *have* the key," replied Fischer calmly.

"Y-you what! YOU HAVE IT? Fantastic! I mean what is it?"

"Persimmion."

"What?"

"That's it, the key word, but I don't know what it means."

Fischer told Eric of all the data thus far accumulated. They agreed that a formal search by the prime computer was in order. Every word stored in the prime memory banks and its auxiliaries would be scanned for persimmon and Persimmion and several other bastardizations. It would take several days to check the seven hundred trillion bits stored as memory sequences.

The data the computer produced was even more puzzling than ever. Except for the references by Jason Oleandre, there was no such word as Persimmion, not in what was supposedly the net record of humanity's achievements. Jonathan Fischer was not discouraged and he said he would try rearranging the word and see what that produced.

Eric watched the orangutan warily. The monkey yawned, tugged at a tuft of hair on its abdomen, and licked its genitals. Dichtysomal looked up at Eric. Eric could not tell if the ape recognized him. This would never do, he thought, the tests must start.

The orangutan was placed in the restraining chair and the electrodes protruding from the skull were attached to the telemetry devices. The lights were dimmed and the simple testing was begun.

Not only did Dichtysomal respond perfectly to the preconditioned signals, but the character series and simple words produced a flood of neural transmissions similar to the old recognition patterns. The new brain functioned perfectly — Dichtysomal was reborn. Jesse and Eric stood in the dark. The greenish light from the cathodic tube cast an eerie glow to the monkey's face, which seemed to hover as if suspended by levitation. Light patterns danced like phosphenes on the black walls. They stood speechless, in awe. It was as if they were the creators of life; but each knew in his soul that they merely were the preservers and transformers of essence.

After several moments of silence (or was it an hour?), Eric turned up the lighting. Dichtysomal looked around as if nothing special had happened. Eric would immediately file a report with the Scientific Committee. This would be followed by a formal journal article which would be in both Eric's and Jesse's names. For the first time, Jesse Horvitz felt he had truly helped make a scientific contribution, something that had the potential to help human kind.

There was not too much time for celebration since, as in all valid scientific endeavor, the experiments had to be repeated again and again. Eric would have to wait, too, for the proper time to try the brain transplant on a human. Although he was elated, he did not share Jesse's blind optimism. Eric flopped down in his chair to record the communication to the Scientific Committee, and Jesse carried Dichtysomal back to its cage.

It was a short, highly descriptive message consisting of only four inches of tape, which Eric placed in the communicator for transmission. He touched the lever marked T. About twenty seconds later, a yellow light appeared signifying that the computer at the Scientific Committee chambers had received his message and stored it. Jesse was cleaning up the laboratory as Eric stepped into his living suite.

Just as he entered, Maggie came in the other entrance followed by toddling Sean and silent Pseudomonius.

"Eric! Through so soon?"

"Yes darling, it is done," replied Eric. His face betrayed the success.

"Oh Eric, it worked?"

She threw her arms around his neck and just looked at him. Finally she said, "This certainly calls for a celebration."

Maggie turned to Pseudomonius and said, "Pseudomonius, for the evening meal, I want lots of lettuce and tomatoes which you can get at the hydroponics laboratory; and pick up several packets of flour and some bread at the distribution center."

"AS YOU SAY DOCTOR SENKA, THE LONGER-HAIRED," rasped the servomechanin who had no concept of sex.

"And get a beaker of lubricant for yourself, my metallic mongoloid," chuckled Eric.

"ILLOGICAL," was the reply.

After the filling evening meal, when Eric was mellow from the draughts of vaporous brandy, he suddenly became very serious. Maggie could always sense this, since, when he was in a contemplative mood, Eric would stare at a far wall and tap his right index finger incessantly.

"What *is* the matter? You should be very pleased today."

"I am, but. . ."

"But what? Tell me!"

"Well, it's just that — here I am at a breakthrough into a new realm. There're so many things to be learned."

"That has never stopped you in the past."

"Perhaps, it's not really that part of the unknown that bothers me. It's — well — the way science was used under the damned Alliance, and that Fields business."

"I don't think that will happen again."

"It must not! That is my worry. My work *could* be used to make possible the very thing we destroyed."

"I don't follow."

"Well, suppose, and only suppose, that I perfect the brain

transplant in humans."

"That would be wonderful."

"Yes, but only under humane circumstances. Suppose someone decides he wants to mold people into classes or something. . .permanently. . .he could use my technique to program minds, and what would be the result? Humanoids like that mechanical imbecile over there."

"I don't think it would be worth anyone's trouble, since robotoids do almost anything now anyway. And they are improving them all the time."

"Perhaps you're right, Maggie. . .perhaps."

Jonathan Fischer's only hope lay in the millions of dusty and worn volumes that were decaying in the deep vaults of the metallurgical complex. These books, considered unimportant or worthless to the Mission, were deposited there before Oleandre originally moved from its Martian orbit, in the days when it was known as Phobos. Even the degenerate Alliance literature took precedence over these books. The mass of the deposit consisted mostly of old romantic novels and grossly outdated scientific textbooks that were printed in the early twentieth century.

After telling Seth Hayakawa of his partial success, and seeing the Commander's excited look, Jonathan Fischer asked for assistance. A hundred volunteers went with him to the great cavern that sat under the nuclear reactor in the metallurgical complex. Among the volunteers were Seth Hayakawa and Ahab ben Jemma. Maggie and Eric would come in the evening hours after the work day.

The moist grotto, continually dripping with carbonic acid, was literally stacked to the ceiling with plastic containers through which could be seen the yellowing paper and cracked leather bindings of thousands of discarded books. Desks and mechanical readers were brought in and a clearing established so that an orderly reading would take place. Those volumes that had been scanned would be taken even deeper into the complex for final storage or destruction. For days, the bleary-eyed and mind-weary readers toiled.

Because of his tactile unit, Jonathan Fischer had an extrapowerful light source brought down for his own use. This was set up at a far corner of the cavern so as not to interfere with the others. The light from the praeseodimium-arc lamp, hidden behind a huge stack of old encyclopedias, cast eerie shadows across the cave. When Eric was down here in the evening, he felt romantically gothic. Jonathan Fischer ate and slept down there and, after two weeks, Dr. Fitzgerald suggested he get out for a while for health's sake. However, one soon got used to the musty atmosphere.

Proving there *was* justice in the universe, Fischer, himself, found the vital work. Very early one Martian morning, a huge blue volume with faded gold-leaf printing caught his eye. The rag pages had been well preserved and showed tinges of yellow only at the extreme margins. He opened the great cover with a crack. The title read, *EPHEMERIS-1908 UNITED STATES NAVAL OBSERVATORY.*

Turning first, as he always did, to the index, his finger ran down the page. At first, probably due to mental fatigue, he passed it. Then he could not believe his "eyes." Situated between the words *Percha* and *Pertan* was *Persimmion*. He checked again. Yes, the spelling was right. Fischer became so excited, he almost sounded a general alert in trying to call the Commander and Eric all at once. But *Persimmion* was there all right. In the days before the middle twentieth century, most asteroids had popular names, often named after the discoverer or his mistress or his homosexual lover. Thus, in the late nineteen sixties, all the minor planets' names were dropped in favor of numbers. The popular names fell into disuse and were ultimately dropped. It would not take much time to find Persimmion's number classification.

From the coordinates given in 1908, the prime computer, coupled with the astrophysical department's data bank, determined that the asteroid known as Persimmion was designated EPT401. There was not much more data available other than the facts that early estimates gave a diameter of about seven miles. The prime computer plotted an orbit for the planetoid. Elliptical in nature, the projected orbit was indeed a strange one. In the next week, Persimmion would pass through the area of spreading radioactive dust that had once been the Earth. If Persimmion indeed held the key to the last Jason Oleandre probe, they must get to it quickly. The absence of the Earth as a mass would have already shifted the asteroid's orbit.

News of Fischer's discovery spread rapidly throughout the colony. It was not, however, greeted with much enthusiasm. Perhaps after years of dejection, people dared not let their hopes be raised again. Ahab ben Jemma, to his disappointment, was put in charge of Oleandre Control, as the Commander himself would lead and direct this operation. The Sub-Orbital Craft was stripped to the barest essentials in about twenty hours, and fitted with a new-type, ion engine. Eric and Jesse would accordingly accompany Hayakawa, and all agreed that it was only appropriate that Jonathan Fischer come along too.

They were almost delirious. The possibility of finding the last probe, coupled with his recent scientific success, was almost too much for Eric to ask. Maggie rarely saw Eric in high spirits. She, too, was feeling the excitement of the times and it was strange that she hadn't the deep foreboding sense of disaster that occurred when Eric had left on previous occasions.

A horrendous blast from the hypergol booster lifted the Sub-Orbital Craft out of Martian orbit. Once the main booster was jettisoned, it sped through the void on ion power. It would take the good part of a day to reach the area of projected interception with the small barren rock called Persimmion. Seth Hayakawa flew the ship himself, while Jesse Horvitz was in continuous contact with Jemma at Oleandre Control and with the prime computer, which continually monitored their course. On a televisor panel that hung next to the environmental control console, the path of the Sub-Orbital Craft from Oleandre was charted in red, while the path of Persimmion was superimposed in green. Dotted, yellow projection lines shot out ahead, and where they crossed was a set of continually changing white digits that indicated the distance and time to the point of interception.

Exactly six hours before the rendezvous, Hayakawa initiated a reverse-thrusting sequence that slowed the Sub-Orbital Craft for its approach to Persimmion, which could not yet be seen on the forward viewing screen even under high magnification.

The yellow intercept lines were nearly one now; and out of the port Eric could see an oblong shaped object suspended in the distance against the background of Orion's stars. Rigel burned white, while Betelgeuse glowed like a red coal. The tri-starred belt of the mythical huntsman ran like a pointer down to Persimmion, which rotated slowly, one side brightly illuminated by the Sun's light. The rocky mass looked very small; but this was illusion since telemetry showed the planetoid to be five-and-a-half miles long, three miles across and two-and-a-half miles thick. It was computed that Persimmion had a rotational period of 3.73 hours. Spectroscopic data was still being computed.

Commander Hayakawa maneuvered to within a half mile of Persimmion. Its lifeless landscape filled both viewing ports. Lack of an atmosphere made its terminator very sharp and distinct. The Sub-Orbital Craft was moved around the asteroid so that its instruments could scan all areas of the surface. A small blip in the incoming telemetry was analyzed as an object of metallic alloy. It was indeed ironic that such a small bit of data could influence the Mission in such a crucial way. Sensors indicated that the object was about three by seven feet and cylindrical in shape. It could no longer be just mere coincidence...they had found the last Oleandre probe. A jubilant Seth Hayakawa sent a robotoid-shuttler down; and, with its magnetic grapplers, the little vehicle returned with the prize to the waiting Sub-Orbital Craft. The cylinder was soon safely stored in the underside compartment, and the group sped homeward at full ion exchange.

An excited Ahab ben Jemma, full of questions, met them at the Oleandre Hoverport, and two servomechanins gently transported the cylinder to the Commander's suite. Eric asked if Maggie could come up, and Seth nodded. Eric quickly called her.

After getting someone to watch little Sean, Maggie arrived five minutes later. The cylinder, its nosecone crumpled and torn, lay before them. Its metal sides bore many dents and minor pockmarks and, in places, the black metal had discolored. Its three crude retro engines were only capable of providing about four hundred newtons of thrust. A critically located dent had jammed the small hatch in the side of the probe; and it had to be cut open with a laser torch. The alloy finally yielded to the intense energy. In a small chamber was a gyroscopic guidance system, a Sun-Canopus sensor, and a single hermitic black box; and in the box was a celluloid envelope containing a lonely microdot card. Beside the envelope was a tape. The tape took any size spindle due to its variable adaptor, and it was quickly played. A metallic monotone spewed forth a series of numbers. The viewing of the microdots revealed that it was only a visual duplicate of the voice.

For the next six months, the best analytical minds Oleandre could muster spent endless, fatiguing hours trying to decipher what came to be known as the Persimmion Sequence.

CHAPTER 9

It never ceased to amaze Klingon Chachevsky that the tiny, wand-like rod he held functioned as a writing instrument. The slightest pressure from its tip on the dark, carbocel panel would leave a white imprint which could be easily erased by touching a static sensor on the floor. The classic blackboard slate and chalk had been eliminated, as had the telltale smudges on coat tails that betrayed one's professorship. Klingon Chachevsky stood in front of the immense board marked with equations and figures and, sometimes, mere doodling. Standing with legs far apart and hands on both hips, he pondered the mysterious symbols that danced before him. "Futz," he grumbled. "Mutterfutz!"

Chachevsky's grey hairline had long since receded. His complexion was mottled, the skin sagged on his face, and he walked with a slight limp, a mere symptom of age, for he was ninety-six. The former Chairman of the Department of Theoretical Neomathematics at the University of the Hague, Fellow of the Loftagrad Institute, and protege of Kurt

Nusbaum had been summoned to Commander Hayakawa's suite that morning. Seth had presented him with a series of numbers, both verbal and visual, and impressed upon him that the entire future of the Mission lay encoded within them. Chachevsky was told that there were two hundred thousand sets of digits, and that there was (must be!) a code hidden there. He was to find it.

After making a preliminary computer scan, he found the Persimmion Sequence to contain not two hundred thousand sets, but two hundred thousand and one. To precision neo-mathematics, a five parts per million error was extreme and unacceptable.

The first experiment would be to scan the entire sequence for simple roots and multiples. This elementary operation, for the prime computer, was completed in two hours with no meaningful results — just a random distribution of these parameters. Next, Klingon tried scanning for the presence of prime Maxwellian sets. . .no luck. Before going any further, he thought, it would be wise to see if the visual and audio sections *were* exactly alike. The audio scrambler stud was depressed and the metallic voice began: "FIVE TWO SEVEN (pause) SIX TWO (pause) FIVE ONE TWO. . ." At the same time, the matching part from the microdot card was put on the televisor screen:

```
******************************
527-62-512*******************
******************************
```

At this rate, Klingon Chachevsky spent ten days of nerve-rending fatigue listening to and watching the sequence. Only then, was he satisfied that the audio and visual series were indeed identical. He also detected no change in the inflection of the voice, so that no clues as to emphasis could be gleaned from it. It was a perfect, mechanical monotone.

While the visual numbers were on the screen, he had the computer "see" each one, there perhaps being subtle differences in the type or printing of the numbers. They, too, were uniform. This tedious work, all very time-consuming, yet vital, presented a real challenge to Chachevsky's analytical mind. An unknown mathematical treatise was contained within the Persimmion Sequence. The thought of this possibility served to heighten his determination and zeal.

It was not by mere chance, nor intuiton, nor luck, nor random experimentation that the solution presented itself. Chachevsky applied the lengthy, but very methodical, analytical theories of the Pre-Cambrian Masters of NeoLobeshevskian mathematics. After forty-five days of ceaseless labor, with hardly any time for rest, Klingon Chachevsky had solved the riddle of the Persimmion Sequence.

Several benches had risen from compartments in the floor and a large, carbocel panel had dropped from the ceiling of the Commander's suite. When all were present, Chachevsky began: "Good day, colleagues. I will explain how, after exhaustive analysis, I have arrived at what I consider to be the solution to the Persimmion Sequence. I tend to speak rapidly and in rather complicated terms, so feel free to stop me at any time.

"Now, in what was called Europe in the Earth-time known as the Middle Ages, there lived a great mathematician. . . Leonardo of Pisa. He is perhaps most well-known as Fibonacci. He, the son of Bonaccio, in his book *Liber abaci*, which dealt mainly with a defense of the superiority of Arabic mathematics over the Roman, presented a trivial problem out of which evolved the Fibonacci series of numbers and their counterpart, the Tribonacci series. Now, I will show you an example."

Klingon raised his wand, and with his shaking hand, printed

out the following set of numbers on the panel:

$$1, 1, 2, 3, 5, 8, 13, 21 . . .$$

"Without much inspection, any fool can see that the series begins with two positive integers, each number thereafter being the arithmetic sum of the preceding two. Look at the third number, it is two: the sum of one and one. The last is twenty-one, the sum of eight and thirteen. You see? I suppose there are an infinite number of these; but this is the simplest Fibonacci series and consists of the first eight Fibonacci numbers. You can also see that the numbers get very large very quickly; for example, only the thirty-eighth Fibonacci number — the thirty eighth, mind you — is thirty-nine million, eighty-eight thousand, one hundred and sixty-nine. Think of the size of the millionth Fibonacci number! That would probably define infinity since it would take eternity to write it out.

"There has been all sorts of mystical significance attributed to these numbers down through the ages. . .from interpretation of ancient Scythian lyrical syntax, architecture, agriculture, number of predicted pubic hairs, and even, in recent hydroponics, growth patterns were thought to follow the Fibonacci series.

"But this is of no matter here! As you know, the sequence from the last Jason Oleandre probe contains two hundred thousand and *one* sets. My beloved computer and I have, through a very practical approach, scanned the sets and come up with the following striking pieces of data. The two thousandth set in the Persimmion Sequence is *one*. The thirty-nine hundred and ninety-ninth set is also *one*. The fifty-nine hundred and ninety-seventh set is *two*. The seventy-nine hundred and ninety-fourth set is *three* and so on. In short, by decrements of one, starting at set two thousand, the sequence consists of precisely a hundred groups of numbers and, those numbers are the first one hundred Fibonacci numbers in order. Do I make myself clear?"

"Yes," said Seth Hayakawa. "Very, *very* excellent work Klingon. I believe I share the sentiments of our colleagues when I say that history as we conceive of it, will see you as a prime contributor."

There was a smattering of applause. Eric Senka rose to speak. "I am certainly impressed, and thankful for your presenting us with a version simplified for our inexpert ears. I have one question, however, and, I might add, a damned vital one. What the devil does it mean, this Fibonacci series?"

"I haven't the foggiest! That is up to you people. I only derived the sequence, not its significance."

"O retro," muttered Jesse, just above hearing threshold.

"What do you mean, 'o retro,' young man?" said Chachevsky in an irritated tone. "Look, we would all like a simple solution; but I am only a humble prophet of neo-mathematics, not a historical, cryptic, coptic wizard, not a master of thought-alchemy, not a. . ."

"I think what Jesse means," Eric broke in, "is that everyone thought the solution of the sequence was the answer. It's obviously not; it is just a clue. We must discuss all ways of delving into the sequence. . .we might as well start now. . .and I will begin. Jonathan, you have compiled a complete resume of all data on Jason Oleandre. Is it possible to put this into a complete psychological profile? If so, could not your memory banks actually *be* Jason Oleandre?

"Yes," said Fischer. "The resume is as complete as it ever will be and, yes, we could cook it up as a psychoprofile. But the final answer is, regretfully, no. The prime computer, advanced as it is, has not the capability to *be* Jason Oleandre, or anyone for that matter."

"*Wait*," shouted Hayakawa almost falling out of his contour chair in excitement. "Eric! Don't you see it? Your work! I just read your paper. It could work! By Leonardo's ass, this is it!"

The thought hit Eric Senka with the full impact of a rolling thunderball. Of course, he thought, his head swirling with ideas, it *can* be done.

What was hoped to be the last stage in the deciphering of the Persimmion Sequence was to be a joint effort. Jonathan Fischer would assemble all the known data on Jason Oleandre into a complete psychoprofile. The key to the whole profile was Fitzgerald's invaluable tape of Oleandre's medical records, the most important part being Jason Oleandre's NPT.

The Neuro Potentiality Tracing was the modern equivalent of the outdated and unreliable electroencephalogram (EEG). The NPT recorded electrical impulses from the brain cells on two thousand frequencies of a varied-channel-analyser. Oleandre's NPT contained transmissions of the most intricate workings of his mind. Coupled with Eric's brain transplantation technique, they hoped to "recreate" Jason Oleandre.

For Project Romulus, as it was now known, success required both a donor and recipient. These were not donor and recipient in the normal ethiomedical terminology. The donor would contribute his blanked brain and, of course, his essence would cease. The recipient would also lose his brain and identity. It would have been so much simpler had the recipient a normal brain. Unfortunately, the only available body had a diseased brain, hence the necessity of a total neural transplant.

Dr. Fitzgerald presented two cases that were the only people available for Project Romulus. The person who could donate a brain was a woman, Herrietta Spatlase, wife of Kierkegaard Spatlase who was attached to the Historiography Division. She had been struck by a landing Hovercraft on the Martian surface, her chest horribly crushed, beyond repair. Kept 'alive' only by artificial means, her brain functioned perfectly.

The chosen recipient was a madman named Clarence Clone. A technician from the Hydroponics Section, he had to be kept restrained in a well-lighted room. Nothing could be done for him. The damage prior orthomolecular-psychiatric treatment had done to his mind could not be reversed. Insulator-sensors showed a gradual but steady decrease in brain myelin content which undoubtedly accounted for Clone's psychic aberrations. Although his mind-brain dichotomy was badly diseased, the body functioned well, although under considerable stress. Clarence Clone was expected to live only a few more days.

Fitzgerald and Seth Hayakawa went to see Kierkegaard Spatlase and he agreed that when the time came, they had his permission to stop all resuscitative efforts and take his wife's brain. It would be a fitting tribute, he thought.

Eric would be ready in two days. The intervening time was spent in self-torture, vacillating between confidence and fits of self-doubt.

In a large, white, rectangular room, Clarence Clone lay alone. He lay dying. On the long table, his naked body was bound so tightly by an ivory, sterile sheet that even if he had the strength he could not have moved. Catheters ran into his body orifices carrying nutrients and removing wastes. The digital clock clicked away the silent minutes of his last hours. . .the remnants of a man lying senseless. The tatters of his mind that remained functioning through the paralyzing hypnosis of the cloudy, neutralizing drugs, fought its eternal battle with the enemies of light:

". . .O Thoth," it screamed, "return the long lost Horus-eye to its rightful orb and restore the light. Defend me, O Thoth as the vile Horemheb would snuff out the symbol of Helios. Restore the royal greenness to the skin of me, thy servant, and deposit my remains in the underworld! Do not allow my tomb

to be defiled! Yea, even as Osiris raiseth Thoth from the dead,
so then shall ye raise Clone. . ."

This uproar of mad emotion caused an equivalent concern
in the computer that monitored his metabolism. It had the
bile-colored body injected with a cathartic and psychic-
neutralizer. The reticular calmer caused his eyelids to shut for
an instant, and the total darkness spun webs of horror.
Uncontrollable shaking fear penetrated the outer defenses,
leapt over great neural escarpments and scaled the
prophylactic parapets of his twisted, yet strangely wise mind,
causing Clone to cry out, "O Anubis, present thy canine
appearance. The darkness, O the *darkness*. . .Aten! Aten, thou
were correct. The darkness cometh to parch the land. Out, ye,
the false Gods of the Lower Nile. . .the Nubian Pretenders.
Septet! O Septet, let me see thy image riseth on the far
horizon. . .inundate me with new vigor and life. Then, only
then, can thy work, O Aten, begin. Only then, can thy warm
and essence-giving disc distribute the benevolent rays upon me.
Give me peace, O Aten! Give me. . ."

The computer responded to his plea by giving more
anesthesia, and this positive feedback caused Clone to be
thrown deeper into the grisly, dark, spiral pit of his fears. Just
before he died, Clone's eyes opened and he stared into the
blinding sterilizer lamp overhead. The God of Lights smiled
down on him and he screamed something that was lost in the
wailing reverberations of the alarm system. Then he was silent.
The chest still moved, but the wide eyes were dull and the
corneas opaque.

Subsequent investigation of his NPT showed the cause of
death to be an overlap of the alpha and epsilon waves in such a
way as to overload the neural circuits. The body was
maintained, but the pathetic thing, Clarence Clone, was gone.
Perhaps Eric's technique could have saved Clone; they would

never know. As it stood, Clone's contribution to Oleandrean historiography would be posthumous. There was no one to mourn his loss, no one to shudder in uncontrollable grief, no one to stand at a symbolic bier.

But on a far distant planet in the Fornax galaxy, the anubian hounds would howl a eulogy that night as the purple winds shrieked over the Mountains of Simbel. . .Aten's prophet is dead!

The death of Clone set into motion the strangest sequence of events ever to occur in that small corner of the Milky Way galaxy. Only in the imaginations of the ancient science fiction writers could such an act occur. Yet, it was true: the re-creation of Jason Oleandre had begun.

Eric Senka's facilities would be very crowded. Two 'living' cadavers lay separated by a transparent partition. Each was completely covered with opaque sheeting. Tubes and wires ran in under the covers. Great sterilizing units were brought in and their bacteriocidal rays were emitted in every direction, requiring everyone present to wear either protective goggles or the standard surgical helmet. Fitzgerald erected metabolic sensors over both bodies. The NPT from the Clone cadaver was flat, but all body functions operated normally. The Spatlase metabolic parameters were null; but the brain, now artifically perfused, had normal NPT readings. Already the electrical storage data was being removed from the Spatlase brain.

While Eric and Jesse worked feverishly to produce a blanked brain, Fitzgerald and his two assistants, Connely and Twi, carefully removed Clone's brain. Being sure to leave nerve stumps intact, the Clone brain was soon lifted out of the skull, leaving a gaping, strangely dry cavity. Taking the brain over to the sink, Fitzgerald made several slices through it with a sharp, crystal blade. Clone had indeed been diseased: many small, pus-filled abscesses and infractions were found. The assistants filled the empty skull with salinated pads, inserted a sterile-emitter, and covered the entire surgical field with sterile cloths.

Convinced that all electrical activity had been removed, Eric and Jesse stepped back to allow Fitzgerald to remove the Spatlase brain. Seth Hayakawa stood at the edge of the laboratory wearing a surgical helmet and watching with great interest. Jonathan Fischer sat behind a transparent barrier at the computer console checking and rechecking the psycho-profile of Jason Oleandre.

Eric had forbidden Maggie's presence and she sat sulking in the very next room.

The brain, glistening wet and hanging with perfusion tubes was finally lifted free. The assistants rolled the cadaver out and down the corridor to the freezing chamber. Fitzgerald held the living, cellularly kinetic mass over its new abode. Eric and Jesse stood next to him, each with a small laser and cryogenic needle.

"Do we imitate the Gods today?" asked Jesse, somewhat melodramatically.

Eric said nothing, his eyes darting behind the visor of his helmet.

"No, no more so than did the first cardiac transplanters back in the twentieth century," said Fitzgerald.

"Let us begin then," said Eric. His voice seemed irritated and he perspired profusely.

After twenty hours of interrupted work, the skullcap was finally replaced and the hairless scalp sutured together.

The computer reproduced Jason Oleandre's NPT exactly. "*Encephalize,*" shouted Eric, and the pulsations were fed into the blanked brain, followed by the entire psychoprofile. Soon it was done, and all the electrodes removed. Except for the metabolic monitor, the brain seethed and lived on its own, or rather, the Clone body containing the essence of Jason Oleandre lived.

When it was finished and all were dismissed, Eric fell into exhausted sleep at Maggie's side. The fragmented words and melody of an old Earth ballad seemed to linger in his mind:

> . . .in my sleepiness, there ain't
> no place I'm going' to. . .my senses
> have been stripped and my hands can't
> feel the grip. . .toes. . .toes too
> numb to step. . .

The preliminaries were complete. Now, the crucial testing would begin.

Clone-Oleandre lay quietly sedated under the thin covering as intravenous catheters carried nutrients to its body. Eric did not believe the creature would actually *be* Jason Oleandre. There was not enough data in the psychoprofile for that. He hoped, however, that just enough of Oleandre's 'self' would be present so that some clue as to the meaning of the Persimmion Sequence could be obtained. They were ready; and no amount of stalling could put off the inevitable. Twi neutralized the sedative.

Clone-Oleandre, still bound tightly to the table, opened its eyes for an instant and then the lids fluttered shut again. NPT registered the proper reaction in the gamma-wave region. It was seeing. Eric bent down, close to its right ear.

"Can you hear me? Can you understand?"

NPT coupled, biphasic audio-temporal sensors indicated that the facility for hearing was present. Voice-pattern recordings of both Clone and Oleandre were simultaneously displayed on a split-screen televisor screen.

"Can you speak?"

"uuuuhh. . .aah. . .y-y-yes. . .yes," said the voice softly, barely audible.

"Jee-suz," muttered Jesse behind his mask.

The voice pattern, like a fingerprint, indicated that the voice was that of Clone, not of Oleandre; but it was not *whose* voice it was that mattered.

Its right fingers, capped by yellowish waxy, artificial-looking nails, clenched into a fist, then relaxed. His heart beating wildly against his chest wall, Eric asked if all was in readiness. It was. He asked the first in a series of prepared questions.

"OLEANDRE. . .you are familiar with that word?"

"Yes," replied the faint monotone.

"Oleandre and you are one. Oleandre and you, you and Oleandre. You *are* Oleandre! Do you understand?"

"Yes."

"You will also be familiar with the word Persimmion. . .P-E-R-S-I-M-M-I-O-N."

"Yes."

The NPT readout went into wild recognition patterns. Jonathan Fischer nodded to Eric in a signal to continue, and touched a volume-recording control. Eric began again.

"There are a series of numbers, a sequence related to the word Persimmion."

"Yes. . .I know them. . .one. . .one. . .two. . .three. . . five. . .eight. . ."

"THAT IS FINE. . .you need not repeat them," said Eric.

"Good God, it. . .that thing *knows* all of the sequence," said Hayakawa in an amazed voice.

"Is there significance to this series?"

"Yes."

"Excellent, I will give you each number," said Eric, looking up to see that recording equipment was in proper condition.

"Then," said Eric, "we shall begin. . .ONE."

"Null," replied the voice of Clone-Oleandre.

"Null? Jesus, what is this?" asked Jesse.

"For Christ's sake, shut up man," hissed Eric. He shot a steely-eyed look at Jesse.

"ONE," said Eric again.

Again the weak monotone replied, "Null."

"ONE. . .ONE!"

"Null. . .three pi cube."

"TWO."

"Two-point-one-four-one-six. . .twelfth root. . .dee ex. . .dee y. . .en log. . .cee square. . .slash four-oh. . .point-one-four."

"THREE."

"Integral pi. . .dee ex. . .dee tee. . .powers matrix coordinates. . .five. . .reciprocal four-oh. . .point-one-four."

"Jee-suz," said Jesse.

For hours the numbers of the Fibonacci series were given and there spewed forth in answer a myriad of complex theorems and equations in matrix theory and topology, the sum total of which represented the most valued piece of data the Oleandre Mission could own. . .the Powers Equation.

When Seth Hayakawa, who had taken over for the fatigued Eric, repeated the one hundredth Fibonacci number, Clone-Oleandre said, "Null."

That was the end of it. All were mentally exhausted, all but the creature on the table whose voice never wavered, whose face remained expressionless the entire time and whose ungodly eyes never once blinked.

Christ, thought Eric, those eyes. One cannot help but think that eyes so black must surely serve a madman. Nothing can have eyes so dark, and deep, and clear, and not be just a little insane.

When they were sure it was done, Clone-Oleandre was again heavily sedated. As the pinkish yellow eyelids, sticky with mucus at the corners, wavered for an instant, then snapped shut, a curious and almost frightening phenomenon occurred.

The face that had not changed expression for many hours suddenly acquired a smile...a slight upturning of the thick purplish lips as if it had done a required task and was now, finally, at peace with itself. This was all very unnerving for those present, everyone but Eric — and Eric knew!

Commander Hayakawa's edict to all Oleandreans praised the team effort and the entire population was thrown into a tumultuous uproar of hope and ecstasy.

But Eric knew!

While the Powers Equation was being dissected and reintegrated by theoretical physicists and engineers alike, Eric brooded.

The Clone-Oleandre had lived many weeks now. Late in the evening of OD-5:240, while Eric played with Sean who ran and laughed, he saw the clear-eyed inquisitiveness of youth in his son's eyes. Only then did he know what must be done.

When he told Jesse the next day, the young man cried out, "NO, no...for God's sake, you can't...all our work...for nothing? You just can't!"

"Jesse it must be done. What we did trespassed into another realm. We should not have delved into that area."

"But it was for science...for knowledge."

"Yes, but was it a necessity? Could we have done it another way?"

"No!"

"Perhaps not; but I won't have my techniques, our techniques, perverted. Christ, Jesse, I feel like a Goddamned, surrealistic Frankenstein."

"But there was no other way...the Mission had to be preserved."

"At what cost?"

"Oh, hell, it's not as if we actually *created* or rather, re-created Jason Oleandre. We just used a human representation. That thing in there is at best, a mushy servomechanin. I'll bet it can't even walk or move much."

"It can walk my boy, it can. And, what's more, it can think — and very well, too."

"What?"

"Yes, I've tested it and the mind is clearer with each passing hour. So you can see what I must do. Are you with me? You have been in the past."

"Yes sir. . .I suppose. . .Of course!"

Jesse obtained a recording of some obscure death via *tremens metabolis*. This metabolic record was placed into the continuous metabolic monitor so that it would seem as though the Clone-Oleandre body had failed naturally and irreversibly. Eric and Jesse took an oath never to reveal what they did that night.

Eric injected the minute amount, two nanograms, of the tetra-ammonium-salt of trifluropurine into the I.V. catheter. Clone-Oleandre went rigid for a second, then relaxed. As it went into the irreversible cardiac arrest, the metabolic monitor wailed; but to no avail. As the artificial life spark oozed from the Clone-Oleandre, Eric and Jesse bent over it in almost worshipful awe. Its eyes were glassy and wide with fear, but from its mouth were uttered words that bristled the hairs on the back of their necks. They would not likely forget them for the rest of eternity:

"Thank you. . ."

When it was over, and death had entered and left, Eric put his hand on Jesse's shoulder and squeezed it as a father does a son's. Jesse understood. With the metabolic monitor's alarm still howling in the background, Eric called the Commander and with every bit of false emotion he could muster, told him that Clone-Oleandre was dead. . .dead forever.

At the autopsy, the brain was found to be in perfect condition, and Eric was elated with this. The transplantation had been a success, so something very positive had come out of the whole ghoulish business. He dared not even tell Maggie of his deed; but while Sean and Maggie were on their way to an outing on the Martian surface, Eric recorded into his journal:

". . .and it must be recorded for other generations that we acted in a way most unnatural. We tampered with the life process. The brain transplantation technique was meant to give longer life to the living, not to restore life to the long dead. That is not the function of science. Science, my science, is meant to benefit and further the concept of the word human. . .human in all its connotations. The practice and aim and actuality of scientific research should be goal oriented, and the best possible results are usually obtained when that goal is both possible and hopefully probable. It is not probable that full and useful and normal life can be returned to the dead. It *IS* possible to extend the useful life of the living. I must interject here that this concept of science can be extended into the social and political disciplines. The Alliance did not see this application. . .had they, we might not have had to be in this situation today. . ."

The Martian day had dawned crisp, cold and clear. As Eric shuffled through the sand in the low gravity, hands in pockets, breathing the purified air of his respirator, he was greeted by a squeal of laughter as Sean rushed up and into his arms.

CHAPTER 10

The Powers Equation was a set of finite mathematical terms which set forth the conditions of traveling faster than the speed of light. They also gave complex applications, equations which were the basis of constructing a propulsion system capable of thrusting Oleandre through the light barrier and into the realm of postphobic travel. It was further theorized, yet not by any means proven in the Powers Equation, that the entire concept of Heintz-Lederberg space was in error.

The universe, according to Powers, was not one finite Mobius strip suspended in something approaching an ethereal void, through which one could travel continuously as long as one stayed within the Mobian reference frame. No, the Powers sets intimated that the structural basis of the universe was pleated in nature, as if one took a ream of celucel sheets and placed them end-to-end, then connected each end with a hinge, and folded them up again in a stack. If one started to travel, one would go up one sheet then back on the next, up on the next and so on.

Light traveled on the pleat and was the limiting factor. But suppose one knew where to cross over pleats? Then, one could, in effect, travel faster than light. In this model of the universe, things such as stars and galaxies were actually much closer if one crossed the pleat or space warp. This gave the universe finite size. But there was one important corollary:

The pleating was continually expanding. Light speed along the pleats was still constant; but as the pleats unfolded, the time-sequential to cross over a given set of pleats, out of the light-reference frame, increased. Eventually the pleating would be fully expanded and the universe would reach a maximum volume. Then, energy-matter coupling would occur, and pleating would begin inward again, and so on, *ad infinitum.*

After building the postphobic propulsion packet, the crux of the problem lay in finding just the right spot to jump off one pleat and onto an adjoining one. The Powers Equation gave derivations to be used in calculating where great magnetic-moment "holes" were to be found in the pleats. Once the location of a galactic pore was established, the transpleating phenomenon could be carried out. The uniqueness of this system was that the slowing of the aging process as one increased speed became irrelevant. Of course, this fact lay not in the time-universe model proposed by Powers; but in the fact that there was no Earth left for comparison in aging. All that was left of the human race would be traveling together; thus, sequential again would be no problem.

The Powers Equation, when it was applied to a functioning galactic engineering system, would give Oleandre the power dreamed of by a generation of science fiction writers and dreamers. . .intergalactic travel at hyperlight speeds. But this boon was also a Pandora's box of responsibility and dangers. Humans had never traveled out of the Sun's system, much less out of the Milky Way galaxy. They had never come into contact with real aliens. Could the human adjust to being the ultimate protean man? Could he deal with other life forms? Could the human evolve fast enough to wipe out his own subconscious evil and racial hatred? These were all situations and conditions to reckon with. They were the unknowns.

Some long-lost historiographer, whose parched white bones were exhumed by nuclear cataclysm and are now part of the swirling, hot, dusty orgasm that was Earth, once said that the history of any world is recorded in the lives of its great men. Not so! The history of man was indelibly etched in toil and sweat and pain and suffering, this done by the men and women whose labor got *them* nothing except an early, worthless grave; but their work lifted civilization just an iota higher. And here, detached from the world they once loved, the Oleandreans would strive for the ultimate historical phenomenon. . .the beginning of the highest human civilization.

The voyage of Oleandre would be the most dangerous and, at the same time, the most exciting mission in the history of humans. Much as the early Earth explorers struck out into unknown, uncharted waters, the Oleandre would be driven by the galactic winds.

No one knew why the earlier explorers were driven to cross the boiling seas at the edge of their world, to dare the Gods, to present themselves at the courts of the Khans. Why? To find pools and fountains of eternal youth? For gold and jewels and fragrant spices? Perhaps, since the sea was there, it had to be crossed, just as mountains had to be climbed, or Lunare landed upon? To exert the ultimate human conviction, that of himself over his environment? No one knew.

They would go in search of a new home, not necessarily a new Earth. They would try to seek out any intelligence in the universe, and the probability certainly existed that there is life elsewhere. The Oleandreans would go to teach those life forms more primitive than themselves, and learn from those more intelligent. They hoped to become wise and extend the essence of humanness to the limits of this creativity and goodness, and to reduce and eventually eliminate all its capability for evil. It would be a monumental undertaking; but the people of Oleandre had destroyed the seat of their intellectual and evolutionary origins and had emerged, after several taxing experiences, as hardened and ardent explorers. With ingenuity, the Powers Equation, and some luck, they would be off to fulfill man's longest dream. . .the exploration of the universe.

Commander Seth Hayakawa sat next to the viewing port of Oleandre's observation bubble. In his left hand was a null-G beaker of black coffee, its vapor vent sometimes fogging the glass. The red Martian disc filled the lower left quadrant of the port. The polar caps had shrunken now and he noticed a white and yellow dust storm slowly advancing across the area of the Sinus Sabaeus near the equator. Being several thousand miles long, the huge dust cloud vaguely formed a giant letter "J." The subconscious impact set his mind to wandering. The Commander sipped on the hot coffee and virtually shuddered at the thought of his responsibility in leading the Mission. Still, it was freedom. . .complete intellectual freedom, within the boundaries of a loose ethical framework. For the time being, common sense and pragmatic philosophy would suffice. Looking out the port and space-dreaming, he saw the companion satellite Deimos just going behind the mother planet. Soon the sunlight would come streaming in. He touched the green panel just under the oval window. A light appeared behind the panel and a solar filter slid down over the port. The Sun's glare was practically nil. He took another long draught of the black brew.

Something had bothered Seth Hayakawa for a long time. . . something about Jason Oleandre. The Commander had always had a nagging question in the back of his mind, something he could not quite put his finger on, an uncomfortable feeling. The recent events had brought the matter to a head. What *was* the connection between the Jason Oleandre he knew, and the now dead creature Clone-Oleandre? Was there even a connection, or was it merely a figment of his imagination? Though he had not been a close intimate of Jason Oleandre, he knew him well enough to have seen certain quirks in the man's personality.

Oleandre worked and thought with almost emotionless, mechanical agility. Seth Hayakawa had been chosen second in command and, when Oleandre was killed, he was the logical choice for the Commandership. Seth always thought him a near genius anyway, and had, therefore, excused some of Oleandre's strange behavior as mere eccentricity. Now, somehow he wasn't so sure. Then too, he always suspected Oleandre of being a Perceptor, a man able to carry out telepathic communication, although it was never recorded that Jason Oleandre underwent a Perceptorship, which refined telepathy and exceeded the witchcraft and black magic science of ESP.

There was almost a mythical aura about the name and the man Jason Oleandre. Soon, he thought, people might be saying, "by Jason," instead of "by God," or "Jasdamn you!"

He couldn't quite decide exactly what bothered him. There was some connection. Something. It was almost as if the voice of the Jason Oleandre he remembered and that of the creature which Eric Senka had created were one in the same. Impossible, this is preposterous, he thought. But is it? His skin crawled at the thought.

Jim Webb of Communications Engineering, in conjunction with C. S. Sepanov of the Transition Metal Crystallography Laboratory, had invented a new form of communications device. Having a thousand times the range, with improved visual and audio clarity over the old televisor system, the device used radiation emanating from a crystal of tetraflurogadolium dichromate, which had been recently synthesized in Sepanov's laboratory. The new system was simply called Dichroic. The Dichroic used the old televisor software so that no dismantling was anticipated. When in operation on Oleandre or between Oleandre and the Martian complexes, no detectable improvement was seen. But when used in an accelerating probe, for example, none of the usual lag in audio-visual communication was noted. The speed was automatically compensated for by varying oscillations in the gadolium-complex crystal. Thus, the Dichroic would, at least in theory, function across the pleated universe *and* through the transpleating maneuver.

She sat naked on the edge of the bed, a sheet pulled sloppily around her waist. Her dark skin was glistening in the soft artificial light as though it were covered with a thin film of oil. Jesse Horvitz sat across from her, thumbing aimlessly through the stack of old papers that threw up a musty odor to his nostrils. After a long silence, he ran his fingers back over his damp head, and making sure his eyes did not meet hers, said, "Jesus Christ, darling. . .you can't, I mean, what good would it do? Everyone's going."

"My mind is made up," said Iridani. "I have decided. It is something I *must* do."

"You'll be so alone. O Christ, *I'll* be so alone. Oleandre leaves in two days."

"It does not matter. I have cleared it with Hayakawa."

"WHAT? You mean he's allowing this?"

"Yes, I told him the circumstances. He understands. He tried at first to talk me out of it, but now he understands."

Jesse looked off into nothingness and his voice became small, only a whimper, "You can't."

After another gaping silence, with the Martian winds shrieking outside, he said, "You could at least give me reasons. . .an explanation. You owe me that much. After all we've meant to each other."

"Let us get one thing straight between us," she said, looking directly at him, her black eyes tearing at his very soul, "*I* have meant much to *you*, you have meant nothing to me. . .nothing permanent that is. Oh yes — do not misunderstand — I am very fond of you, Jesse. It may even approach your concept of love. . .that which means nothing to me."

"B-but why must you stay?"

"I do not fit, I cannot be part of a band of celestial wanderers, nomads of intergalactic space. I could not adapt to that way of travel. Besides, I do not believe your Powers Equation or formulas or whatever they are, will work. Truly, I think you have doomed yourselves, but this is your concern. I must have ground underfoot, even if it must be this wretched red soil."

"You'll be killed anyway." His voice was steady and solemn, "When they start up the great engines, the gamma radiation emitted will be so intense as to kill off an entire planet at this range. The Oleandre population is protected by the reflector shield of ultradense Tholium-hydride, but you. . .you'll die.

"Oh, no, Jesse, you cannot con me with that! Hayakawa told me all about *that* danger and, if I stay deep in the metallurgical complex, in the cavern under the nuclear reactors, I shall be safe. When you are very far away, then I will emerge."

"How will you live?"

"The Commander has left a food synthesis unit along with a complete environmental control system. I could live here or down in the complexes for many lifetimes. I. . ."

"O Christ," he broke in, "I didn't mean *that*. I meant how will *you* live, survive. You will surely go mad from the loneliness and desolation of this place."

"Perhaps I will, but it is not certain. Jesse. . .Jesse. . .Jesse, how can I make you understand that I would certainly go mad if I go with you. Perhaps you can adjust to living in a metallic sphere for most likely, all your lives. I could not even withstand those few years we were out. I was losing control; and if," her voice was softer now and she reached over and lightly touched the top of his hand, ". . .if I had not found you, I would have surely perished. Go into the unknown. Go and find the new Earth. And you *will* find it, because wherever you go, you take the evil that is human with you. You cannot escape yourselves. You are all alienated. Your actions are not your own. You are the victims of illusion; and while under the illusion of doing what *you* want, you are driven and twisted by forces that are separated from your selves, working behind the masks of your existence.

"You are strangers unto yourselves, just as your fellow men are strangers to you, Jesse. You experience yourselves not as what you really are, but as foggy images, distorted by the unconscious powers which operate in them. You have lost yourselves as center of your experience; you have lost the sense of self. I do not have to run, because I know what I am. I know what I was meant to do. I must stay. I must write my poetry *here*. I would ask you one favor, my friend."

"Anything," he replied, suppressing the violent heaving within his body that threatened to burst forth and cover her with pity and despair.

"I will leave all my works sealed in a cylinder and placed under this very shack. Would you note the location somewhere in the Oleandre Prime Computer?"

"Of course," he said, looking around at the dingy, stained metal walls of the hut, "you know I would do anything."

"Perhaps, if the Mission is successful, you or someone might return here someday. . .someday, someone may want to know what I wrote here. . .someday, long after I am gone."

He stood and, taking her hands, pulled her up to him. The sheet dropped away as she came into his encircling arms. He could feel her breasts rising and falling in irregular tempo against his chest, and looking down into those dark, crystalline eyes for the last time they told him she was sorry. . .sorry to be hurting him so.

"Go," she said softly, "before it is too late. You are the last one."

Iridani pressed a folded piece of yellowing manuscript into his unfeeling hand.

His trembling lips touched the moist black hair at the base of her neck where it fell away in unkempt whorls, and the tears welled in his eyes.

Then he was gone.

She stood in the doorway as he ran stumbling down the windswept path, jerking the respirator over his face. He did not look back. A few minutes later, she heard a roar over the next hillock and the small Hovercraft blasted into the distance, its afterburners spitting angry, red despair at the Martian sphere.

He was gone and she was alone, as alone as any human could be and still be called human. And as she watched the vermillion glare of the Hovercraft's engines grown dimmer in the purple Martian twilight, she was aware of a sharp pain in her lower abdomen that was gone as quickly as it came upon her. Only months later would Iridani discover the twin embryos now growing in the liquid warmth deep within her.

The work involved in preparing Oleandre for this, the final flight, was staggering. Yet, it proceeded very smoothly. Webb already had the Dichroic-master-oscillator installed, with units working in every cubicle on Oleandre. Engineering was proceeding in the development of the transphobic propulsion system. The metallurgical complex had been stripped of all necessary equipment. The food synthesizers were brought up into Martian orbit, assembled there, and then moved into Oleandre. The date set for propulsion out of the Martian influence was seven hundred hours, OD-6:1. There was no doubt of the justification in starting the Mission now. A vote had polled all Oleandreans after a neutral briefing by Seth

Hayakawa and Senka. With but one abstention, all voted to go. The absentee would remain, to everyone's surprise, then horror, on Mars.

The rocky vault that surrounded Oleandre was to be jettisoned. Great cuts were made with laser torches and controlled explosions ripped off huge chunks of matter which were taken and either put into lower orbits or propelled down into the thin Martian atmosphere to burn up or further scar the land. Soon a new star appeared in the heavens as Oleandre floated like a shining silver sphere in the void. Only the protrusions of the Hoverport, the engines and the observatory marred its perfect symmetry.

Max Lacquerer and his crew in Propulsion Engineering had put the matter-antimatter interconverters through a series of extensive tests. They were ready. Oleandre would move out of orbit and proceed on a course that was a straight line from the Sun toward Arcturus. About three fourths of a light year out on this course, the Powers Equation demonstrated the presence of a galactic pore that would allow them to initiate the transpleating maneuver. It would take them about eight years to reach the pore area using the antimatter engines. By this time, the engineers and scientists aboard Oleandre would have perfected the transphobic propulsion system. Once through the pore and onto the next pleat, the Powers Equation predicted they would be only two months away from a star known to have a planetary system. . .61 Cygni.

Most Oleandreans were already moving into their quarters. Much of the scientific work was not even disturbed since only the fabricating and production groups had originally moved to the metallurgical complex on the surface. Five hours before orbital detachment, Seth Hayakawa ordered a general alert and reports from all levels and sectors within levels. Heads of all groups and departments reported: AFFIRM-GO.

A flurry of Hovercraft darted in and around Oleandre, making last-minute inspections. Then all was made secure on its surface and the glimmering metal reflected only the far distant Sun that it would soon see fade. Oleandre would not feel a warming radiation on its hull for many years and its only life-force would be the steady pulse of its antimatter engines and the collective heartbeat of its inhabitants.

At detachment (D) minus thirty minutes and counting, the Commander entered the bridge of Oleandre Control. Crew members scurried about below him, carrying out their assigned duties. Eric Senka and Maggie came in behind him and he bade them come up to the bridge. On the floor of Oleandre Control, Ahab ben Jemma sat at a console that was high on a milky white pillar in the center of the room. Around him, a great curve of blinking white, red, blue and green and yellow lights flickered. Gradually, all the lights were changing to green as crews deep in the ship made their own last-minute countdowns. When the last of forty-eight thousand indicators changed from yellow to green, ben Jemma swung around in his cradle chair and, with the Dichroic wand in his hand, looked up at Seth Hayakawa in the bridge. Ben Jemma raised the wand to his thick, purplish lips and announced throughout Oleandre, "DEE MINUS SIX ZERO SECONDS... COUNTING."

Simultaneously, all indicators flicked red, then blue, then yellow. Then all but one changed to green as a built-in Prime Computer double-checked all systems. Only the red indicator that sat next to Seth Hayakawa's left hand remained lighted. He watched the digital counter dissipate the numerals and his fingers raised the celucel cap that protected the engine power-stud. Ben Jemma's deep voice erupted over the Dichroic again: "DEE MINUS TWO ZERO SECONDS...COUNTING...ALL PERSONNEL, CRADLE POSITIONS."

"DEE MINUS TEN ZERO."

"NINER. . .EIGHT. . .SEVEN. . .SIX. . ."

The Commander's finger tightened on the stud ring, perspiration spotted his wrinkled forehead.

"THREE. . .IGNITION. . .ONE. . .POWER."

The stud was depressed and a cluster of fifty boosters slowly pushed Oleandre out of Martian orbit.

"ORBITAL DETACHMENT. . .SEVEN HUNDRED HOURS. . .FOURTEEN SECONDS. . .OH DEE SIX DASH ZERO ZERO ONE."

The boosters belched forth tremendous energy as chemical bonds sheared and reformed with amazing rapidity. The roar was not heard within Oleandre, but its power was felt. The boosters cut out.

"BOOSTER STAGING. . .DEE PLUS ONE MINUTE FORTY SECONDS. . .FLUX CONVERSION POWER. . .ALL PERSONNEL, POST-STAGING PROCEDURE."

Once again, all systems reported in, and only a few minor mishaps had occurred during the critical period of orbital detachment. Oleandre abruptly moved up and out of the Martian plane of orbit. Ahab ben Jemma looked up from his duties for an instant. He saw Seth's face in the clear ozmyglass partition that separated the bridge from Oleandre Control. Seth was smiling. Ahab gave him a wink, a thumbs-up, and a big, toothy grin. In front of ben Jemma, the great curved panel pulsated with incoming information. The huge Dichroic screen that was split into two sections, each about twelve by twenty feet, showed fore and aft telescans. Behind them was the Sun's dulled sphere and the red Martian disc in waxing phase, just fading from the bottom right of the screen. Ahead, in the center of the Dichroic screen hung a bright pinpoint of light. . .Arcturus.

This was indeed a momentous day in the history of man. It is remarkable that everyday repetitive events can occur within such a sphere seething with expectant humanity, with each singular deed or action contributing to an overall phenomenon of the universe. On the day of the orbital detachment fourteen babies were born, and twenty-two Oleandreans died either of old age or irreversible disease; there were no accidental nor deliberate deaths. On this Day of the Mission, three young females were initiated by their respective panting lovers into the human sexual rite. In this infinitesimal period of time, marking the start of the run toward the galactic pore, ten thousand tons of solid fuel were consumed by the huge boosters and six tons of human fecal wastes were processed into organic fertilizer. For the second time in less than a decade and in less than a millipicosecond in the life of the expanding universe, a satellite of Mars left its orb, and eight-point-seven tons of edible carbohydrate were synthesized. On this, the day marking the end of the interim and the beginning of the new civilization, over a million words of pointless, meaningless curse were uttered, and over a million harmless twinges of body pain were felt. Untold billions of koinoprotons interacted with equal billions of antiprotons, and the resulting energy of their consumption drove the ship and generated new pairs of matter-antimatter.

With power throbbing, the ark named Oleandre accelerated out of the Solarian System, away from a minor, innocuous, G-type star called Sol. Their beacon lay ahead, orange-yellow Arcturus of the ancient constellation Bootes, a cooler K-type star. Arcturus was merely a guiding point of light, not a goal, a navigational source, not a culmination of dreams. The end of the journey hopefully lay in the planetary system that spun around 61-Cygni. This was the destination. Many years of energy-consuming work lay between them and a new home, a new Earth. No one could say for sure they would make it; but they had the host of human knowledge and ingenuity at their command.

Long after ben Jemma's return-to-normalcy order, Jesse lay in the reclined motion cradle. A folded sheet of pressed fiber burned through the breast pocket of his acceleration tunic. In the preceding days, he had not the fortitude to open the paper Iridani had given him in their last, emotion-rending seconds together on Mars. It sat in his pocket, a sensuous living thing. He knew not why his feelings should change so radically at that instant, but he felt a sudden, almost heated release permeate his body. Perhaps it was that he was finally and irrevocably away from her, gone with no hope of return. He pulled out the paper which was yellowing, slightly brittle, and crumbling on the edges. It was crude handmade paper, an example of a lost art. It was written in her distinctive, sprawling script. Jesse's eyes darted over the words:

This is for you, Jesse, the poem you asked about. It is called ILLUSIONS.

One day, while comprehending a Dalian landscape
  With mind suspended by a good red wine
I launched a mind-probe to escape
  Into the swirling misty realm of time.
Like a rising tide it sped
  Through eternity, stopping only once
To contemplate a dead
  And a dismal and wretched sphere.
A world whose orb carries it 'round
  A minor star of the inner galactic arm, and near
Its scarred surface comes only the sound
  Of the frightened and howling winds.
It was once a place where love of self
  Flourished, and scorn was placed on mediocrity.
There was a vibrant and dynamic fortitude
  In an Eden that worshipped creativity.
But there arose a class of mindless evil
  Beings, whose sole existence was
The theft and perversion of that world's
  Only commodity of worth. . .ideas.
" 'Tis for the State," was the cry

Of propaganda slogans that
Made men sell their very souls and die
 While still among the living.
The looter's end was near, since
 Evilness had made the bureaucracy
Top-heavy and the pendulum of time
 Swept down and crushed their vile images.
In violent, rending holocausts
 The thermonuclear clouds
Dissipated oceans; the land is now
 Unfit, even for the Gods.
Now out of limbo, the mind-probe
 Rushes back at me in hot, orgasmic flashes
And the illusions it unfolded
 Have returned to whence they came. . .the ashes.

This is what the human race has done. This is the evilness in us all, maybe even in you, my innocent one. Some of the words are illusions, and are archaic. But that is the point. Perhaps it was a better time when words like " 'tis" and "whence" were used, perhaps not. Carry this with you in the universe, Jesse, or, if it's too painful a remembrance, carry this in your heart: I have felt for you a great affection — I may have even loved you — but sometimes, something other than love for another must take precedence. . .love of life, of existence.

Go into the unknown, Jesse, and may Hadem watch over you. I too, shall be with you.

 I.

He could bear it no longer. The paper vaporized in the shimmering stream of positrons. He walked up the bright corridor, fists clenched, breath coming in irregular heavings.

The Sun had grown visibly dimmer in the aft Dichroic screen. Eric and Maggie stood speechless. He squeezed her shoulder. Inside, Eric felt the pangs of grinding nausea that beset earthly explorer and galactic traveler alike when they faced the empty void. . .the unknown.

TOWARD THE NEW WORLD

> . . .thus, it is written that in the
> fourth millenium of the Vulcupea Empire,
> intelligent life-forms from a
> planetary system surrounding the minor
> star Necros in the beta arm of our
> Centoris Galaxy came forth out of
> their orb into deep-void, not having
> perfected a method of hyperquark drive.

> — A TEXTBOOK OF GALACTIC SECTORIAL HISTORY,
> H. Q. Zsu, Editor, 193rd cinematic
> edition.

CHAPTER 11

The humble star called Sol lay in the spiral arm of the Milky Way galaxy. Composed of a hundred thousand million suns of many spectral types, this pinwheel of myriad specks of light was eighty thousand lightyears across and was surrounded by a halo of shimmering star clusters, so that the entire galaxy was a hundred-thirty thousand lightyears in diameter. The Milky Way was part of what was called the Local Group, sixteen other galaxies all within two million lightyears; and the Milky Way, itself, was a member of a triple system.

Local Group was an antediluvian term, long fallen into disuse. It was now called the Hypogalactic Group, and was thought to be part of a vast, flattened cloud of galaxies, sixty to eighty million light years in diameter. This was known in these times as the Local Hypergroup. But the Local Hypergroup was only a minute section of the expanding universe. Other galactic groups were known, so massive that the Local Hypergroup was a mere pittance in comparison. A particularly striking case was the Cetan galactic group composed of over ten thousand swirling spirals which, in turn, contained a million-million burning, gaseous spheres. Surely intelligent life was to be found in the Cetan system.

Thus came Oleandre, away from one insignificant atom of a universal grain of sand washed by the ether of time, bathed in the cold energy of the void.

Over eight years passed, and they had traveled many billions of miles. Yet, this was but an inconsequental and practically immeasurable distance compared to the swiftly receding clouds of stars at the edge of the universe. . .galaxies so far that their distances were incomprehensible to humans. . .galaxies lost in the vast, endless abyss and infinite vacuum.

But for many of the Oleandreans, lifetimes had ended and begun, and for them time still held its very special human meaning. It was true, however, that time, as it effected the Mission, was beginning to acquire a new connotation. The *meaning* of time, its very concept, was losing its former significance. Primitive as they were, the Oleandreans were out in the universe now, where eternity stretched into infinity and an infinite number of eternal time sequences intermingled among themselves.

But eight years! Much had been accomplished in this period, much still remained to be discovered and perfected.

It would be too time-consuming to list all the discoveries made during the long voyage of Oleandre to the region of the galactic pore. One major achievement was the perfection of the brain transplant technique.

Sometime in the first decadays of OD-8, Eric Senka turned over the procedure to two of Fitzgerald's best students. After months of painstaking instruction, Eric and Jesse witnessed the first successful human neural transplant. In the next years, the practice became more or less routine. If prizes such as the Nobel or the Frelmann existed at that time, Eric Carnovon Senka would have surely been awarded one. As it was, he was made Chairman of the Department of Neurological Chemistry of Oleandre University, succeeding the aged Hans Tishler.

For him, this was accolade enough, but as temporal rewards went, Eric received extra space, a two-room suite opposite his living quarters and laboratory. One of the new rooms was expanded into another laboratory, the other was used as an office and micropoint library. He moved in his computer to make more room in the old lab. The office was also Neurological Chemistry's lecture room, because the University had evolved into a loose system, having no formal set of class rooms and other things usually associated with the old university concept. Classes were held in the areas of the instructor's own section.

Eric had a new assistant, Jules Nemo, son of the recently deceased Hektor Nemo who had made some valuable contributions to the field of high-vacuum tribology. Jules was young, about seventeen, and had the wild optimism and limitless energy of youth.

Jesse Horvitz attended the University full time and finished the Class-I sequence in a year. He came back to Eric's department to work on the Class III, the equivalent of the old

Doctorate. On OD-10:107, Jesse completed his work; and the Council, upon reviewing his research, awarded him the Class III. He was now Jesse Horvitz, III. Technically, he was Dr. Horvitz, although the title had all but disappeared on Oleandre. Jesse's dissertation dealt with the mediation of cyclic-guanidinemonophosphate with the sequencing of lipids in the process of long-term memory.

Having successfully developed the neural transplant, Eric turned to more academic horizons. He sought the molecular basis of the storage of data in the nervous system. Aiming generally at an understanding of mental disease, he started in the broad area of memory neurochemistry. He hoped to work not at the molecular level, but at the subatomic level. Seeing the development of atomic biology evolving out of the old twentieth century molecular biology, Eric carried the process one further step...into the realm of electronic biology. Perhaps, he surmised, the key to disease and to life itself, was held in the milieu of the swirling electron clouds.

It was not long after he began the new projects that Eric was elected Chairman of the Basic Medical Sciences Section. He sat on the Council next to Fitzgerald, who was Head of Applied Medicine, a dichotomy of leadership that would cause friction among researchers and practitioners, as it had in the past.

On OD-10:314, Commander Seth Hayakawa died peacefully in his sleep. There had been no warning, and he had been pronounced in perfect health only one week earlier in a routine physical. At sensorelectronic autopsy, it was found that the late Commander suffered a massive coronary. Had it occurred during the normal working day, he might have been resuscitated and saved, yet, as it was, he was dead over eight hours before being found, and the cellular necrosis had been much too advanced.

Not only was there a great sense of personal loss among Oleandreans, for Seth Hayakawa was probably the only one aboard whom everyone cared for, but the Council was faced with the monumental decision of selecting the new Commander. The possibility of a Commander's death in mid-Mission was never thought to be an impossibility and steps *had* been taken to assure an orderly selection. Still, it was a shock. The Council met in open session and after much debate and downright bickering the decision was made. Ahab ben Jemma, the most likely candidate, was Commander.

Jemma quickly assumed his duties. He had been prepared for just such an emergency by Hayakawa himself, years ago, at the beginning of the Mission. All the late Commander's files, except those vital for the running of Oleandre, were deposited with Jonathan Fischer in the Receptacle.

Several years passed, and Ahab ben Jemma was faced with a crucial decision early in his career. He was advised one "afternoon" by Navigational that Oleandre was galactically off course. It had been checked and rechecked, and there was no error. Oleandre had indeed strayed off its project flight path. According to the Powers Equation derivation, they were on course, but navigationally, they were not. The discrepancy was found by Chachevsky to be a minor mass-moment integral in the Powers Equation that had to be readjusted as one got further from the Sun. On the basis of this information, Jemma decided on the proper course change theoretically designed to get the ship to the great magnetic flux of the nearest galactic pore. The maneuver was made two years before they would arrive.

The mid-course change was accomplished, but the most vital aspect of the Mission still was unsolved. The combined efforts of Applied Physics and many engineering groups had failed, thus far, to come up with a workable model engine based on the derivations of the Powers Equation. The construction of the physical plant that contained the engines was complete, although only a pilot model. The trouble lay in the kionomeson-antimeson generator. Every time the pilot system was tried, the energizer would undergo magnetic collapse and recycle itself before full pulse-power was reached. At that time, no solution was in sight.

During this period, Jesse Horvitz married Sue Rafferty in a short ceremony, officiated by Ahab ben Jemma. Jesse had long since stopped brooding over Iridani, although he could never, would never, forget her. The flowing gracefulness of her lyrical verse would haunt him for an eternity. But he saw in Sue the kind of devoted love a man needs, for she had stood by him while, in her eyes, he had made an ass of himself with an older woman. He too, eventually saw this, and his admiration for Sue Rafferty grew to affection and then, after much mental anguish, he loved her.

The rigidity of their relationship did not immediately loosen and warm just because *he* decided he was indeed in love with her.

They were standing alone together, waiting for the axio-plasmic flivver to take them to their University classes. He had proclaimed his feelings about her weeks ago, but she was still hesitant.

"But how can you possibly return the love I have for you? *She* has drained it from you. O Jesse, I want to have your babies, start your sonosager, operate your servomechanin — all these things — but I want your total love."

"She hasn't drained anything. But it is true that I can never forget her, just as you could not forget the other lovers in *your* life. You shouldn't forget them. That would be unnatural."

"There have been no others. You are the first and last."

He took her face in his hands and gently rubbed his thumbs over her cheeks. She looked up at him, her eyes blinking rapidly and irregularly. He smiled, thinking, O balls, she's such a hyper-romantic, there's always more than one love in a person's life. "Suzi. I *do* love you. Believe me! When you're down and crying, I'll be there to wipe away the tears and comfort you in troubled times. If your happiness falls into ruins around you, I will help rebuild your hope. I love the Sun, and you are that radiance. Please, please think on that."

The flivver arrived and they parted, for their classes were on different decks. Jesse went to Radslekovski's lecture on the lipoidal regulation of hypothalmic function, while Sue Rafferty attended a laboratory session in applied linguistics.

There was never any economic question as to the practicality of their marriage since, in effect, economics did not exist on Oleandre. There were no salaries and, for that matter, no money. Everything was available to everyone. Only in an atmosphere of creative thought could a system like this work. There was not even an administrative bureaucracy, and Oleandreans lived in a setting that was almost utopian. To them, it was. Eventually, in the new world, wherever or whatever that was, the enterprise system would be reestablished, although probably on a new basis. That one function in the discipline a person did best was the only rule that applied on Oleandre. No lethargy would be tolerated. Since Jesse and Sue now functioned as students, they were entitled to all the benefits and privileges that applied to Commander ben Jemma. This utopia functioned because there were no uneducated, unmotivated masses to bog it down with apathy, despair and fear. It operated because it had no malignant bureaucracy to become so top-heavy as to topple in upon itself. It proceeded because gifted humans had taken painful, violent steps to perceive its inception, and had given their lives to ensure its completion. Whether it would survive was another question, the answer to which no one could foretell.

When it became pretty much common knowledge that the construction of the postphobic propulsion system was not going well, all sorts of new ideas came forth. Most were so farfetched as to border on the ridiculous.

Commander ben Jemma dredged up something from the preAlliance period on Earth. A vehicle designed for a voyage to Proxima Centauri had been conceived. The Aldebaran Project — no one knew why it was called that — employed a powerful system of lasers that sent out a beam of concentrated light toward the destination. The space vehicle was attached by means of miles-long cables to a great sail a square mile in area and a mere sixty microns thick. The pulse and energy of the laser wind would catch the sail, dragging the ship behind. Preposterous as it sounded, the theoretical speed attained by a vehicle weighing two thousand tons was over forty thousand miles-per-second after ten years travel. The ship would then break off course and go into orbit around Proxima Centauri, do the necessary exploration and set up another laser unit there to drive it home again.

The Aldebaran Project had been given feasibility-clearance, but the evolution of the full-scale Asian Mainland Wars took away most of its funding. This, of course, was in the days before the invention of the first, crude matter-antimatter interconverters, similar to the refined version now driving Oleandre.

This idea was finally rejected since the size of the astrosail required for a craft of Oleandre's dimensions was out of the question, and no one had even the slightest idea if a laser would work in the galactic pore or if, in the postphobic transfer, even the concept of the laser was valid. To determine this mathematically required a greater task than had producing the complex calculations that led to the Powers Equation, more than a decade in preparation. The Council was in agreement: work should continue toward completion of the postphobic propulsion system designated in the Powers Equation.

Early on OD-13:85, sensors picked up a great magnetic force field that lay directly on the projected course of Oleandre. Even though a year's travel still lay ahead, the field registered over four on the Gauss Scale. It was, indeed, very powerful. In this sense, the Powers Equation had been correct!

The celestial view ahead was unimpeded and only slight shifts in the star patterns could be seen due to Oleandre's change in position. Yet a magnetic flux of unimaginable power lay directly ahead.

Deceleration began. Oleandre spun on an axis and retrofired the exchange engines. The arrival at the vortex of the magnetic field on OD-14:13, occurred without incident. Still, no aberrations were detected in the visual images coming in.

Oleandre was motionless, a dull, blue-silver spheroid suspended in limbo.

It had been a number of years now since Maggie Senka had observed the weird, rhythmic pulsations emanating from that strange pulsar. During the voyage, she had been concerned with the raising of her son, now age twelve, and with a prime Astrophysics Department project: a detailed spectroscopic study of the small and large Magellanic Clouds, companions to the Milky Way. She was studying their effect on the spiral-potential field of the galaxy. From time to time, however, she looked over the tapes she had made of the first contact.

Was there a message? she thought. Maybe a code. . .oh, not another. Perhaps that is the function of life: discover something, break another sequence, a genetic code, the Persimmion Sequence, the Faldurbarr operon series. Perhaps. Perhaps the only advancement of civilization is the solving of the riddles put to us by Nature. But what was the worth in that? Did Nature even know the answers to her own enigmas? Or was man being used by Nature, used as a tool by an omnipotent, malignant intelligence to delve into the universal mysteries under the guise of improving the human condition? But then, who really cared; what did it matter? The quest for truth and knowledge had to be held almost in revered awe, for it was all a human had. Otherwise, he might as well have never crawled from the mire, never have been born.

Maggie had not been able to do much investigating into the mystery of that special pulsar, or fluxar, as she called it. Careful, intricate astrophysical measurements could not be made while aboard a sphere hurtling through space. But now, with Oleandre in a 'Hold' condition, she could begin some preliminary work.

It was soon obvious that the fantastic magnetic flux in the area of the galactic pore not only did not interfere with astrophysical measurements, but improved their accuracy. The number of galaxies visible with the Rasai instrument was triple the number seen when observations had been made near Mars. There was no explanation. It was not that they were merely closer, since a few billion miles were inconsequential when compared to the distance of these hitherto unseen galaxies. A whole new physical principle was at work here, opening new vistas. The phenomenon was remotely akin to the revelation and impact felt by Twenty-first Century Earth astronomy when the 180-inch orbiting telescope was first put into use in July, 2004 — and later, when with its 420-inch companion on Lunare, it gleaned much new data on galaxies that had been unobservable up to that time because of the eccentricities and unstableness of the Earth's atmosphere. Now, almost a century later, astrophysicists would be able to study the fine structure of galaxies with a resolution never imagined and gather much evidence as to the evolution of galaxies, investigating the curvature and scale of the very universe itself.

It was here that Maggie Senka embarked on a personal crusade that would not end for twenty years. When it was through, humans would never be quite the same.

Although he was only twelve, Sean Senka had already become something of a minor legend. Sean Senka was a genius, not in the usual connotation of eccentricity, for he had the rare ability to have foresight into a vast number of disciplines. At the age of thirteen, when Oleandre began its 'Hold' at the magnetic flux field, Sean Senka entered Oleandre University and accomplished the Class-I in only three months.

It was a sensation, in a society that held knowledge and creativity above all else. Although Eric and Maggie had prodded him occasionally during his early education, Sean's talent was a natural thing. Abstract concepts and their applicability to reality came easily to him. He leaned heavily toward theoretical physics although, because of his tremendous capacity for retention, and he devoured literally thousands of textapes on every imaginable subject, from conceptual historiography and comparative philology to psycho-autoimmune phenomenon and extensor-antimatter conversions. Even at fourteen, he was more "well-rounded" than most adults.

Sean was not outwardly concerned with his genius — he had work to do, things to accomplish. And though his feats may well have been those of genius, he knew he would die the death of a genius: never quite finished with one's dreams. Death, in all its varied manifestations comes to all humans; and in death the mongoloid is the genius' equal. Perhaps earlier than most men, Sean had stepped from the painfully sweet twilight of youth into the stark, still painful but blatantly real world of manhood.

Easily adapting to the social problems that befall brilliant young humans in an adult environment, Sean applied, at his father's urging, for Class-II and III work under Joi Chou-Li, a subatomic kineticist whose interests lay in the creation of the universe. . .theoretical cosmology.

During the five years Oleandre was stationary, waiting for the breakthrough in the development of the postphobic propulsion system, Sean Senka completed his formal education and, at the age of seventeen, began his own work in the area of galactic evolution. Despite the gap in their ages, he and Jesse Horvitz became friends and, eventually, inseparable compatriots. There was a period when he spent more time at Sue and Jesse's quarters than he spent with his parents.

The lines of worry and age, if the two are separable, etched Eric's face. The dark purple furrows under his eyes pulled the skin tautly over his cheekbones giving added strain to his already sallow countenance. Although he was only fifty-five, Eric bore the internal scars of a millenium of human conflict. Now that the possibility of success was in sight, he sighed a cautious breath of relief.

He had been recording into his computerized journal for over an hour: ". . .thus we have brought all that remains of what is called human to an area that is, for us, deep in the hyperspace. We come to continue. . .no, to *propagate* our civilization. It has often been said that invention and innovation come only out of turmoil, urgent hot turmoil. In the example of our former Earth, this seemed the case. No real change came calmly to her. Historically, only violent upheaval, both natural and social, wrought the progress of human civilization. We of Oleandre, by our acts and accomplishments — and by the very fact that we have thus far succeeded — are testimony that civilization *can* proceed without the gradual apocalypse that permeated the Earth's historical experience. It is ironic, indeed, that in order for the concept to work, the ultimate destruction had to be dealt with by us, those humans dedicated to the peaceful renewal. We must revive the ancient Aristotelian concept that man was not born merely *as* something, but born *for* something. . .not for evil and destruction, but for a creative dialogue with the Universal. By whatever is holy, we must succeed! Otherwise, other. . . oth. . .er. . .O G-God. . ."

A distinct rustling noise, along with a wheezing gasp, was heard in the tape, followed by the steady whirring of a blank spindle. Then silence.

"That's all there is," said Sean sleepily. Yawning, he stretched his arms and arched his back. He tilted his head to one side, the air rushing between his teeth.

"Buy why did it end so abruptly?" asked Diahna.

"Died. . .died right there. . .recording. . .those were his last words." His brain recoiled under the dull, rhythmic thud of a hangover headache.

"OH. . .oh, I'm sorry Sean, I didn't realize," she said, her surprised look turning into one of solemnity.

"It's no matter now. . .been a long time now. They say he died of the stress of the Mission, probably as did Hayakawa."

"He was a great man, Sean, and you should be very proud."

"I am at times; and I'll tell you something, girl," he said, rubbing his temples. "His greatest contribution was not in the development of the neural transplantation and the later psychic experiments. Eric Carnovon Senka will be listed with the Contributors because of these very tapes we've been listening to all night. They will give all Oleandreans a basis for reviewing their heritage and the reasons for its destruction. They will give them encouragement and, at the same time, impose upon them the greatest sense of responsibility for carrying out the Mission."

"Sean," said Diahna, squeezing his arm, "I'd really like to tell you. . ."

It was at this point that the Dichroic sounded with the announcement that at nine-hundred hours that morning Sean

Eric Senka would be elevated to the grade of Scientific Fellow and sit on the Council.

Sean shrugged his shoulders, smiled at Diahna, and ordered the servomechanin Claudio to bring them a beaker of cerebral detoxicant and two hot breakfasts.

POSTEPILOGICA

TYYLON

A thousand light years from the Sun, in a spiral arm of the Milky Way galaxy lay an unspectacular star called Alpha Signoris. A single, banded planet whirled around Alpha Signoris in a perfectly circular orbit.

The bluish star was called Ecterus by the inhabitants of the planet Tyylon. The sphere that was Tyylon, was nearly covered with a dark red liquid which abounded with non-intelligent life forms and, upon which, the intelligence of Tyylon depended for nourishment. On the planet's only land mass, on the rugged continent of Ra, stood the magnificent, terraced megalopolis of Logistikon. Purple and lavender vaporous clouds drifted over the sphere in wispy, finger-like patches.

The rotation of Ecterus had long ago been adjusted by the Conceivers to have periods of equal light and darkness. The burning blue disc of Ecterus had just disappeared below the mountainous Tyylonian horizon. The dark purple hue of twilight quickly gave way to the dense black period of night; the red oceans lapped peacefully at crystalline magenta shores. The great white domes of Logistikon opened their dark slits and the magnifiers swung their snouted lenses toward the heavens. Being perfectly stable and transparent, the atmosphere of Tyylon was particularly well-adapted for extraTyylonian investigation.

The being called Nomos made its way carefully across the clay flats. Bubbles of hydrogen gas from subTyylonian pits occasionally erupted at the surface with explosive force. He had to be extremely cautious. The starlight glistened on its metallic skull, and Nomos picked up the flowing white, togan robe so that it wouldn't drag in the muck. He was traveling across the most treacherous part of the clay flats now, and his long, hairless, bony foot ending in two nail-less toes stuck in the red mud, held tightly by vacuum. As he pulled it up with a sucking noise, a fluorescent green vapor discharged around the foot and quickly dissipated. Nomos muttered something, a Tyylonian oath.

He made his way up a steep stone stairway of ornately carved blocks — white, and stained red and blue, and a multitude of intermediate shades resulting from mineral contamination. The observatory was situated high over Logistikon. Nomos' psychic energizer opened the entrance under the great dome. Most of his colleagues were already present, and a good deal of excitement seemed to permeate the group. Nomos discarded his soiled white garment which flashed into nothingness in the disposar, and he donned a fresh robe from the pile that lay next to the regional omniscanner tube.

"...E haih fe ko kokum xaahx secum sa hahi e fornicum eet...!"

Free translation into Mundanlingua was as follows:

"...And Hier has discovered a momentous thing in the area of the Xaahx sector...!"

"What is the nature of this discovery?" asked Nomos, shuffling up to the group.

Hier croaked, "I, that is, we were observing the sector near the star Xaahx, a minor yellow star known to possess a planetary system. Positronor scans show a cataclysmic explosion in the region of the third planet. It is evident now that the planet was destroyed in some kind of nuclear holocaust, primitive, yet effective. We may be in danger!"

"Then," said Nomos, "there is but one thing to do...we must send the Investigators."

All six metallic heads nodded gravely.

POSTEPILOGICA CONTINUUM

MARS

On this vivid chromatic Martian afternoon, the sunlight filtered through the distant, gently swirling dust clouds in daggered slashes and yellow shafts, then changed to coiled, golden serpents that appeared, only to vanish in the continually shifting air. The winds buffeting down the twisting

Valley of Prophecy, slicing over the jagged outstretched rocks in the Ancient's Crater, produced a whining melody that accompanied the light beams in dramatic counterpoint. But the rare aesthetic moment was to be short-lived in this hostile world — a single static thunderclap announced the return of the violent season.

The biting cold winds howled and roared in off the Haganaah Plains, bringing with them the ever-present, piercing dust storms. On the sunlit side, just ahead of the advancing terminator, Iridani Beshiva walked, a light webbed pack slung over one shoulder. Her eyes squinted into the setting ochre sun. "Hadem," she said, and shaded her eyes with the back of her tanned hand. Behind her and a little to the right walked two children, hand-in-hand. Both were dressed in silver-leaf suits with hoods and insulated boots. They were twins. The girl, Seegara, was fair of skin and brown-haired. Jesse, the boy, was as dark as his mother, and his obsidian eyes reflected the conflict of his being.

On the way back to the dilapidated shack, Iridani stopped to harvest some grey-green lichens growing wild on the gentle slope of a small sandy knoll. Impulsively, she stopped, grabbed a fistful of the primitive plants, and with the clotty soil still clinging brought them to her lips. Their velvet texture penetrated her soul and her eyelids drifted shut as she deeply inhaled the sweet-pungent odor. She smiled.

Over a rise they had traveled a hundred times in the last eight years, they came upon a strange set of what appeared to be footprints. . .deep and long, with two toes.

High above them, although they did not see it, a streak of brilliant gold light broke out of the Martian atmosphere and pulsed at full power across the Perseus arm of the galaxy.

The winds shrieked and the reddish Martian soil slowly covered the alien tracks. The sun was down and the full beauty of the starry sky erupted before them.

Boiling suns of infinite galaxies had their violent birth, evolved, and burned out into slow gravitational collapse.

Only time was eternal.

The Oleandre Trilogy is continued in *The Winds of Heliopolis* and concluded in *The Oleandre Solution*.

For those books not available at your local newsstand please order from:

Apollo Books
30 Hazel Terrace
Woodbridge, Connecticut 06525

Please send the books checked below. I have enclosed my check for _____

☐ *Wellspring* $0.95 plus $0.10 postage and handling.

☐ *Beautiful People* $0.95 plus $0.10 postage and handling.

☐ *Stop It! I Love It!* $1.00 plus $0.10 postage and handling.

☐ *Astrology and Horoscope* $1.50 plus $0.15 postage and handling.

☐ *Discover Your Sexual Personality* $1.00 plus $0.10 postage and handling.

☐ *Ransome Castle* $0.95 plus $0.10 postage and handling.

☐ *House of Deadly Calm* $0.95 plus $0.10 postage and handling.

☐ *Beware of the Cat* $0.95 plus $0.10 postage and handling.

☐ *The Agent Orange Affair* $0.95 plus $0.10 postage and handling.

☐ *Behold the Upright* $1.25 plus $0.10 postage and handling.

☐ *Mystic Sciences* $1.00 plus $0.10 **postage and** handling.

☐ *The Ultimate Weapon* $0.95 plus $0.10 postage and handling.

☐ *You Don't Have To Be Jewish To Be A Good Cook* $1.00 plus $0.10 postage and handling.

☐ *The Doctor's Handbook for Parents* $1.50 plus $0.15 postage and handling.

☐ *Rain for a Dusty Summer* $0.95 plus $0.10 postage and handling.

☐ *Prisoners of Devil's Claw* $0.95 plus $0.10 postage and handling.

☐ *The Adultress* $0.95 plus $0.10 postage and handling.

Name _____

Address _____

City _____ State _____

Zip Code _____